For Mis:

You are

of everyones [...]

Mike Tuck

Aquarius Falling

ʔ

A novel by

Michael J. Tucker

ISBN-10: 1475042124
ISBN-13: 9781475042122
Library of Congress Control Number: 2012905000
CreateSpace, North Charleston, SC

Acknowledgments

I T IS TRULY DIFFICULT to accomplish things in life without help. I've been exceedingly fortunate to have friends help me bring to fruition *Aquarius Falling*. A special thanks to Robin Crouch for making it a better story, and to her brother, Dale Jones and his photographic memory, for some of the specific details of Ocean City in 1964.

Thanks to Lauren Carpenter for fixing my syntax, grammar, and punctuation. Without her help you probably wouldn't understand what I was trying to say.

And a big thank you to Lloyd DeBerry for capturing my vision and making it a reality.

Aquarius Falling

By

Michael J. Tucker

Chapter 1

May 11, 1964
A Ride to the Beach

Filled with rage, rage and self-loathing, I slammed the door behind me with a resounding crack that echoed like a rifle shot in the empty corridor. Walking out the main door onto the commons with knuckles white from clenched hands, my right hand gripped the handle of my suitcase. My left hand was a fist. I crossed the red brick entrance and walked through the wrought iron gates, looking back at the gray stone Jesuit edifice that overlooked the Potomac. I had failed and could blame only myself.

Stepping onto Wisconsin Avenue, I started hitchhiking with no idea of a destination, just to leave this town. Each time a driver asked where I was going, my stock answer was, "As far as you'll take me." The random rides led in an eastern direction out of Washington, D.C., eventually reaching U.S. Route 50 and the Maryland countryside. Rather than engaging in meaningless conversation with the car's driver, my mind replayed the conversation with Monsignor McLaughlin.

"Thomas, my son, actions have consequences." His words repeated again and again in my head. He always called me "my son," and I always addressed him as "Father Sean." To me, those words—"my son" and "Father"—meant much more than simple salutations. Monsignor McLaughlin, Father Sean, was the first person to greet me when I arrived at Georgetown University as an eighteen-year-old freshman. I was a child without a family, but he would make me forget that. He seemed to know my thoughts and fears. He gave me guidance, which was his job, but he gave me so much more. I thought of him as my father, the father I never had, and I liked to think the celibate priest thought of me as the son he never had. Just a few short hours before, he had spoken his last words to me.

"Thomas, the girl almost died because of your actions—your actions here on campus, *in your room*. And it has put the school in a terrible position. We don't believe there will be a lawsuit, but her father is an alumnus and has provided important financial support to the university. Your actions have put that financial support in jeopardy. I'm sorry, Thomas, but the board has revoked your scholarship, and you are expelled from the university, effective immediately. You must accept responsibility for your actions. Always remember, Thomas, my son, actions have consequences."

I knew in my heart that Father Sean was right. At the same time, I wondered if my consequences would have been different if I had had a father who provided important financial support to the university. My reality was that I didn't have a father. Nor did I have a family. My family was Georgetown and Father Sean. My hope was for a secure future that my education would provide. Now all of it was gone. My life was in my small suitcase. My fortune was the few dollars in my pocket.

At crossroads, decisions have to be made. This one came at Annapolis, and the choice was to go north to Baltimore or east to the ocean. The decision was easy. It would be east the ocean. It was midday, with a cloudless blue sky; I stood on the side of the road, waiting for my next ride of chance. The scent of honeysuckle dominated the air. Across the road, pink and white azaleas bloomed. The oppressive humidity of central Maryland was still a few weeks away. The air was freshened by a breeze that made the treetops dance. The sun beat on the asphalt, causing distant objects to shimmy and float. The wiggling object now coming toward me on the horizon would be my next ride.

Hitchhiking is about the element of uncertainty or possible danger. You have no idea who is stopping to pick you up or why. When you climb into a stranger's car, you are saying, "I don't know you from Adam, but I trust you." Deserve it or not, you relinquish any control of your destiny. And so it was when the red Austin Healey pulled onto the shoulder.

The car's top was down, and the driver, a guy in his late twenties with a blond crew cut and round face, smiled as he looked back at me.

"Where you headed?" he asked.

"Ocean City." That would now be my destination of choice.

"You're in luck. Get in. I'm going all the way."

I hopped into the two-seater. "Thanks. Really cherry car you've got."

He accelerated through the gears as I wedged my suitcase between my legs, not very comfortable but thankful for my last ride of the day. By the time he hit fourth gear, we were outpacing the other traffic. He glanced at me, then looked ahead and said, "Charlie MacGuffin's the name, lived in Ocean City all my life. What you planning on doing when you get there?"

"Tom Delaney," I said. "I'm looking for work. Planning to work the summer at the beach, Charlie. I want to see what happens, then make some decisions about what to do when fall comes. Maybe go back to college or stay and become a permanent resident."

"You go by Tom or Tommy?"

"Just call me Delaney."

"Well, Delaney, Ocean City's dead after Labor Day. Tough to get any job there then. What kind of work are you looking for?"

"Anything. Any suggestions?"

We chatted like that for the next sixty miles with little of significance in our conversation. He made it clear he was from a family with old money. They owned several hotels and businesses in Ocean City. Then he asked, "How 'bout your family?"

It was the wrong question, asked at the wrong time. I felt my molars clamp down and my jaw clench.

"I don't have a family, Charlie. I don't know who my parents are. I was raised in an orphanage, a Catholic orphanage where I busted my ass, got top grades, served as an altar boy, and earned a scholarship to Georgetown until I fucked that up and got kicked out." I was actually yelling with anger, but the roar of the engine through the thin firewall and the rush of air in the open sports car masked it.

"What did you do to get kicked out of school?"

"You ever hear of alcohol poisoning?"

"No."

"Neither had I, but apparently if you drink too much, the excessive alcohol in your bloodstream can kill you."

"Really? I just thought you could drink until you puked or passed out."

"Yeah, me, too. I had a girl in my room, we were drinking, and she had too much. She got pretty sick. Anyway, the shit hit the fan, and now I'm out of school early." I calmed down after getting the words out, and I don't think Charlie even noticed my anger. "I'm sorry, Charlie. I don't know why I just spilled my guts to you like that. I'm usually a more private person."

"That's OK. You needed to get it out. Besides, it's always easier to talk to strangers about really personal stuff. You don't have to worry about being judged. We'll most likely never see each other again."

It was the trill of the tires on the metal grates as we drove over the bridge on the Choptank River that seemed to signal a change in mood and atmosphere. Driving through the Eastern Shore town of Cambridge, I got to see the dark side of friendly Charlie.

"That there is the worst town on the shore. It's filled with those uppity niggers that want to integrate schools and restaurants, take jobs from the whites. Really bad place. They had race riots there last year. That stuff is bad for business. Costs us money. Folks up in D.C. and Baltimore think the shore is like that, and then they don't want to come to the beach. A couple of troublemakers come in trying to rile things up. One of 'em from New York or someplace up north, his name was Hamson or Hansen—something like that—he led a bunch of local high school kids and college kids from Morgan State. Morgan State's up in Baltimore, but they come down here just to make trouble. Some white people came with 'em. They were just as likely to be Jews from New York. Probably all commies."

I felt beads of sweat trickling down my back, and anger began to well up inside me. There was no such thing as segregation in the orphanage. I can't remember how old I was when I realized our skin color was different, but I grew up with the knowledge that skin color was the only difference between Bobby, Lawrence, Philip, and me. I lost track of them after I went to Georgetown, but they were like my brothers, if I had had any brothers. I also remember being shocked the first time I read propaganda against the Catholic Church, and I put Charlie's rant in that context. I'm Irish and had been dumbfounded to learn that a century earlier, there was harsh discrimination against the Irish. I'd wondered how anybody could hate me without knowing me. Could people hate me just because I was Irish or Catholic? I was certain that Charlie didn't know any Negroes or Jews from Cambridge, Baltimore, or New York. Why did Charlie have that hatred? Where did it come from? I just didn't understand it.

"Anyway, Hansen got the shit kicked out of him by some locals. Then the mayor had Hansen arrested for disturbing the peace." Charlie laughed. "Then the dummy up and does it again, only to get the shit kicked out of him once more and get himself arrested again."

Charlie continued his tirade about American race relations while I sat quietly listening. It was with some irony that Smokey Robinson and the Miracles were singing "Shop Around" on the Austin Healey's radio.

"Now, I don't want you to think I hate them all. Some of them are not bad, but most are lazy. Half of them in Cambridge don't work. But there're good ones. You take Marvin Gaye, Mary Wells, Ray Charles—they're good. They work hard."

It occurred to me that the reason half of them didn't work was that people like Charlie wouldn't hire them. I decided to keep that thought to myself. In fact, I had not once responded to any of Charlie's racial opinions. I really didn't want to continue the discussion and regretted sharing my personal history. We were on the last sixty miles to my destination; there was no point in starting an argument and getting kicked out of the car. I silently stared at corn and soybean fields as we rolled through the flat countryside. Soon there was only the hum of the rubber on pavement and the smell of fertilizer filling the air. These were strange sights, sounds, and smells for me that simply made me feel more alone.

When we finally got to Ocean City, Charlie pulled up to a mustard-colored, three-story clapboard house with a tin roof.

"This is Millie's Rooming House. Her rates are cheap, and it should do you till you find steady work. She can tell you how to find the state employment office."

Breathing a sigh of relief, I thanked him and was glad to see him drive off. I thought, *You son of a bitch, you talked like your family owned half this town, and you tell me where the state employment office is! You couldn't suggest a job in one of your family businesses? Asshole.*

I climbed three steps to the porch, knocked on the door, and was greeted by Millie, a small, thin, mousy woman who must have been somewhere in her late forties or early fifties. She had a Marlboro between her lips with a quarter-inch of ash about to fall off the end. Her grayish black hair needed combing. She wore a pink housecoat with no hose and bedroom slippers.

"Cheapest bed I got is in the dormitory. Come on, I'll show ya." Her deep, raspy voice belied her stature and echoed years of whiskey and tobacco.

The steps to the dormitory were outside the house and led to what was probably once the attic. Inside were two rows of single beds with three-inch-thick mattresses. Each row had five beds, which were really cots, and a footlocker at the end of each bed. There was a six-foot-wide aisle between the two rows. The roof pitched down to the head of the beds, so if you jumped out of bed too fast, you might knock yourself out. A slight hint of mildew crept into my nostrils and reminded me of the orphanage.

"It's three bucks a night, paid one week in advance."

I paid Millie the twenty-one dollars and counted what money I had left. It came to forty-nine dollars and some change. I needed to find a job soon. The dormitory was empty and no one else had checked in yet, so I picked a bed in the middle of the room, tossed my suitcase on it, and decided to look for something to eat. Millie's was on St. Louis Avenue between Second and Third Streets, which consisted of buildings similar to Millie's but tended to rent rooms and apartments for the entire season. Passing these buildings, I made my way to Baltimore Avenue, the main drag, and walked by souvenir shops, a drugstore, and a mom-and-pop grocery store before finding a Tastee-Freez on Fifth. A dollar got me a hot dog, fries, and a Coke. Then I walked to the beach.

Even before reaching the boardwalk, my senses took in the salt air of the ocean, the creosote of the boardwalk decking, and waves crashing on the shore. At the boardwalk, I leaned on the railing looking east and stared at the sand, then gazed at the breakers, breathed the air, and felt the wind from the sea against my face. Watching a seagull suspended in flight overhead reminded me of the aerodynamics at work, but it amazed me how a bird can face the wind and effortlessly float on air. We were still weeks from Memorial Day and the formal opening of the summer season. A few restaurants were open, but the arcades and the T-shirt and souvenir vendors were still shuttered. For now, the boardwalk was a quiet place where cries of gulls, the beat of the surf on sand, and the whistle of the wind dominated.

Looking in both directions, I could see no more than a dozen people on the boardwalk, and all but one were several blocks away. A woman wearing a solid black muumuu walked in my direction. She was adorned in jewelry, rings, bracelets, and a gold necklace. Her gait was casual and her posture erect, tall like a model on a runway. She moved as though balancing a book on her head. She looked at me with a broad smile as if she knew me. The ocean breeze was whipping strands of her long black hair so that it looked like velvet ribbons blowing in the wind.

"Hi," she said.

"Hi." I tried to match her broad smile and wondered if she had mistaken me for someone else.

"Lonely out here at this time of evening," she said.

In the approaching twilight, her skin was white as milk, and I guessed her to be a new arrival like me. Zodiac symbols hung from her necklace.

"Yeah, I guess this place doesn't liven up until Memorial Day."

"Right. You're not local, are you?"

I fixated on her with every word she spoke. Her husky voice reminded me of the actress June Allyson. She had a wide mouth with full lips that I wanted to hear say the words, "Kiss me." Her eyes had a magnetism that I was sure could make me do anything she wanted.

"No, I'm not local. Did you think I was someone you knew?"

"No, I just thought I'd say hi. My name's Misty." She extended her hand.

I was impressed—not many women did that—and I responded by shaking her hand, saying, "My name's Delaney." Her handshake was firm but delicate. She held on a little longer than I expected, as if she didn't want to let go. I liked it. I liked her. "I just got here a couple hours ago."

"Where are you staying?"

"Oh, a little boarding house a couple blocks from here, place called Millie's. How about you?"

"You have your own room?"

"No, I can't afford that. I'm sleeping in her men's dorm. It's only three bucks a night."

8

"Hmm, yeah, OK. Hope to see you again." She turned and continued her walk down the boardwalk.

"Hey, wait a minute. Where are you going? Can I see you again?"

She looked back at me with a smile that made me feel special. "Yeah, you'll see me again. In fact, I'm sure we'll see each other again. It's written in the stars." She turned her back to me, and I watch as she walked away, her black hair buffeted by the breeze.

I wondered, *What just happened?* She was coming on to me, or so I thought, and just as quickly dropped me and left. I didn't know what to make of her parting words.

Streetlights came on. It was getting dark. Time to head back to Millie's.

As I walked back to Millie's, I thought about my long day. It had gotten off to a horrible start with losing my scholarship to Georgetown, but more important, my relationship with Father Sean was over. I couldn't see a way to redeem that. And then the ride here was tedious at best . . . that bigot MacGuffin spouting off about Negroes and Jews, implying he was better than they were. He could have offered to help me find a job with one of his family businesses but instead pointed me to the state employment office. Then the strange encounter with that girl, Misty. Could things get any lower? I was at rock bottom. It had to get better. It just had to.

As I neared the top of the stairs at Millie's, a loud and collective chant of "ooh ah, ooh ah" came from the dormitory. A radio was booming out Sam Cooke's voice to "Chain Gang," but the *oohs* and *ahs* were coming from several loud voices in the dorm. I stood frozen at the top of the steps and listened. When the song got to the line where Sam sings, "Give me water," the voices from the dorm chanted, "Give me beer." I no longer had the dorm to myself.

Chapter 2

May 11, 1964
I Meet Sal and Dean
Evening

THE LAUGHTER WAS LOUD and boisterous as the song ended, but the room fell silent as I opened the screen door and all eyes turned to me. Four guys in various stages of dress were guzzling cans of Pabst Blue Ribbon and sizing me up.

"Hi," I said.

"Hey, what's up, dude?" said the glassy-eyed guy closest to me.

"Hiya," came from another as he swayed as if on a boat in a rough sea.

A gray cloud of cigarette smoke hung from the ceiling, and the smell of beer replaced the mildew odor. They were well on their way to drunkenness, and they watched me as I walked between them toward my bunk.

A short, husky guy with a two-day-old beard in the bunk to my right said, "Hey, I'm Sal Paradise, and this is my buddy, Dean Moriarty." He motioned with a sweep of his right arm to one of the guys sitting on a bunk across the aisle. Sal introduced the other two with names I immediately forgot because I was busy rifling through the file cabinet of my mind for the Sal and Dean reference. I knew Sal and Dean were not their real names. Schoolboy giggles and glances confirmed it. Then I saw a paperback book with dog-eared pages on Sal's bed, and it hit me. The names were characters in Jack Kerouac's semi-autobiographical work, *On the Road.*

"So what happened to Jack Kerouac? Couldn't he make the trip?" I smiled. "I can read hip literature, too." I picked up the book from Sal's bunk, waved it in front of him, and tossed it back on the bunk.

"Ho-ah, way to go! We can't fool this guy, Nick. He's cool," Sal said to Dean, whose real name was apparently Nick.

My quick response made me immediately accepted. Everyone was laughing. "Sal" shook my hand and gave me a beer. He seemed to be the leader of this bedraggled gang by the way he spoke for the group and the fact that he had assumed "Sal" as his *nom de guerre,* which Kerouac used to identify himself in the book.

"So, Sal, what's your real name?"

"Johnny Walker," he replied, drawing more laughter.

"Oh, bullshit. How many names will I have to go through before I get to your real one?"

"No, seriously—that's my name. I'll show you my driver's license."

Sure enough, there was his picture next to the name John E. Walker. And it was John, initial E, not Johnny. With a quick glance, I saw he was from Frederick, Maryland, and was twenty-four years old, three years older than I.

John E. explained, "Dad's first name was Herman, and he hated it and swore none of the kids would have a name like Herman—only names he liked. Dad had taken to drinking Johnnie Walker Scotch whisky during the time between when he and Mom got it on and when I was born. So he insisted on calling me John E. If only he had been drinking Jim Beam at the time. Then I'd be Jim Walker." Laughter filled the room.

"At least you should be thankful he wasn't drinking Four Roses," I said. "You wouldn't have wanted to grow up being called Rose." Everyone, including John E., thought my comment hilarious and cracked up.

One of his friends—the tall, skinny one with shoulder-length hair—was laughing loudly and said in a voice reminiscent of Goofy the cartoon character, "Yeah, Rose, Rose. Hey, Rosie." John E. was between me and the Goofy guy, so when he turned and looked at Goofy, I couldn't see the expression on his face, but I could see Goofy's. His laugh stopped and his stupid grin froze, and there was an expression in his eyes that resembled fear.

Turning to me with a smile, John E. said, "Everyone calls me Jack. I really don't like the John E., so call me Jack."

"And you can call me Delaney."

Jack was an inch or two shorter than my five-feet-nine-inches, but he was a muscular 200 to 225 to my 155 pounds. His head was large and very round, reminding me of a pumpkin. His dark brown eyes were pinched together and out of proportion to his round head, and he had a scattering of freckles on his tanned face. He had a pronounced brow and jutting chin, and his fingers were stained yellow with nicotine, the nails bitten down to the quick.

I had a couple of beers with the group and learned they were all from the Frederick area, a small town in a rural area west of Baltimore. They were an odd lot. Scruffy, unshaven faces and long, uneven hair, except for Jack, whose hair was short, like a military cut. They seemed poorly educated, used bad grammar, and talked like farm boys. Jack, the oldest and better educated than the others, directed all the action and the conversation.

Jack gave me a proper introduction to "Dean" as Nick Novack. Nick appeared to be the same age as Jack, mid-twenties, but taller and slimmer. Nick had a confident air, and you could tell he had been around and knew how to handle himself. The other two looked to be eighteen or nineteen, a few years younger than I, and were clearly tagging along. Jimmy Conner was the Goofy guy, skinny with shoulder-length red hair and wearing a paisley shirt with the sleeves torn off, cutoff jeans, and no shoes. Bob Jordan was short and thin and was making a weak effort at a surfer look with bleached blond hair covering his ears, baggies, and bare feet.

There was a knock at the screen door. A girl looking through the screen asked, "Ain't nobody naked in there, is there?"

She was introduced to me as Susan—nothing more, just Susan—and she didn't offer a last name. Susan was Jimmy's girl-friend and had made the trip with the guys. Skinny like Jimmy, her long brown hair hung straight over both shoulders to her flat breasts. Jimmy and Susan were both going for the beatnik look. Maybe they were influenced by Jack's copy of *On the Road*, but both were out of their element.

While everyone talked, Susan clung to Jimmy as if he were her life preserver as she struggled in water over her head. I saw her whisper in his ear, and a few moments later, during a break in the conversation, Jimmy said, "Hey, me and Susan are gonna take a walk."

They left, and the screen door closed with a bang. The room was quiet, and as the sound of their footsteps on the stairs grew fainter, I heard Jack say, "Pussy." Nick and Bob chuckled.

About five minutes after Susan and Jimmy left, I heard another bang of the screen door. A new boarder had arrived. He was tall, over six feet, and slim but muscular. His rust-colored hair was curly and tight, forming a widow's peak. His side-burns made me think of Elvis, and his clothing made him look as though he had stepped out of a Marlon Brando motorcycle movie from the mid-fifties. He wore a tight-fitting white T-shirt with a pack of cigarettes rolled up in the left sleeve. His right sleeve was also rolled up to his shoulder, showing off his biceps. A thick black leather belt with a large shiny silver buckle held up a pair of Levi's that were rolled and pegged over his black leather motorcycle boots. He gave us a nod with a scowl as his only intro-duction. A cigarette hung from his lips, its smoke drifting across his face. He carried only a navy-colored gym bag that could hold only a change of underwear and a shaving kit. His boots made a loud clomping sound as he walked to the back of the dorm. He picked a bunk against the far wall, as far away from the rest of us as he could get, and that was OK by me.

Things quieted down when we ran out of beer. I stripped down to my underwear, got in my bunk, and secured my wallet under my pillow. I stared at the ceiling while my stomach churned from a combination of anxiety and hunger. An uncertain future awaited me, and my hope for tomorrow was to find a job that included a room so I could get away from this crew. For now, things would have to be day by day.

Chapter 3

May 12, 1964
Jack: An Unlikely Hero

MORNING CAME WITH SNORES, snorts, occasional grunts, and heavy breathing from my new friends, who were in a deep morning sleep. I slipped into the bathroom, showered, shaved, splashed on some Aqua Velva, squeezed some Pepsodent onto my toothbrush, and brushed my teeth. I wanted to get dressed and out of the dorm before anyone else awoke. I walked out of the bathroom and saw the Marlon Brando guy standing at the head of my bunk. He was dressed, had his gym bag in one hand, and had his other hand by my pillow.

"Hey, get away from there," I said.

He turned, looked at me, and then started for the door. My wallet was in his right hand. I dropped my shaving kit, ran, and grabbed his shoulder. He spun around, hitting me in the head with his gym bag and pushing me back. I fell over an empty bunk, my head hitting the floor and my feet pointing to the ceiling. All I could think of was kissing my money good-bye.

I got up in time to see Jack kick the guy in the nuts and follow with an uppercut that put the tall man on the floor.

"Hey, buddy, don't fuck with my friends." Jack was a welcome sight, wearing just his boxer shorts, his fists clenched, and towering over the downed man. It looked like a scene from an old photo of bare-knuckle fighters. Jack picked up the gym bag, walked out to the stairs, and tossed it over the railing. He came back in the room and pulled the guy up by his short, curly red hair. Jack pushed him through the doorway and said, "Get the fuck outta here." He walked back into the room, picked up my wallet, and tossed it to me.

"You need to take better care of this, Delaney."

"Thanks, Jack. Man, I can't believe that just happened."

"Yeah, well, this place is full of thieves."

"No, I mean I can't believe you just kicked the shit outta that guy and got my money back. I really owe you, big time. The little bit of cash in this wallet is all I have."

"Don't worry about it. All in a day's work." Jack's wide grin told me he thrived on this kind of cowboy stuff. I knew then that we were as different as cats and dogs. I could usually talk my way out of problems. Jack, no doubt, just fought his way out. His confident air told me he usually won his fights.

The others never got out of their beds. They were propped up on their elbows with a relaxed posture that made them appear to be resting on chaise lounges, watching television. Goofy Jimmy and bleached-blond Bob were wide eyed and open mouthed, while Nick acted as though he'd seen this movie before.

"Jack, man, come on. It's too early for this shit," Nick said as he rolled over on his side to go back to sleep.

Jack walked over to Nick's bunk and put his foot on Nick's butt and, with a push, rolled him onto the floor. Nick got up laughing and said, "All right, asshole," as he tossed his pillow at Jack.

"Delaney, have breakfast with us."

"I'd like to, Jack, but I gotta find a job."

"Come on, man, ya gotta eat."

How could I say no? I had planned on eating alone, but I was obligated to Jack. If he hadn't dropped the guy, all my money would have been gone. The consequences of that were beyond my imagination. In my best conjuring, the only outcome I could see was begging for nickels and dimes.

The boys didn't do much in the way of cleaning themselves up. Nobody shaved, and Jack and Nick brushed their teeth. Bob and Jimmy did nothing more than put on the same clothes they wore the previous day. On the way out, we gathered up Susan. I watched as Jimmy greeted her with a long kiss, and I wondered what she thought of his morning breath.

Jack led the six of us to the corner of First Street and Philadelphia, not far from Millie's, to a place called Melvin's Restaurant. A large white sign in the window offered a bacon and egg breakfast for ninety-nine cents. At this time of year, the restaurant catered to locals. Waitresses in pink uniforms hustled from table to booth, refilling coffee and taking orders on little notepads. The faux Tiffany overhead lights were out of place with the knotty pine walls and the red-checked pattern on the curtains and vinyl tablecloths, but the smell of bacon and fresh coffee stoked my appetite. I was starving.

There were just two four-tops open, one near the front door and the other further back, close to the kitchen. Jack directed Bob, Jimmy, and Susan to take the table by the door. Then he led Nick and me to the table in the back. We sat down, and a pink uniform with a pot of coffee appeared as if by magic. "Coffee?" asked the waitress. She doled out menus, poured the coffee, and disappeared. I added cream to my coffee while Jack and Nick read their menus. After I counted my pennies, the ninety-nine-cent breakfast special was all I needed to know about the menu.

Our waitress came back to our table. I noticed her nametag said Harriet. She was short, and the pink, single-piece uniform she wore hid any concept of her body. A little cap with two pointy ends sat atop her dark blonde hair, which was tight with curls, and made it look like she was wearing a football helmet.

Her glasses had black plastic frames with batlike wings and small, thick lenses.

"Hi, hon, wha'ya havin'?"

"The bacon and egg special for ninety-nine cents," I replied.

"Ya know that comes with only one egg, hon?" Her jaw was moving a mile a minute as she chomped on gum.

"Ah, how much for two eggs?"

"That costs another quarter."

"OK, two eggs."

"How you want 'em cooked, hon?"

"Over medium."

"Right." She scribbled the order on her notepad. "How 'bout you, hon? What ya want?" She was talking to Jack.

He offered his best toothy smile and said, "Hi, Harriet," as if she were some long-lost friend. "How are you?"

"Fine, hon. Know what ya havin'?"

"No, I'm not sure," he said slowly. "You have any recommendations?"

"No, everything's good. Everything on the menu is good. Whatever you want is good."

"How are your pancakes?"

"Pancakes," she said and started writing on her notepad.

"Wait a minute. I don't know if that's what I want. Are they good? Is the griddle hot? Pancakes aren't any good unless they're made on a really hot griddle."

"Our griddle's burnin' up, hotter than hell's fire. I'll bring you the cakes. You'll love 'em." Without waiting for agreement from Jack, she moved on to Nick. "How 'bout you, hon? What ya want?" Nick quickly ordered a Western omelet, and then Harriet vanished.

"She's awfully grouchy for someone as young as she is. What do you think, eighteen?" Jack asked.

"Jack, old buddy, she's grouchy because of people like you jerking her around," said Nick.

"What if I don't like my pancakes?"

"Jack, you wouldn't dare."

"Yes, he would, Delaney. You don't know this guy."

Noise filled the busy restaurant—the clatter of dishes and silverware, the drone of voices with just a word or two from an indecipherable conversation, a sneeze, a cough, the ringing bell and slamming drawer of the cash register. Nick studied his coffee as if he needed to describe the shade of brown in his cup, his index finger drawing invisible circles on the placemat. Our food came, and Jack ate his pancakes without protest. When we finished eating, Nick pulled out a cigarette from a Lucky Strike pack, and Jack sparked a Zippo, putting its fire to a Camel. Like a rehearsed dance, they inhaled deeply, then blew smoke to the ceiling, relaxed their shoulders, and returned to their coffee.

"Jack, Bob and me were talking about going back home today," said Nick.

"We just got here yesterday," relied Jack.

"We can't score here. The place is dead, Jack. We can come back after Memorial Day. There'll be more going on, more people, better chances."

"Let's give it a couple more days."

Harriet appeared, slapped down individual checks on the table, and said, "Pay the cashier in the front."

"Thank you, Harriet," said Jack as he snatched my check before I could pick it up. "I got this, Delaney."

"Jack, no, man. I should be paying for yours."

"Don't worry about it. I'm flush with cash right now." Jack paid the cashier, and we went out to the street, where we were joined by the other three.

"Let's go to the beach, Delaney. Come on with us."

"No, Jack, I gotta get a job. I'm not flush with cash, as you would say." I held my hand out to shake his, and he took it. We both gave a firm grip, like long-time friends. "But thanks, anyway, and thanks for breakfast—and that other thing this morning. Thanks for that, too."

"No problem, Delaney. We'll see ya later." Jack looked me in the eyes and nodded as though we connected on some level of understanding. But the meaning of it was lost on me.

Chapter 4

May 12, 1964
A Day of Hard Labor

THIS WAS TURNING into my lucky day. Jack rescued my money and bought my breakfast, and the people at the state employment office got a job for me at a place called the Castle in the Sand Hotel. This was a beachfront hotel around 37th Street, beyond where the boardwalk ended. I hitched a ride and was there in no time.

The hotel appeared almost as a mirage. I immediately understood how it had gotten its name. It was designed like a castle, with a white square turret that stood six or seven stories tall, towering over the main building. Though remote, or perhaps *because* it was remote, the setting hinted of romance, which added to the hotel's beauty and conjured images of Moorish castles. The surrounding area consisted mostly of dunes, a few beach houses, and a couple of smaller motels further south. This was a family destination and far removed from the more raucous party atmosphere of Ocean City proper. I approached a tall man who was tending some ornamental shrubs near the front door. He wore a green, sleeveless T-shirt and Levi's. His arms and legs displayed well-defined muscles and thick, ropelike veins that popped from his forearms. He looked like a sailor with leathery skin, as if he had spent a lifetime in the sun.

"Excuse me, do you know where I can find Mr. Johnston?" I asked.

"You found 'im," he responded, his voice deep and gruff. "Reckon you'd be the boy from the employment office."

Gee, do I still look like a boy at twenty-one?, I wondered.

"Yeah, that would be me," I said.

He scanned me from head to toe and back to my head. Then he glanced away and shrugged his shoulders as though he didn't like what he saw. Mr. Johnston was an impressive figure for a man I guessed to be in his fifties. His hair was a gray crew cut with specks of black. His sharp, beaklike nose accented his cold blue eyes, reminding me of pictures of predatory birds.

"Well, come with me," he said with a sigh.

His attitude gave me the feeling that he didn't think I could do the job, which made me more determined to prove him wrong. I wanted a job at this castle. There wasn't a cooler-looking place than this one. I followed him around to the ocean side of the hotel, where a coal shovel leaned against the wall. He picked it up and handed it to me.

"Want you to shovel all this sand outta here. Just get it off the patio areas and back onto the dunes. That'll be a start for today."

I looked down the length of the hotel, which appeared to be about two hundred feet. On top of each of the ground floor patios was two to three feet of sand—sand that winter storms had pushed from the dunes against the building, covering patios like snowdrifts. Some of the grains of windblown sand had pushed their way through tightly sealed sliding glass doors onto the carpeting of the ground floor rooms.

I began my work with great enthusiasm, hoping to impress Mr. Johnston and perhaps catch on for the summer as a desk clerk. The sun was well off the ocean but not yet at full strength, but the white walls of the hotel kicked light into my eyes, causing me to squint. I could see my shadow bending to the task. Grains of sand are tiny and light in your hand, but fill a shovel with them, and they get fairly heavy. Each load got heavier than the last. I tossed some sand as a strong gust of wind blew and tossed it back into my face. My mouth tasted the grains, and my teeth bit into the grit. As the hours wore on, the sun grew hotter, the wall and sand brighter. My pace slowed, and my arms, shoulders, and back screamed for me to stop. My mind wandered and thought about beautiful bodies lying on sandy beaches, little children filling buckets of sand, sand castles waiting for incoming tides to wash them away one grain at a time.

The day seemed endless. The sun was hot. I was hatless and shirtless, my body glistening with sweat. Every shovel of sand I tossed to the dunes found a gentle breeze that managed to flick a few grains back onto my now-sunburned face, chest, and back. Around noon, Mr. Johnston came back and seemed marginally satisfied with my progress.

"Time you knocked off for some lunch. There's a spread for you in the lobby. Just help yourself. You can wash up in the men's room."

The air conditioning was not turned on, which made the lobby warm and stuffy, but at least I was out of the sun. The water from the faucet was cool and refreshing on my blistered hands. When I looked in the mirror, my red nose reminded me of a drunken Irishman's. The "spread," as Mr. Johnston called it, was sitting on the registration desk and consisted of a package of baloney, half a loaf of Sunbeam bread, some sliced tomatoes, a jar of mayonnaise, and a jar of mustard.

My hands trembled from exhaustion as I spread the mayonnaise on the white bread. The blond-haired, blue-eyed Little Miss Sunbeam at the desk watched me eat four slices of baloney and two slices of tomato while I stared back at her.

I was sitting on the floor of the lobby, my back against a wall and my head on my knees, almost asleep, when the lobby door opened.

"Get enough to eat?"

"Yeah."

"Well, let's get back outside."

The rest of the day was a repeat of the morning's labor, only now the sun had moved to the west side of the building, stopping the wall's reflected glare and providing the relief of shade. It was getting close to four o'clock when I saw a green '57 Chevy coupe pull into the parking lot. A young guy, who looked to be about my age, got out and walked up to Mr. Johnston. I heard Mr. Johnston call him Matt. They smiled at each other and shook hands. Matt was tall and lean, with muscles. He wore a sleeveless T-shirt and cutoff jeans and work boots. When I saw the work boots and the greeting he got, I had a bad feeling.

A few minutes later, Mr. Johnston came up to me and said, "That'll be all. You can call it a day." He pulled some cash out of his pocket and handed me a ten-dollar bill. "Here you go. This is for today. I won't be needin' you no more after today."

The job wasn't even halfway finished. As much as I hated the hard work, I looked longingly at the sand piled on the remaining patios. "But don't you want me to finish the job?"

"No, don't need you. One of my regulars from last summer is here now. He'll finish the job."

I took the ten and gave him the shovel. Ten bucks for seven hours' labor, just a little more than the buck-twenty-five-an-hour minimum wage. He popped my balloon, but at least he was fair.

Sunburned, blistered hands, aching body, dirty and exhausted, I trudged across the parking lot, the day's heat rising off the macadam to greet me. Worse than the physical pain was the feeling of defeat and rejection and the demoralizing thought that I would have to start my job search all over again the next day.

Chapter 5

May 12, 1964
An Eventful Evening

"WOW, WHAT HAPPENED to you?" Jack asked. "You look like shit."

He was stretched out on his bunk, a Pabst Blue Ribbon beer in one hand and his dog-eared copy of *On The Road* in the other.

"Just another day at the beach, Jack." My grin belied the pain and depression I felt.

"You look like you could use one of these." He pulled a PBR from a cooler beside his bunk and tossed it to me. I pressed the ice-cold white can with the blue ribbon to the side of my face as I sat down on my bunk.

"Ahhh, this feels so good."

"Yeah, wait till ya drink it. Then you'll feel even better."

I got the church key and popped the can, chugged half of it, and looked around the room. Nick and Bob were on their bunks reading the *Baltimore Sun* and drinking their beer. Nick had the sports pages while Bob's face was in the comics.

"Where's Jimmy?"

"He and Susan are somewhere swapping spit," Jack said.

Jack asked about my day, and I gave him a short version of my labors at the Castle in the Sand—how I worked my ass off but got fired anyway. I finished off the beer, then grabbed a change of clothes and made for the shower. The hot water took its time to climb to the third floor, but that mattered little to me as the cold water flushed away the sandy, sweaty grit along with my body's heat. Finally, I felt refreshed and new again with a light buzz from the cold beer.

"Hey, Delaney, we're gonna go back to Melvin's for supper. They got a steak dinner for five bucks. Why don't you join us?"

"What the hell, why not? It's just half of my day's pay." The baloney sandwich just didn't cut it, and I figured a steak dinner could knock out my depression. Besides, one always sleeps better on a full stomach.

The six of us paraded over to Melvin's, where Harriet was our waitress again. She gave Jack a scowl when she asked for his order, and that seemed to put him in his place. The meal was uneventful, and we each paid our bill at the register and walked out into the twilight. To the west, the sun appeared as a ball of orange fire as it dipped into the tree line on the other side of the bay.

"Hey, guys, I've got to pick up some stuff for my blisters. I'll see you back at the dorm."

"No, man, we'll stay with you," Jack said.

I didn't argue, and they followed me to the next block. We saw a drugstore in the middle of the block on Philadelphia. "This place should have what I need."

"We'll wait here on the corner," Jack said.

I glanced back at them as I was about to enter the open doorway. It was a funny sight, the five of them loitering on the corner, smoking cigarettes and looking at their feet. A middle-aged, red-haired woman was tending the cash register by the door. She looked as if she were sucking on a lemon. She offered no greeting but kept reading a *True Romance* magazine while a cigarette hung from her lips. The only other customer was a mother with a little girl who looked about six years old. The drugstore was more like a general store that seemed to sell everything. T-shirts hung from the rafters, beach balls, children's sand shovels and buckets, fishing rods and reels—everything imaginable was for sale in the store. I wandered aimlessly up and down the narrow aisles. It was hard to find what I wanted among all the sundries. I came across work gloves and tried on a couple before finding the right fit. The gloves could come in handy on the next job. There were baseball caps—Senators and Orioles. I picked a Senators cap. I then found the Band-Aids and picked up a box. Before I got to the Coppertone, Jimmy and Susan came into the store, with Bob about ten seconds behind them. I was sorting through the sunscreens when I heard a crash.

"What was that?" the cashier yelled.

I looked up and saw Jimmy and Susan standing over a display of postcards that was now lying on the floor. They shouted, "I'm sorry! It was an accident!"

The cashier ran toward the fallen postcard display, saying, "It's OK. I'll get." As she did, Bob went to the register, hit a key, and grabbed the cash. The cashier heard the sound of the cash register opening and turned in time to see Bob run through the open door. Jimmy and Susan then bolted past the shocked cashier and followed Bob in a sprint down the street.

"Those bastards! I've been robbed! Somebody call the police!"

Then she realized she was the one who had to call the police. She went to the phone, dialed, and told the operator to send the cops. I walked up and dropped my merchandise on the counter.

"Can I pay for these, ma'am?"

"Did you see that?"

"Not much. I just heard the crash. I've got to get these Band-Aids to a friend. Can I pay you now?"

"I don't know if I got change."

"Well, let's just see what it comes to, OK?"

I just wanted to get out of there before the cops arrived. I'm a terrible liar, and I didn't want to have to answer any questions.

Her hands were shaking, but she punched the prices into the cash register. The mother and child scurried out while my sale was being rung up.

"Total's $7.23 with tax."

"Here." I laid out a ten. "Keep the change. You need it after what happened."

I heard the approaching siren and gathered up my purchases without waiting for her to bag them. My heart was racing as I walked north on Philadelphia, the flashing lights and piercing siren of the police car behind me.

Chapter 6

May 13, 1964
I Took the Money

I T WAS THE click of a lighter's strike that woke me. I kept my eyes closed, trying to guess the time as I heard someone exhale, then seconds later smelled the cigarette smoke as it floated over me. I opened my eyes to a vision of Jack in his boxer shorts, cigarette in his left hand, his right hand teasing the left nipple on his hairy chest. He belched, then looked at me.

"You're awake," he said in a soft voice.

The sun was up, but I could tell by the gray light in the room that it was early and the others were still sleeping.

"Barely."

Jack took a deep drag off his cigarette and blew smoke rings as he exhaled. I thought about the previous night. I had come straight back to the room after the great cash register robbery, never bothered to even try looking for Jack and the boys, and didn't want to be around them. It was a couple hours later when they came lumbering up the steps, giggling and laughing. Their booty was a case of beer, purchased with some of the stolen

31

money. They insisted I drink some of the beer. I drank two cans, and with every swig felt like an accomplice.

"Why'd you do that, Jack?"

"Do what?"

"You know what fucking what," I said, my voice just above a whisper.

"You mean stealing that cash? That was Bob, Jimmy, and Susan."

"Who are you kidding? Those dumbasses don't take a shit without checking with you first." Jack was inhaling as I spoke, and his laughing response to the comment made him cough out the smoke. When he finished choking, he just looked at me with a wide grin. With his pumpkin-shaped head and upturned smile, all I could think of was a jack-o'-lantern. It was not a comforting image.

I got out of bed and went to the bathroom, showered, and shaved. When I went back into the dorm, everyone was awake and either partially dressed or sitting up in bed. Jack and Nick were sitting across from each other on their bunks, talking with serious expressions. I opened my suitcase, pulled out some clean clothes, and dressed while they talked.

"I thought we were staying down here for the summer," Jack said, "let things cool off for a while back home."

"I know," said Nick. "It sounded like a good idea, but I think it's stupid. We don't know nothin' about this place, and we can't keep doin' shit like last night."

"I'm with Nick. I don't like it here, and livin' in this shithole is for the birds," said Bob.

"Really, Bob? You got it that much better in that trailer back in Frederick?" asked Jack. "How about you, Jimmy? Where do you stand on this?"

"I'm with you, Jack. Susan, too. The beach is cool, dude."

"How are you and Bob planning to get home?"

"What if you let us take the car?" suggested Nick.

"Oh, yeah?" challenged Jack.

"Hear me out," said Nick. "Bob and I take the car and deliver it to the chop shop in Baltimore, like we've done with the others. We can get Luke or somebody to come down to pick us up there."

"What about my share and Jimmy's?" asked Jack.

"I'll send it to you by Western Union."

My foot was propped up on the end of the bunk. I was watching Jack as I tied my shoe. He looked to Jimmy, then Bob, and back to Nick before he turned to me and said, "What do you think, Delaney?"

"Hey, man." I raised my hands with my palms open like a stickup victim. "This is none of my business."

"You're a good judge of character. I'm interested in your opinion."

"My opinion?" I looked at Jack, then at Nick, and then back to Jack. "They're your friends, Jack. Why wouldn't you trust them? I'd love to stay and talk some more, but I gotta find a job. I'll see you all later, or maybe I won't." Jack followed me out the door and down the stairs.

"Why'd you pull me into that, Jack?" I asked.

"I'm just jerking those guys around. I just wish that dumb-shit Jimmy and his skank Susan would go with them. I'm gonna give Nick the keys. He'll make sure I get my share. I just wanna clear the air about last night. We weren't trying to set you up or anything like that. We were just talking, and someone—I don't even remember who— came up with the idea. Before I knew it, they were headed for the store, and there was no stopping them."

"Really?" I asked skeptically.

"Honest to God's truth."

"Bullshit." I turned to walk away.

"Wait a minute. Here, take this." Jack held a ten-dollar bill in front of me.

"What for?"

"Just take it. You deserve it. We put you in a bad spot last night."

I looked at the ten in his hand and slowly reached out and took it. "Thanks."

"Good luck today. I'll see you tonight."

I walked away with the ten in my pocket, knowing that it came from the drugstore's cash register.

Chapter 7

May 13, 1964
Pyramid Photos

FINDING A JOB was my priority. My goal was to make enough money to be able to pay my own tuition and try to get back into Georgetown or some other school if Georgetown wouldn't take me back. But that was a long-term goal. My biggest concern right then was having enough money to pay the rent and eat. I decided to skip going to the state employment office and instead try to find something on my own. Shops and restaurants of all kinds lined the boardwalk and the streets. All of these places needed help for the summer, so I started going door to door, getting rejected at each one. It seemed like if I had been a white girl, I could have gotten a job as a waitress; if I had been a Negro woman, I could have been a cook; if I had been a Negro man, I could have been a dishwasher; but as a white man, it looked as if I could get a job only as a lifeguard or a cop, neither of which I had qualifications for.

As I walked along Somerset Street, a dark mood, fed by fatigue and hunger, flowed over me. Looking up, I saw a giant blue replica of a pyramid-shaped telescope hanging over a doorway. In the window and inside the office were blown-up pictures of smiling children, families, and couples, all of whom were either cute and cuddly or strikingly beautiful or handsome. There were no pictures of ugly people or fat people. There also weren't any pictures of groups of guys. A really big man, standing six-foot two-inches and weighing at least 260 pounds, completely baldheaded with a florid complexion and veiny, bulbous nose was behind the counter shuffling some papers. He was an intimidating presence.

"Hi," I said.

"Yeah?"

"I'm looking for work."

"Do you know anything about photography?" he asked.

He spoke with a booming voice. It was as if he were talking to someone across the street instead of someone standing in front of him.

"I can aim a camera and click it."

"Have you ever used an SLR camera?"

"I don't know what an SLR camera is."

"I guess then you don't know anything about aperture adjustments or film speed, either, do you?"

"No."

He was making me feel pretty stupid, and I was just about sure he was going to send me on my way out the door when he said, "No problem. Our cameras all have an autofocus feature, so any dummy can take a picture. But this is really a sales job more than a photography job. You need to convince tourists that the best way to capture and preserve memories of this wonderful day they are having at the beach is with a Pyramid photo. It's a memory of a lifetime. Sell them on it. Got it?"

"Yes, sir, I got it."

"I pay straight commission, so if you don't produce, you don't make any money. I'll give you a week to try it out, and if you don't like it, you can quit. If I don't like the job you're doing, I'll tell you to quit. I can start you today, but just one thing—it'll be slow for a couple of weeks. It won't pick up until after Memorial Day. That OK?"

"Sure, no problem." It's a job! I'd figure out a way to get by until Memorial Day, get an evening or night job if I needed to. At least this was a start.

"Here, fill this out. It's an employment application, that sort of paperwork. While you're doing that, I'll get you a camera and a Pyramid Photos T-shirt. Wear that while you're working. My name's George Devorak. Everyone calls me Mr. D. What'd you say your name was?"

"Thomas Delaney."

Mr. D came out of the back room with a camera in one hand and a blue T-shirt with white lettering in the other hand. He tossed me the T-shirt and then started my training.

"OK, Delaney, here's the camera. It's a Nikon F SLR. The SLR means it's a single-lens reflex camera. Basically that means what you see through the viewfinder is exactly what you capture on the film, unlike these Instamatic cameras that Kodak started selling last year. Those cameras are easy point and shoot. Loading the film is simple because the film is encased in a cartridge. But because the viewfinder and the film don't share the same optical path, what you see in the viewfinder is not really what will show up on the film. The SLR solves that problem. It's a trick with mirrors, but no point in going into those details. Here, look through the viewfinder and point it at the cash register. Line the cash register up with the circle you see in the viewfinder, then click the shutter release, and voila, there's your photo. I've put this on automatic focus so all you have to do is point and click. Don't mess with the focusing ring—that's this thing on the lens barrel—and don't touch the aperture setting, the indicators right here. To load the film, you open it this way, then take the film roll out of its canister, hook the lead on this spool, turn it to set it, then insert the film roll here. Close the back of the camera and listen for it to snap. Then advance the film until you see the number one in the exposure counter window. Then you're ready to go. Got it?"

"Yes, sir."

"One other thing: be careful with the film, especially when removing it from the camera. If you expose the film to sunlight, you'll ruin every photo you've taken. Here, I'll show you how to remove the film and return it to its canister without ruining it."

Mr. D proceeded to show me how to remove the film, and then he gave me more instructions on important administrative functions of the job, such as writing the customer's name on my customer pad—basically a small notepad—recording the time taken and, most important, the canister number and exposure number. Then he explained how to write the same information on a card that had the office address on it so when the customers got to the shop, they could easily be matched up with their photos.

"All right, now, the important part. When you're on the beach, look first for families with a small child or children. They're the most likely to buy. They know time goes fast, and before they know it, the kids will be grown and gone, so they want memories. Always remember that is what you're selling—a memory, not just a picture. Also look for young couples who might be dating or newlyweds.

"When you approach people, don't start by asking if they want a photo; start off by complimenting them. For instance, if the kid is building a sand castle, you could say something like, 'Hey, that's a great looking castle. It would make a great picture with your son showing off his engineering skills.' Or if it's a couple, you could say, 'Wow, you two look like you should be on a magazine cover. Mind if I take a photo?' Always direct your pitch to the woman. Women are the ones who think about memories. Guys don't give a shit—they just live in the moment. And you can forget about older married couples. They've seen enough of each other and don't need a souvenir of the moment. Same thing for single guys or groups of guys—they don't buy nothin' but beer with their money. That changes if you see a couple of fags. They're just like a guy and girl couple and they might buy one, but don't let that be your priority.

"All right, it's after one o'clock. Get out on the beach and see what you can do, but get back here by four. Tell your customers, if you get any, to come by between five and eight tonight for their Pyramids, or they can come by tomorrow."

I left with the instructions swirling in my head and made for the beach. My enthusiasm fell through the cracks in the boardwalk when I saw the nearly empty stretches of sand. There were people on the beach, but few, and they seemed to be seated a hundred yards apart. I trudged and handled one rejection after another until I approached two girls. One was in the usual sun worshipper position, flat on her back, while the other sat with her arms around her knees and seemed to be hiding from the sun under a broad straw hat and a white flower-patterned muumuu.

"Hi, you two look like you're enjoying yourselves. Would you like some memories to take home with you?"

"Oh I think I'll have plenty of memories to take home. Hey, don't I know you?"

"This one of your friends, Misty?" The sun-worshipper's voice was grating and sounded like the squawk of a parrot.

"Misty! Yeah, we met a couple of nights ago on the boardwalk. You even said we'd meet again. If I remember right, you said something like it was written in the stars."

"Oh, yeah...I remember." She looked to her sun-worshipping friend. "That was when I went for that walk." They giggled at each other as if the walk was some sort of private joke. I kept talking about getting a Pyramid photo, and they finally agreed. Misty's friend had light brown hair that might have passed for blond in some circumstances. Instead of a bathing suit, she wore very short cutoffs and a halter top that showed off her ample breasts. Her face, while pretty, reflected a hardness. I learned her name was Sylvia. She seemed more enthusiastic about posing for the photos than Misty and scooted next to her, placing her arm around Misty's shoulder.

"Misty, would you remove your hat and sunglasses?" I asked. She removed her hat, and her black hair fell to her shoulders like silk threads. I wanted to touch it and run the strands through

39

my fingers, hold it next to my face and smell its fragrance. "And your sunglasses." She removed the sunglasses and revealed an expression of tolerance, as if indulging a child. I posed them and took photos from different angles. "Great. That should do it."

"No, wait, one more," Sylvia said. "Take this one." With that, she turned Misty's head and kissed her on the lips." I snapped two quick shots before they fell away from each other with laughter.

"That one should be a winner," I said.

I told them where to pick up the photo but doubted that I'd make a sale. It felt like they were just playing with me. I moved on and got a couple to pose. I found that Mr. D was right about making the pitch to the woman. Another couple wanted a picture of their six-year-old son playing in the sand. Things seemed to be picking up.

"Hey, Mr. Photographer," came a shout from the boardwalk. When I looked, there was Jack and the gang. They hopped off the boards and came across the sand toward me.

"Nick—Bob—I thought you two were leaving."

"We are in a couple of hours. Just wanted to get in some beach time before we left," said Nick.

"Looks like you got a job," Jack said. "Hey, Delaney, take some pictures of the gang before we split up."

Jack took control of the posing, first a group photo of all five, then just the guys, then Nick and Bob together, and then Jimmy and Susan. Finally he insisted on individual photos of each person. I didn't think they would buy any—maybe Jimmy and Susan but not the others—and worried about Mr. D getting upset that I wasted film. Finally we finished the photo session and said our goodbyes. The rest of the day went pretty fast, and I turned in the camera and film before the four o'clock deadline. Mr. D seemed surprised by the number of pictures I'd taken. I just hoped some of them would sell so he wouldn't fire me for wasting film on Jack and the gang.

Chapter 8

May 13, 1964
Evening
Cowabunga's

I WAS LYING ON my bunk, reading *Live and Let Die*, a James Bond novel by Ian Fleming, when Jack walked into the dorm. He tossed six blue Pyramid telescopes on my chest.

"You ever see your handiwork?"

"No, these are the first ones." I picked one, held it up to the light, and looked into the small end. "Hey, this is good of Nick. What'd you do, buy every shot I took?"

"Yeah, I wanted you to get off to a good start with the new job."

"Jack...well, all I can say is thanks, man. Nick and Bob leave?"

"Yeah."

"What about Jimmy and Susan?"

"I don't know. I ditched them, but they're still in town if that's what you mean. Hey, I found this really cool locals bar just a couple blocks from here. Let's go hang out there for a while. Draft beer's only a quarter."

Millie's was on St. Louis Avenue, between Second and Third Streets. We walked south on St. Louis until we reached the bridge, where we had to do a zigzag to go under it, then through a parking lot to Talbot Street. We turned toward the bay, and I saw the bar's sign, "Cowabunga's" written in neon script atop a neon-shaped wave. As we walked to the door, Jack said, "It's a really cool place with a surfer theme, but I don't get the name. Wasn't that something from the Howdy Doody show?"

"Yeah, Jack, but it's a surfer phrase now. It means...like, wow."

We went through the door, and my eyes lit up in amazement. To say it had a surfer theme would be an understatement. Cowabunga's was a heavy-duty surfer bar. The walls were filled with posters of Duke Kahanamoku, Miki Dora, Phil Edwards, and Nat Young, along with photos of big wave action at the Pipeline, Waimea Bay, and Sunset Beach. And the music was unlike anything I'd heard in Ocean City. Just as we walked in, Jørgen Ingmann's version of "Apache" was beginning, the staccato drumbeat picked up by Ingmann's twanging guitar. Half-naked people dancing, laughing, screaming—it was loud, it was rockin', it was hellacious. Jack looked at me with a big grin. We knew we'd found a home.

We grabbed two empty stools at the end of the bar and ordered two drafts as Ingmann's guitar riff mellowed down. No sooner did it end than the driving beat of Dick Dale's left-handed guitar playing on his Stratocaster fired off with "Misirlou," and then the place really went crazy. Jack and I just looked at each other and smiled.

We got to know the owner, Butch, who also tended bar—a bald ex-Marine with the USMC's globe-and-anchor tattoos on his Popeye-like forearms. He wore a black wifebeater undershirt to show off his biceps. Butch's two waitresses, Betty the blond and Charlene the brunette, both worked their butts off, and it showed as they carried the look of worn-out waitresses everywhere: slumped shoulders, hair in their eyes, and downturned mouths. Russell was the cook. Beads of sweat glistened like sparklers on his black forehead as he popped his head through the window between the kitchen and bar and shouted to Betty and Charlene when their orders were ready. Goldie was the lowest on the Cowabunga food chain: combination dishwasher, busboy, and general grunt. He took orders from everyone. When he wasn't washing dishes, Butch was telling him to clean the restrooms, or Betty or Charlene would tell him to bus this table or that table, or Russell would yell for him to empty the grease from the fryer. If someone spilled a drink, Goldie mopped it up. If someone puked, Goldie got the cleanup job. He was tall—I guessed six-foot two-inches—but his hair fanned out from his head and made him appear six inches taller. The hair also accentuated his gaunt look, as did his sunken eyes, prominent cheekbones, and protruding teeth. He reminded me of photos of starving African children.

Jack started talking about Kerouac's *On the Road* and how cool it would be if he and I took to the road together. He rambled on, talking over the music, about going south after Labor Day. His idea was to get jobs in Miami, hang out on Miami Beach until February, then go to New Orleans for Mardi Gras. I considered it his pipedream and nothing more than beer talking.

We drank until last call at 1:45. By that time, the crowd had thinned out, and things were calming down. As we finished our last round, I noticed two girls by themselves sitting in a booth. One wore a sleeveless muumuu with a white and black flower pattern. She had jet-black hair in a Prince Valiant style, with bangs that touched her dark eyebrows and black eye shadow that made it look like someone had punched her in the eyes. In addition to the large gold necklace that featured zodiac symbols, she also wore several bracelets with different zodiac signs and rings on every finger. I realized it was Misty, but she looked so different with the heavy eye makeup and jewelry. Sylvia was easier to recognize with her brown hair in a ponytail, a sleeveless blouse that brought attention to her large breasts, and a very short, tight skirt that showed off nice legs. Misty seemed to hide her body, drawing attention only with small accents, while Sylvia treated her body as an exhibition.

"Hey, Butch, who are those two?" Jack asked.

"Those two chicks over there?"

"Yeah."

"They're whores."

"What? Really?" I said.

"The one in the muumuu looks like a freak. Why do you wear a muumuu if you're trying to get dudes to pay to have sex with you?" said Jack.

"I don't know, but that one thinks she's some sort of witch or something," Butch responded. "Thinks she can tell the future. Wanted to know my birth date so she could make some sort of chart. Told her I don't need that shit—I make my own future. I made a deal with them: they can hang out here, but they can't solicit. I'm not losing my liquor license for running a whorehouse, so don't you two get any ideas about propositioning them."

"Don't worry, Butch. We don't have to pay for sex," Jack said.

With that, we settled our tab and called it a night. We walked back the same route we came. I couldn't get over the thought of Misty and Sylvia being whores. We were under the bridge when Jack said, "I've been thinking—those whores need pimps."

"What?"

"You know, pimps."

"Yeah...and?"

"They need a couple guys like you and me."

I shrugged off his comments. He was half blitzed. It was just his beer talking.

Chapter 9

May 14, 1964
The Sands Hotel

"THERE HE IS—MY newest super salesman!" Mr. D was beaming when I walked through the doors of Pyramid Photos.

"What?"

"Delaney, every photo you took sold, even the one with the two lesbians. How'd you get that one, anyway?"

"Lesbians?"

"Yeah, here's the proof on that shot." He showed me the proof of Misty and Sylvia kissing. I couldn't help but smile.

"They came in and bought that one? Of them kissing each other?" My head was spinning. When they posed for the kiss, I didn't think anything of it, just playfulness. But then I found out they were prostitutes. And all that time I thought Misty was interested in me. Well, I guess she was in a financial way. I never thought of them as lesbians, but who knows?

"Yeah, even the one with the group of guys with the girl. One of the guys came in and bought every photo of that group. I told you not to waste time with groups of guys, but maybe you can teach me a thing or two. Just don't know how you did it."

In spite of the good start with Pyramid Photos, it was still a part-time job. The pay would cover my rent and food, but there would be nothing left over at the end of the season. I was going to need another job if I wanted to have money for tuition in the fall. I had already stopped at the state employment office and picked up a lead on a desk clerk job at a small, older hotel up on Fourteenth Street. After I picked up my camera from Mr. D, I headed straight for the hotel. I thought it was ironic that the hotel was called The Sands. The fact that sand was once again in the name made me a little nervous, but the desk clerk job seemed more in line with my capabilities.

The hotel owners, George and June Closterman, were a friendly, down-to-earth couple. George was round in every way. He was about five-feet eight-inches with a very round head, face, and body, and with short brown hair and a bald spot on his crown. If he had had a white beard, you would have thought he was Santa. He even smiled. But the khakis and Hawaiian shirt would have been out of place on Santa. June was thin and slightly taller than George. She had the disappointed look of a housewife who had come to realize this was as good as it would ever get. There was no need for her to wear makeup anymore, so she didn't. She wore shorts, showing off skinny legs and knobby knees, and she tied her flowered blouse in a knot, exposing her midriff.

The Sands Hotel was nothing special. It was an older hotel with three levels, only the second and third levels having rooms. There were no elevators or bellhop services. Guests would need to struggle with their luggage up a narrow stairway to their floor and down a hallway to find their room. The ground floor consisted of only a small lobby and the Clostermans' living quarters. The Alibi Lounge, a dive bar that was not associated with the Sands except to share the building, took up the remainder of the ground floor. The Safari Motel stood between the boardwalk and The Sands, and as a result, none of The Sands' rooms had an ocean view. Those deficiencies didn't matter to me when the Clostermans offered me the job at $45 a week, including a room shared with the other two desk clerks.

"The seven to three shift is taken," Mr. Closterman said. "That goes to a retired man named Sam Sparks who has worked for me the past two years. You can have either three to eleven or eleven to seven."

"I'll take three to eleven." That shift would give me both time during peak beach hours for Pyramid Photos and party time late after my shift ended.

"The only hitch is we're is not yet ready for guests, and we don't have anyone booked until next weekend. But you know what? You could still work here doing some manual labor if you want. I got some stuff that needs to be done. It's waxing the floors. You could move into the room now and start working on the floors. Interested?"

"Sure, I'll do it." After shoveling sand, how bad could it be? "Do you mind if I do that work after four o'clock? My job with Pyramid Photos is over by then."

"That'll be OK. I'll pay you $1.25 an hour. Just make sure the waxing is finished before next Friday."

This was great. Not only did I have two jobs but a free room on top of it all. I was counting my money in my head and figuring out how much could be saved by the end of the summer. My goal would be to save my pay from The Sands—$45 times twelve weeks would add up to over $500. Plus, I wouldn't need to spend all my Pyramid Photo money on food. Add that in and I could go back to D.C. with over $600.

After the Sands interview, I went back to the beach to sell photos. It was a slow day. By three o'clock, I'd gotten only a half dozen photos of couples or families. I turned in the film with the camera to Mr. D and then headed to Millie's to pack up and move to The Sands. As I climbed the stairs, I saw that Jack was perched in a precarious position—sitting on the railing at the top of the steps, a cigarette in one hand and a bottle of PBR in the other.

"Jack, what the hell are you doing? Aren't you afraid you'll fall?"

"How'd things go today, Mr. Photographer?"

"Good news and bad news. Things were slow on the beach with the photos, but the good news is I've got a second job, and it includes a room. I gotta get to the new job right now." Jack followed me into the dorm and watched me pack my stuff as I told him about the floor waxing and desk clerk job. His expression didn't change much. He didn't seem happy for me as I thought he would be.

"I was hoping we could go back to Cowabunga's tonight."

"We still can, but I probably can't get there until ten or so."

Chapter 10

May 14, 1964
Evening
Misty and Sylvia

"**P**IPELINE" BY THE Chantays blasted from the speakers, and the dance floor was packed. I told Jack I'd meet him at Cowabunga's around ten, but I didn't see him at the bar. My eyes scanned the booths and found him sitting with Misty and Sylvia. Unbelievable, but at the same time typical of Jack. Something only he would do. I weaved through the dancers and walked up to the booth.

"Hey, what's up?"

"Hey, Delaney, let me introduce you to my new friends. This is Misty and Sylvia. Girls, this is Delaney."

"Yeah, well, actually we've already met, haven't we?" I said as I sat down. Jack was sitting next to Misty. I took the open seat next to Sylvia but didn't put my legs under the table. Instead I sat half in and half out of the booth. When people looked at me, they couldn't tell if I was coming or going. The girls just nodded and smiled—or maybe it was a grimace. Sylvia tapped her index finger on the tabletop like a woodpecker pounding a tree while Misty appeared bored and irritated. Charlene came by.

"I'll have a Miller High Life," I said.

"Bring me another National Boh, Charlene," Jack ordered. Turning back to us, he said, "What are you talking about? You all have met before? When'd I miss that?"

"Pyramid Photos. I took their picture," I said. "I saw the one you girls bought. Very nice." They both looked at me and sneered without comment. The girls' drinks looked like daiquiris and were half empty.

"Delaney, I was tellin' Misty and Sylvia about our plans to go to Miami and tryin' to get them to go with us."

"You two should leave tonight," Misty said. "You know, get a head start on everything. You should go right now. I'll even pick up your bar tab if you leave now."

This was not the same Misty I'd been talking to. The makeup and jewelry seemed to change her personality, or maybe it was something Jack had said or done before I arrived. She was not smiling. She was wishing us out of their lives that instant. But after finding out they were whores, my attitude toward them changed also. Jack ignored her comment and continued to ramble on about the money we could make in Miami and New Orleans if the four of us worked as a team. The word "pimp" was never mentioned, but it seemed like that was his point.

My eyes went to a rip in the vinyl booth behind Jack's head and focused on a dirty piece of cotton sticking out that exposed the plywood backing. In my mind were two thoughts: 1) there was no way I was going to go to Miami with Jack, and 2) I wanted as little to do with the whores as they wanted to do with us. When I had first met Misty, I liked her and thought she was interested in me. But after learning about who and what she was, I wasn't going to get involved with a prostitute. As Jack's voice droned on, I was lost in my own world. I looked up to see that Misty was staring at me. The black eye shadow, eyeliner, and long lashes with dark eyebrows acted as a magnet to draw my attention to her hazel eyes. Her eyes were cold but held a promise of pleasure beyond knowledge, of a world one would never want to leave. Her thin, straight nose pointed to full lips covered with lipstick that looked like it was made from maraschino cherries, accentuated by skin white as marble. I couldn't feel myself breathe. It was as though she had hypnotized me. Her lips were moving as if in slow motion. What was she saying?

"What?" Misty said.

"What?" Jack said.

"What?" I asked.

"You people are crazy," Sylvia said.

"What are you talking about?" I asked.

"You were staring at me, Delaney. Do I look funny to you?"

"No, Misty, I don't think you look funny, and I wasn't staring at you. You were staring at me."

"Why would I stare at you?"

"Hey, hey, what's this all about? We're havin' a nice pleasant conversation. No need to be arguin'," said Jack.

Misty blew smoke in Jack's face and said, "I'm not arguing, but your friend is staring at me like I'm a freak. Do you think I'm a freak, Delaney?" She raised her eyebrows as if to mimic my earlier gesture.

She wasn't a freak, but she was something, and I had no idea what. She had confused me the first night I met her, and I was even more confused now. Turning my legs in under the table as if confirming a decision to stay, I took a swig of my Miller's, looked into Misty's unfathomable eyes, and said in a very soft voice, "No, Misty, I don't think you're a freak. You're very attractive. In fact...you're stunning."

Suddenly Sylvia stopped her tapping, came to life, and said, "Oh my, oh my....It sounds like you have an admirer, Misty."

"Come on, Sylvia, time to go home. Outta my way, Jack. We're leaving."

We stood up to get out of their way and watched them make for the door, Misty in her muumuu and Sylvia with her ass waving like a matador's cape.

"What the hell just happened? What was that all about?" Jack asked. "How well do you know those girls? Have you been holding out on me?"

"I don't know, Jack. The woman scares me. I swear she hypnotized me just now. It was like I was frozen. I couldn't move, couldn't think. What are you trying to do with them, anyway? Do you want to get laid?"

"No, man, we don't need them to get laid, but we could pimp for them and split the money. We could get 'em business they can't get for themselves. This could be the beginning of a whole new life for us, Delaney."

Goldie came by to clear off our table. He picked up Jack's National Boh, and Jack grabbed it back.

"Hey, what the fuck you think you're doin', man?" said Jack.

"Whoa, man. It's last call, and I thought you was done, that's all," said Goldie.

"It's last call to order, dumbass. I'm allowed to finish my beer."

"You don't need to go callin' me no dumbass, I jus'..."

"I'll call you whatever the fuck I wanna call you..."

"Jack, be cool, man." I tried to defuse the situation. "It was just a mistake. Goldie, it's OK. Go on, man."

Goldie started walking away but kept staring at Jack, with Jack staring right back. Then Goldie said, "It's not OK you callin' me a dumbass."

"Yeah, how 'bout I call you a dumb nigger?"

I jumped up. "Jack, shut your mouth. Goldie, ignore him. He's the dumbass."

I was now standing in front of Goldie, Jack still sitting in the booth with his smirk. I leaned into Goldie's face and said, "Ignore the motherfucker. Goldie, don't get yourself fired because of him. He's not worth it."

Goldie got real cool, stepped back, and said to me, "OK, Delaney, but that motherfucker's gonna be sorry he ever said that to me." He turned his back to Jack and walked to the kitchen.

"What the fuck's the matter with you, Jack?"

"He pissed me off takin' my beer like he manages the place. He's just the fuckin' busboy or dishwasher. He fucks with me again, I'll snap his skinny neck like a twig."

I could picture Jack doing that. The fight would be as fair as a bear fighting a giraffe.

"Jack, why do you wanna mess with that poor kid? He has the worst job in Ocean City. Well, maybe a garbage collector has it worse..."

"He tried to take my beer. I don't let nobody do that until I'm finished."

"Jack, it's not about the beer, is it? It's about Misty and Sylvia walking out the way they did."

"What are you now, Delaney, my shrink?"

"Come on, Jack. Let's split. Butch is closing down. I hope he didn't see this shit. If he did, he'll probably ban us."

Chapter 11

May 15, 1964
Wendy

JACK CALLED TO tell me he had gotten hired as the bell captain at the Majestica Atlantica Hotel, and he was starting that night. An important duty for the bellhops at this ancient queen of all the Ocean City hotels was the night fire watch. As Jack explained it, this required taking a type of clock device on a sweep of the hotel every hour. At a number of stations throughout the hotel, there were keys that somehow fit into this clock. This would confirm that someone was going through the hotel and making sure there were no fires or other problems. His first night on the job would be to learn the procedure and then train new bellhops. All, including Jack, would work a rotating shift.

After finishing my floor-waxing chore at the Sands, I cleaned up and went out for supper. I grabbed a burger at the Alaska Stand at Ninth Street and the boardwalk and continued walking south. There was a sock hop at the Ocean City Pier Ballroom. I climbed the stairs and paid the quarter admission. The interior of the ballroom reminded me of a high school gym with hard-wood floors and a high ceiling with rafters. A giant mirrored ball was rotating from the ceiling, reflecting flashes of light around the semi-dark room. A DJ played Mary Wells' "My Guy," and about twenty couples were dancing. I never understood why they called it a sock hop. People always had their shoes on at every one of these things I'd ever been to. The room was about half filled with people who appeared between their mid-teens and mid-twenties. The next song was the up-tempo tune "Love Me Do" by the Beatles, which drew out more dancers. Three girls were standing at the far end of the room along the wall. One stood out more than the other two. She had blond hair that just touched her shoulders with bangs that fell midway on her forehead. I couldn't tell you what the other two girls looked like—she was a stone fox, and she had my full attention. As I started to walk in her direction, the Beatles song finished, and the DJ started playing "Surfer Girl" by the Beach Boys. Two guys approached her friends for a dance, leaving my blond standing alone. Perfect.

"Wanna dance?"

"Sure," she said, stepping into my arms.

She wore a white sleeveless shell, madras shorts with boat shoes and no socks. Her only jewelry was a gold pin in the shape of a circle that was pinned above her heart. A healthy tan contrasted with her white teeth and very blond hair, and her small nose turned up at the tip like a miniature ski jump. Her high cheekbones and pointed chin created a heart-shaped face. As we danced, her hair brushed against my face and tickled my nose. I smelled peaches. She had to have weighed less than a hundred and have been no taller than five-feet one-or-two-inches. I felt as if I were dancing with a bird.

As we moved to the Beach Boys' harmony I asked, "So are you a 'surfer girl'?"

"Yes, actually, I am."

"I thought surfing was mostly a guy thing."

"It pretty much is. For every one chick there are probably fifteen to twenty dudes."

"So do you have a surfer boyfriend? Sounds like women have a lot to choose from."

"Most of the surfers think they're really hip, but they're not. They're flakes, and I'm just not into them. They think they can drop in on me because I'm a chick."

"What do you mean? Do they go to your home?"

She laughed. "No...no....You're not a surfer, are you?"

"No, but I'd like to get a board and learn."

"Well, then, you need to learn the language. Right now, you're just a hodad, a nonsurfer that just hangs out on the beach. When you do start to surf, you'll be a gremmie because you won't be able to surf very well. And it's not a board—it's a stick. And 'drop-in' means a dude who gets on my wave after I'm already on it. So I really don't care for most of the dudes that surf. Besides, there are lots of chicks around. They're called beach bunnies if they don't surf. You see them sitting on the beach while the dudes are surfing. They're either dating one of the dudes or they want to date one." Her voice was soft and feminine with a lyrical rhythm. I could have listened to her talk all night.

"My name's Tom Delaney, but everyone calls me Delaney. What's your name?"

"Wendy Morrison."

The Beach Boys song was winding down, but I wanted to keep dancing and talking to Wendy. The DJ started playing "The Stroll" by the Diamonds. Not good for talking but a fun dance, so I said, "Let's stroll," and we did. As we started to walk off the dance floor, the Drifters started singing "This Magic Moment." We looked at each other and simultaneously said, "Cha-cha?" We danced the cha-cha to the Drifters, and when the song finished playing, Wendy was laughing and smiling. We left the dance floor holding hands, went outside, and walked to the edge of pier. There was no moon yet, and the sky was filled with more stars than I'd ever seen. We looked to the horizon where stars vanished into the black sea. We listened to the music from the ballroom as it blended with the crash of the surf against the pilings of the pier.

"Are you still in school?" I asked.

"No, I just graduated high school. I've been accepted at Hood College. I'll major in French and Spanish. I want to be an interpreter at the UN. What about you?"

She tilted her head and fingered a strand of hair, smiling while I gave her my story of Georgetown and my current jobs.

"When do you do your surfing?"

"I work part-time in my daddy's law office. so I don't get to surf every day. Usually Tuesdays and Thursdays—and weekends, of course."

"Where do you surf? I've never seen anyone surfing in this area. You don't try to 'shoot the pier,' do you?"

"Yeah, 'shoot the pier'—that stuff is fiction. Only dudes wanting to commit suicide do that. No, you can't surf here."

"Too many people?"

"Yeah, I mainly surf on Assateague Island."

"Where's that?"

"You've never been to Assateague? Oh, it's really cherry. It's a barrier island that's a national park. There's no development allowed—no hotels, no houses, almost no tourists—just some campers and a few people surf fishing. Oh, and of course, the ponies."

"Ponies?"

"What? You mean you've never read *Misty of Chincoteague*?" She laughed.

"I assume that wasn't written by Chaucer."

Laughing again, she said, "Noooo, there are wild ponies on the islands. Chincoteague is the island south of Assateague, and these ponies run wild on both islands. It's really cool to see them just roaming free like nature intended."

"So you go surfing on this island of the wild ponies."

"Yeah. Well, here's another cool thing about Assateague: you need a four-wheel drive vehicle to go there, which helps keep out a lot of people. For my sixteenth birthday, Daddy bought me a Jeep so I could surf there."

From the ballroom, the Beatles were singing, "She loves you, yeah, yeah, yeah..." while Wendy was talking, and I thought, *Hope she does.* I took her hand in mine and said, "Let's dance some more." We walked hand in hand to the ballroom and danced every dance.

"I've had fun, Delaney. Seems funny calling you by your last name and not Tom or Tommy. But I have to go. I have a forty-five-minute drive, and my parents don't like it when I'm on the road late at night."

"I'll walk you to your Jeep." We held hands as we walked to her car.

"Can I see you again? I'd like for you to teach me to surf."

"Yeah, that would be fun. I've never taught a dude to surf before. I'll call you. How can I reach you?" she asked as we reached the topless Jeep.

We were holding hands when she turned to face me. Putting my arm around her, pulling her toward me, and kissing her felt like the most natural thing I'd ever done. Her full lips were moist, soft, and welcoming. She pulled back, climbed into the driver's seat, and asked again, "So how can I reach you?"

"Call The Sands Hotel. I don't even know the number, but it's in the book. Just ask for Delaney."

She started the Jeep and shifted into first gear. As I stepped back, she looked at me and smiled, saying, "I'll call you. It's been fun." Then she said, *"Bonsoir, mon amour,"* and drove off. I watched the glow of the red taillights fade into the night and wondered what her last words meant.

Chapter 12

May 16, 1964
In a Good Place

SLIVERS OF LIGHT pushed their way past the blinds to say morning had arrived. I was on my back staring at the ceiling, running those French words through my head and wondering if she really would call me. Why hadn't I gotten her number? She told me she lived in a little town called Princess Anne. It sounded like a made-up name. Wendy was in my head, and there was no getting her out. I got out of bed, showered, brushed my teeth, put on my surfer baggies—red with a white palm leaf pattern – and a white T-shirt, grabbed my sunglasses, and headed to Melvin's for breakfast.

The rough pattern of the boardwalk made itself rudely known to my tender bare feet. Splinters threatened, and protruding nails flashed a warning with their shiny heads. Walking in sand offered safety as the cool grains filled the gaps between my toes and massaged my arches. My feet sank slightly with each footfall and then sank deeper into the cooling relief as I pushed off for the next stride.

More businesses were taking down the plywood that pro-tected their closed stores during the off-season and were getting ready to reopen. The pedestrian traffic on the boardwalk was still light but heavy with sounds of workmen's saws and hammers. At Melvin's, I took a seat at a small table. Harriet came around to fill my coffee cup. She didn't seem to recognize me from my first visit with Jack and Nick. Her businesslike manner was unchanged—gum-chewing, efficient, and slightly curt.

"Pancakes, no butter, and a side of bacon."

"You got it."

I did get a big smile from her, showing off nice teeth with thin lips, something I didn't see the first time. Her smile was either flirting or just working for a tip; I couldn't tell. After fin-ishing breakfast, I left a quarter for Harriet and paid the sev-enty-five cent bill at the register.

I wandered about and found Bobby's Surf Shop at the corner of Worcester Street and Baltimore. Inside, the smells of Copper-tone, wax, and glue mingled together. New T-shirts and surfer baggies hung from racks while surfboards nine and ten feet long stood straight like giant sentries circled to protect the soft goods. The scene and scents made me think of Wendy, the little surfer girl. Was she really going to call? Was she serious about teaching me to surf? I looked at posters on the walls of beauti-ful models in bathing suits, and my memory told me Wendy was prettier than these girls. A tall guy in his mid-twenties came from the back of the shop. His bleached blond hair hung over his ears and curled up the back of his neck, but dark roots pushed up from his scalp. He wore a bright blue Hawaiian shirt with a floral pattern of red, orange, and yellow flowers over solid dark blue baggies. The shirt was unbuttoned and revealed a shell necklace on his chest. He had some kind of ropelike bracelet on his left wrist.

"Hey, dude, need any help?"

"Nah, just looking."

I admired a Bing surfboard. It was a redwood board sanded and stained light with a two-inch royal blue stripe, which ran from nose to tail. Between the blue stripes, a one-inch stripe of natural redwood ran the length of the board, with the outline of an eye intersecting all three stripes in the area where you put your back foot.

"You like that board?"

"Yeah, it's really cool looking."

"The eye in the center gives the board good karma. You don't have to worry about sharks attacking you with this one. Its only $120."

"That's three weeks' wages, man. It makes me a looker, not a buyer."

"That's a pooper, dude. Too bad."

Life—it always came down to money. The thought of money reminded me of Pyramid Photos. I decided to get an early start on the job and made my way to the shop.

"Here's your shirt and camera. Today should be your best day yet. Weekend warriors are in," Mr. D said.

"Weekend warriors?"

"Yeah, early birds coming in just for the weekend, before the holiday. They get in Friday night, hit the beach all day Saturday, and then leave sometime Sunday. So this should be your first big day, but next weekend will be even bigger. And then the following weekend is Memorial Day, and you'll go crazy taking pictures. That weekend will be a big money weekend."

I took the camera and headed out, dollar signs in my eyes. On the boardwalk at Wicomico, the Alaska Stand employees were doing their prep work. Hot dogs sliced in half sizzled on the grill, and hamburgers hissed as they were flipped. At Thrashers, the early crew dumped spuds into the peeling and cutting machine. The smell of hot peanut oil permeated the area along with the sound of gurgling as the first potatoes were dropped in the fryer. I stopped at Kohr's on Fourth and bought a frozen custard for a dime. The weekend warriors, as Mr. D called them, began to stroll the boardwalk, mostly couples, some with children, all with pasty white skin that announced they were tourists. I moved to the beach, looked for photo opportunities, and found Mr. D was right. I was having my most successful day. It seemed almost every couple or family wanted a Pyramid photo.

Morning passed to afternoon, and walking on the sandy beach from customer to customer offered a new challenge as the strengthened sun heated the grains of sand. I took a break, went to the shoreline, and felt the firm, ocean-cooled sand under my feet. Gulls hung in the sky and cried while killdeer scurried on the beach. The incoming tide rushed cold water and foam over my feet and then drew away and back out to sea. My feet sank into the softened sand, and the moving water created the illusion that I was moving sideways with the outgoing water. The illusion made me feel dizzy, but at the same time I was happy and knew that I was in a good place. Coming to Ocean City had been the right thing to do; this was where I was meant to be. I had two jobs, I was making money, and maybe, just maybe, I had a new, beautiful girlfriend.

It was a little after three o'clock, and I hadn't eaten since my pancake breakfast. The smell of food cooking on the boardwalk created a gnawing in my stomach. I decided to get a quick bite to eat, turn in the camera, and then get back to The Sands to wax the floors. I'd just sat down at the counter of Ponzetti's Pizza when I heard someone call my name. It was Jack.

"Hey, Jack, what're you up to?"

"Just gettin' something to eat. How about you?"

"Same thing. I was just going to have some pizza and a Coke. Join me?" Jack took the empty stool next to mine.

"How'd things go with your fire watch last night?"

"Ah, that was simple, but hey, I gotta tell you about Jimmy." Jack was snickering. "Jimmy's in jail down in Snow Hill. The dumbass was arrested trying to bag a woman's purse on the beach. I ran into Susan on the boardwalk about a half hour ago. She was looking like a flower child and begging tourists for money so she could bail Jimmy outta jail. She told me what happened and asked if I would help her. I told her I'd give her ten bucks if she gave me a blow job."

"You what?"

Jack laughed hard. "Yeah, I told her if she gave me a blow job, I'd give her ten bucks toward Jimmy's bail." Jack was still laughing but obviously not joking.

"What'd she say?"

"She just called me an asshole and walked away," said Jack with a big grin. "They are both such dumbasses. I couldn't care less if Jimmy ever gets out of jail."

So much for looking out for your friends, I thought, but what did I really know about their backgrounds and relationships? Jack's attitude wasn't related to Jimmy's guilt or innocence; he just didn't seem to care that his friend—or maybe more appropriately his acquaintance—was in jail. His negotiations with Susan surprised me. But then Jack seemed full of surprises...some good, some not so good.

After we finished eating, we walked out to the boardwalk and sat on a bench. Jack lit a Camel cigarette.

"I'm the bellhop captain at the Majestica Atlantica," he said.

"Yeah, I know, Jack. You told me that yesterday."

"It's a big deal. The Majestica is one of the oldest and biggest hotels on the beach. It has a pool, restaurant, bar, valet parking, an elevator, and obviously bellhops to carry your bags. And it's right in front of the pier."

"Jack, I know where it is, and I know what it's like. It's the exact opposite of The Sands. What are you doing...trying to rub it in?"

"No, just thought maybe you'd like to be a bellhop at a classy place instead of a desk clerk in a dump." He took a drag off his cigarette and blew the smoke upward. I watched as a breeze gathered up the smoke and carried it in streams toward the ocean. When I looked back at Jack, he was smirking.

Chapter 13

May 17, 1964
Slow Dancing

THAT WEEKEND WAS a moneymaker for me. Mr. D's prophecy about weekend warriors came true—plus, the hourly pay for waxing floors made me feel rich. The only downside to the two days was that Wendy never called. I didn't have much spare time to spend with her, but still, I thought she was going to call. But maybe she wouldn't; maybe it was just wishful thinking. Jack had flipped his shift to a new bellhop he'd trained on Saturday night. He was working the three to eleven, and the plan was to meet me at Cowabunga's after he got off. I walked into the place a little before ten. Duane Eddy's "Rebel-Rouser" played while a dozen couples danced. It was a light crowd, typical for a Sunday night. Across the dance floor, I saw Misty and Sylvia sitting in the same booth they had been in Thursday night. On an impulse, I walked to their booth. As I got there Charlene walked up with a fresh pair of daiquiris.

"Charlene, I'll have a Miller High Life when you get a chance." She nodded in response, and I sat down next to Misty.

Maybe I was pissed because I hadn't heard from Wendy, or maybe it was confidence from making some money. Whatever it was, I felt I could pull it off.

"Do you always crash places where you're not welcome?" Misty asked. Sylvia let out a giggle and put a cigarette to her lips.

"Isn't that the definition of crashing? Come on, Misty, you were very friendly that first time we met. Remember? On the boardwalk—it was my first night in town."

"Yeah, I remember. That was when I thought you might have your own room and some money."

Sylvia let out a burst of laughter and slapped the table with the palm of her hand. I looked into her bloodshot eyes and knew she was drunk. Misty looked sober and seemed to have her wits about her.

"Don't think of me as a customer."

"Client. The word is client."

"OK, client, whatever. We can just be friends, can't we?"

"I have enough friends. Speaking of which, where is that asshole friend of yours? Did he leave for Miami?"

"It's his dream. He wants to be another Kerouac. But he's…"

"Who's Kerowhat?" said Sylvia.

"He's a writer," said Misty.

"As I was saying, not an asshole." I thought about how he'd stopped the guy from stealing my wallet. "He can be a loyal friend. He's a straight shooter, and he doesn't beat around the bush." At that point, Sylvia erupted into laughter and started slapping the table again.

"That's so funny. I'll bet he doesn't beat around the bush. I'll bet he goes straight for the bush," she said.

I looked at Misty. Her lips turned up at the corners, suppressing a smile. "Sylvia, settle down before we get thrown out. Not so loud." Misty's mood softened, and looking at me, she smiled. "You're blushing."

Just then, Charlene arrived with my beer. I welcomed the break and took a swig from the bottle. Misty sipped her daiquiri while Sylvia giggled. Misty pulled a cigarette from a pack of

Parliaments that were on the table. She held the unlit cigarette between her fingers with a limp wrist and a smile as she looked at me. *Finally,* I thought, *I'm actually starting to get somewhere with this woman.*

"Are you a gentleman?" she asked.

"Of course. Haven't I been a gentleman to you and Sylvia?"

"Not really. A real gentleman would have lit my cigarette by now."

"Oh...well, sorry." I reached for the matches, struck one, and put the fire to the end of her Parliament. "I'm not a smoker."

She inhaled off the light and then exhaled, blowing smoke in my direction. "Thank you. You're very naïve, Thomas Delaney. Do you know that?"

"I'm not naïve."

"That's OK. I like naïve. It's refreshing." She was smiling, not the cynical or sarcastic smiles that she flashed before, but a warm, sincere smile that showed in her eyes. Once again, I found her eyes captivating, and I was drawn into them in some magical way. I heard the signature guitar opening to a Beach Boys song, and then Brian Wilson began to sing "In My Room."

"Let's dance," I said, fully expecting her to laugh at me, but she surprised me. We got out of the booth and moved to the dance floor, leaving Sylvia behind with a glazed smile on her face. I put my arm around her, and we began our dance. She easily followed my moves, and we danced as though we'd danced together all of our lives. Her petite frame was light, with a fragile feel that reminded me of Wendy, but the comparison ended there. One had a tan from days spent in the sun, the other a whiteness of skin that spoke of a life at night. Wendy's upturned nose and heart-shaped face, free of makeup, implied she would surf the waves that came into her life, while Misty's straight nose, square jaw, and jutting chin suggested her desire to control the waves of life. One's blue eyes expressed a childlike innocence; the other's hazel eyes said she had seen what the world had to offer but was not yet weary of it. Wendy's blond hair was wispy, airy, and tickled like feathers, while Misty's shiny black hair was thick

69

with body and velvety to touch. And I did touch her hair, and when I did, she looked up at me and then repositioned her body, and I became aroused. She knew it and smiled, giving more of herself.

"Does this mean we can be more than friends?"

"Only in your wildest dreams, Delaney. Unless, of course, you're prepared to pay," she laughed.

"In My Room" stopped and was followed up with "Little Deuce Coupe," again by the Beach Boys. The up-tempo song changed the mood. We turned to go back to the booth and saw Jack sitting next to Sylvia. Misty's mood took another dive.

"I'd hoped you'd gone to Miami," said Misty.

"No, that's not until after Labor Day. I'm sure that by the end of the summer, you two will go there with me and Delaney."

The four of us stayed until closing time, Jack and Misty trading barbs while Sylvia, with half-closed eyes and a lolling head, gave an occasional giggle but was close to passing out. As we were leaving, I laid a dollar tip on the table as the others walked to the door. I turned in time to see Jack bump Goldie while he bussed a table. Jack looked at Goldie with a scowl and said something, but I was too far away to hear his words. Goldie stared after him as he walked out the door behind Sylvia and Misty. I caught up with them, and we walked the girls to their boarding house.

There was no holding hands, no invitations to visit their room, and no kisses good night. It was just a casual walk, with occasional action to keep Sylvia from falling off a curb. We left them and continued to the boardwalk, where I would turn north to The Sands and Jack would go south to the Majestica Atlantica. Before we went our separate ways, we sat down on one of the boardwalk benches. Low clouds had moved in, and a cool, northerly breeze chilled the night air, making me shiver. I crossed my legs and folded my arms for warmth. Jack put a Camel to his lips and sparked his Zippo, cupping his hands to light the cigarette. He sucked the smoke deep into his lungs, and when he exhaled the smoke, it quickly disappeared into the wind.

"I saw you dancing with Misty. She likes you. I can tell. Keep on her, Delaney, and before you know it, we'll be partnered up with 'em."

I looked toward the ocean. The overhead lights cast a glow on the brown sand, giving it a pasty look that extended only a short distance before fading to black. Beyond that was total darkness.

Chapter 14

May 19, 1964
Learning to Surf

I WAS ASLEEP WHEN the phone in the room rang. No one had ever called the room before.

"Hello."

"Delaney?" spoke a feminine voice.

"Yesss?"

"*Bonjour.* It's *moi*, Wendy."

"Wendy!"

"Were you expecting someone else?"

"I wasn't expecting anyone. This is the first time the room phone has rung. I didn't even know if it worked."

"I told you I'd call you. So do you want to learn to surf today?"

"You bet. What time is it?"

"It's seven o'clock. I'll pick you up at eight-thirty at your hotel, OK?"

"Why so early?"

"The wind and tides dictate the time and place, my little gremmie."

"Great. I'll see you then."

I shaved, found my cleanest T-shirt, put on my surfer baggies, and headed next door to Safari's coffee shop to grab a coffee and a roll to go. I was standing on The Sands' porch when a red Jeep with a surfboard sticking out the back and the world's most beautiful girl driving it pulled into the parking lot.

"Ready for your big day?" She smiled.

"You bet," I said, jumping into the passenger seat. Wendy wore a blue short- sleeve, button-down Oxford shirt that looked like a man's. It was unbuttoned to reveal her two-piece top and firm stomach muscles. She wore cutoff Levi's and was barefoot. Her hair in a ponytail, she pulled out of the parking lot and turned north on Philadelphia.

"Where are you going?"

"What do you mean?"

"I thought we were going to Assateague to surf."

"Oh, I thought we could do that next time. There's someplace special that I want you to see near Bethany Beach. It's actually in Delaware. Have you ever seen or heard of the World War II watchtower?"

"No."

"I didn't think so. You'll like it. Guys always like war stuff. Besides, it's a good place to learn to surf. Not many people there but also close to civilization; not so desolate like Assateague."

So we headed north. As we passed the white turret of the Castle in the Sand, it occurred to me that had I worked there, I never would have met Wendy. Maybe things do work out for the best. The Jeep's radio was playing, and I heard Gene Chandler singing the last lines of "Duke of Earl." Then the DJ said, "And now, the Beatles," and the Liverpool four began "I Want to Hold Your Hand." Wendy provided a full-throated sing-along. When Wendy and the Beatles finished, she looked at me and said, "Aren't they wonderful? No, fabulous—that's the word for them. Oh, not to change the subject, but see that huge hotel?"

I looked to my right toward the ocean and saw a hotel more than twice the size of the Castle in the Sand. It was also more than twice as isolated.

"That's Robby Roberts' Sea Circus Hotel. Have you heard of that place?"

"Yeah, I read about the hotel in the *Post* when it opened," I replied. "And I read about Roberts' scandal in *Life* magazine last year.

"Scandal? I don't know anything about that. Anyway, the hotel is the biggest and best in Ocean City. I've never been in it, though. And it's so far from town that it's hard to believe we're still in Ocean City. Heck, we're almost to Delaware."

"OK, you were saying you like them better that the Beach Boys?" I asked.

"Oh, yeah, way better."

"But you're a surfer girl. Don't you like the Beach Boys' surf music?"

"Surf music is not the point," she argued. "Don't you like the Beatles?"

"They're OK, but they're not as good as the Beach Boys. In fact, I don't think they're the best British band."

"Oh? Who's better?"

"Dave Clark Five."

"Oh, yeah, the DC 5 and 'Glad All Over,' better than the Beatles...right! No point in arguing with you. I give up. Thankfully we're here and I don't have to continue this absurd argument with you," she said as she steered the Jeep into some dunes. "There's the watchtower I told you about."

Rising above the green scrub bushes and dunes was a medieval-looking gray concrete silo structure that stood fifty feet tall with two horizontal slits near the top for viewing. We got out of the Jeep, and Wendy pulled her surfboard out of the back. I attempted to carry it for her, but her smiling response was, "Get outta here. I got it. It's my stick and I'll carry it."

We walked up to the tower and looked into the ground floor opening. There was debris from a fire someone had built, empty beer cans, and graffiti on the walls. A spiral staircase led to the top observation deck, but the stairs had long since been cut off about halfway from the top, presumably so no one would go to the top and fall off in a drunken stupor.

"This was an observation tower during World War II. Volunteers would man it twenty-four hours a day looking for German submarines. I guess they were afraid the Germans would pick Bethany Beach to invade us. I don't know."

"Whatever. It's still pretty neat."

I thought about the men who had manned this watchtower staring out at the horizon, looking and waiting—how cold they would have been in the winter, how harsh it would have been during a nor'easter when rain off the ocean would pelt its way through the lookout slots.

"Did they ever see a U-boat?"

"I don't know. Come on. Time for you to learn to surf."

We walked to down to the beach about twenty feet from where the foam of the surf was ending, and Wendy laid down her long surfboard.

"Aren't we going in the water?" I asked.

"First you need to learn how to stand up on the board. You can learn that on dry ground better than on the water. Here, lie down like this."

Wendy demonstrated by lying facedown on her board with her feet nearer the back. She was so small, she didn't cover half the board.

"Bring your hands back close to your ribs, and raise your chin and chest. Then in one motion, your left foot replaces your belly button on the board. Like this."

As quick as a cat, she was on her feet with her left foot leading and pointing at a forty-five-degree angle while her right foot in back pointed at a ninety-degree angle. Her knees were flexed, head and arms pointing forward.

"OK, now you try it."

"Wait. Let me see you do that again—only do it slower this time."

"No. I can't do it slower. You have to be quick."

"Please do it again."

She repeated the demonstration, and then it was my turn. On my first try, I threw my right foot too far back, and it came down half on and half off the board. I fell backwards with my butt landing on the sand. Wendy laughed. "Come on, not like that. Do it again," she commanded. After about a dozen tries, I started to look good—at least on dry land.

"OK, you're ready for the ocean," Wendy said. She then peeled off her shirt and dropped her cutoffs to reveal the bottom of her red two-piece bathing suit. My heart raced. She looked great in every way—petite, tan, and well proportioned with curves in all the right places. How lucky could a guy get?

"Just wade out a little ways with me. I'll paddle out, catch a wave, and ride it in. You can watch and get an idea of what I'm doing. OK?"

"OK."

Wendy paddled out while I stood in waist-deep water. She caught a small wave. Just as it broke, she paddled, got momentum, then popped up on the board. She made it look pretty easy.

"OK, your turn," she said, pushing her board to me.

Climbing on and flattening out on the board as instructed, I paddled out to sea and bounced over a couple of waves that broke in front of me. Then I turned around to face the shore. The first wave came, and I paddled furiously to stay in front of it until the wave's momentum pushed the board forward. The time was right to make my move. I hopped up, felt the board push out from under me, and fell backward into the water. It took me more than a dozen falls, including one headfirst, before finally getting the hang of it, but I still looked feeble compared to Wendy.

On the drive back, I commented, "Those waves were really small—not at all like I imagined they would be."

"How long have you been in Ocean City? You've seen the waves here. Did you think we would magically have a ten-foot wave here or on Assateague?"

"No, I was just thinking out loud. Do you ever get big waves here?"

"Sometimes we'll get six-foot waves when there's a storm offshore. Of course, on the rare occasions when we have a hurricane, it will get very rough and we get some big waves then. But those waves are rollers with wind off the sea, not good for surfing, and there's often a dangerous undertow."

When Wendy said the word "hurricane," she pronounced it like it was spelled "hairicane."

"Wendy, what's a hairicane?"

"Don't they teach you anything at Georgetown? You don't know what a hurricane is?"

"I know what a hurricane is, but I've never heard of a 'hairicane,'" I said, mocking her. "At Georgetown, we spell it h-u-r, not h-a-i-r." I saw her blush for the first time.

"Go ahead make fun of my Eastern Shore accent," she smiled.

"I'm hungry. Why don't you pull into the Tastee-Freez up here, and let's get something to eat."

We both ordered cheeseburgers and split an order of fries. She had a Coke, and I had a vanilla milkshake. We finished our burgers and fries sitting in the Jeep, and then we pulled out and headed toward The Sands. She turned on the Jeep's radio, and the Crystals were singing "Then He Kissed Me." Once again, Wendy sang along to every word as though she were part of the girl quartet. As we pulled into the parking lot of The Sands, I joined her in singing the chorus, "And then he kissed me," at the top of our lungs. She stopped the Jeep at the front door as the song ended, and we were laughing.

"You can't carry a tune, can you?"

"No, I can't, but that won't stop me from singing."

"Well, somebody should stop you from singing," she teased as she leaned her head toward mine, her lips inviting a kiss. I pressed my lips to hers and again met those soft, moist, heavenly pillows.

When our lips parted, I said, "That was just like the song."

"What do you mean?"

"You kissed me like I've never been kissed before."

"*Au revoir*," she said as I stepped out of the Jeep. "I'll call you." She put the Jeep in first gear and pulled out.

Chapter 15

May 20, 1964
Telling Jack about Wendy

"LET'S GET SOME Thrasher's fries," Jack said as we walked out of his room and toward the boardwalk. We were half a block away when we first smelled the frying potatoes. I wasn't hungry until the aroma hit my nose.

"I need to tell you something."

"Yeah, what?" he asked.

"I think I'm in love."

He laughed and without looking at me said, "Yeah, so am I. I'm in love with every girl I lay."

I stopped walking and took hold of Jack's forearm, making him stop and look at me. "No, really, I'm serious. I really like this girl."

"Are you talking about Misty?"

"No, not her."

"OK, OK. Well, who is she, and why haven't I seen her?"

"Her name is Wendy. She lives in Princess Anne. I met her the other night at the Pier Ballroom. You were working that fire watch shift." We continued our walk to Thrasher's.

"You fall in love pretty fast. Is that the only time you've seen her?"

"Well, yeah, it's pretty quick to be in love. Let's just say I'm in serious like. I was with her yesterday. She's just as beautiful in the daylight as she is at night. You know, the light at night can fool you sometimes. You think, wow, this babe is a fox. Then in the daylight, it's like, whoa, where'd that nose come from, and those pimples? Anyway, we went surfing, and..."

"Surfing!" Jack interrupted, stretching out the word. "I didn't know you surfed."

"She's teaching me."

"Oh, this is a goddamn fairy tale," he said as we approached Thrasher's counter. "Hey, Louise. How ya doin', sweetheart?" Jack shouted in a singsong manner. Louise was a dark-haired, big-boned girl, about twenty years old. Because of the high counter and her white uniform, you couldn't make out much of her body other than that she was large, maybe fleshy.

Louise smiled and said, "Hi, Jack. What are you having today?"

"Well, since you only sell fries and Cokes, I guess that's all we can get. Give us two fries, Louise, and make sure they're fresh ones right out of the fryer."

"Come on, Jack. Thrasher's fries are always right out of the fryer. And what size, dummy?"

"I like it large, Louise," Jack said with a smirk. Louise blushed and giggled.

"I'll stop by your place tonight after I get off work, Louise," Jack said as she served us the fries and Cokes.

"What the hell was that all about, Jack?" I asked as we walked away.

"I forgot to tell you, Delaney. I have a 'serious case of like' going on with her." He chuckled and added, "When I was in the Army, I had a sergeant who used to tell the recruits, 'I don't like you 'cause liking leads to loving, and loving leads to fuckin', and I don't want to fuck you guys.' So you know where this is going... my liking has led to fucking her."

I couldn't help but laugh. "Jack, you're too much."

We walked north on the boardwalk with no particular purpose. With Cokes in one hand and fries in the other, we had to dip our heads to the french fry cup and pull a fry out with our teeth to eat it.

"Actually, Louise is already in love with me."

"She told you she was in love with you?"

"Not in so many words."

"Well, exactly what kind of words?"

"Last night we were in her bed, and..."

"Last night? How long has this been going on? You're giving me shit about Wendy, but you've been keeping this Louise business from me."

"Yeah, well, what can I say? Things have a way of happening really fast at the beach. Anyway, she looks at me and says, 'Jack, I'd do anything for you.'"

"What'd you say?"

"I said, 'anything?' And she said, 'Yes, anything.' And I said, 'Will you give me a blow job?'"

"Jack, you're a pig."

"Yeah, I know, but what can I do? It's my nature. I'll tell ya, having sex with Louise is not that pleasant. She smells like a deep fryer. Fucking her is like fucking a giant french fry."

I nearly choked on a fry laughing at the image. We made our way to the edge of the boardwalk and sat with our legs over the edge and our bare feet in the cool sand.

"How can you stand vinegar on your fries?" I asked. "I see people doing it all the time. It's tart, sour. I think it ruins the fries."

"It's just the way I like them. Obviously I'm not alone. Thrasher's must go through a hundred bottles of vinegar a day."

"I don't know, Jack. I just think there should be condiment rules. Rule number one: no vinegar on french fries. Rule number two: ketchup on hamburgers only—not on hot dogs. Rule number three: mustard on hot dogs only—not on hamburgers. Rule number four: never mix mayonnaise with ketchup or mustard."

"You're a ditz, Delaney. I put ketchup, mustard, and mayonnaise on my burger."

"You make me puke."

Jack had successfully steered the conversation away from my discussion of Wendy, and it was just as well. He didn't want to hear about her, and it occurred to me that the less he knew about her, the better. I promised myself to not mention her to Jack again. The beach was starting to get active, and more people were filing in, laying out towels in the sand, pouring lotion on their bodies to make their skin brown. I was really enjoying the vibe when a nagging thought crept into my head. Jack's comment about the Army reminded me that my draft status would be changing. No money and possibly getting drafted and sent to Vietnam...another thing to keep me awake.

"Jack, I didn't know you'd been in the Army. I was just thinking about my draft status. Since I dropped out of school, I'll probably lose my deferment unless I go back in the fall, but I'm not sure I'll have enough money for that."

"Yeah, I don't have to worry about that anymore. I've got a dishonorable discharge."

"You're shitting me. What happened?"

"I went in the Army after high school and got shipped to Vietnam right out of Basic. 'Nam wasn't hot yet. Technically, we were there in an advisory and training capacity. Nobody was shootin' at me. I worked in supplies and got busted for stealing phones."

"You stole phones? What could you do with phones?"

"I would give them to my brother-in-law, who would sell them on the black market in 'Nam."

"Brother-in-law? Jack, you're like an onion. I keep peeling a layer off you only to find something new. So you're married? Where's your wife?"

"Oh, she's Vietnamese. She's back in 'Nam. So is my daughter."

"Your daughter!"

Jack set his fries down on the edge of the boardwalk and pulled his wallet out of his hip pocket. He handed me a photo of a cute Vietnamese-American baby.

"I'm speechless."

"Yeah, pretty cool. After I got to 'Nam, I met Suzy. Actually, Suzy's real Vietnamese name is Dung."

"Dung...that means shit."

"Not in Vietnamese, you dumbshit. It means almost the opposite in Vietnamese. It means beauty, or nice appearance. My daughter's name is Hung, and that means pink rose. We called her that because her skin is more like mine. When she was born, she was kinda pink."

"Dung and Hung?"

"Yeah. Anyway, I Americanized Dung by calling her Suzy. One thing led to another. Next thing I knew, she was pregnant and we were getting married."

"Wow! But what's the deal with the dishonorable discharge?"

"Oh, yeah, well, to make a long story short...so my wife's brother—Duc was his name—tells me..."

"What does Duc mean?"

"Ah, physical...or exercise...something like that. Anyway, I was sayin', he's got friends that can sell things on the black market. Everything is real crazy over there. You can't buy anything unless it's through somebody who knows somebody. Everyone is corrupt. Anyway, he wants to know what I have access to on my job. I give him a kind of inventory. At the time, we had a ton of telephones in the warehouse. Somebody screwed up and over-ordered telephones. The military is always like that. They always have too much of what they don't need and not enough of what they do need. I figured no one is gonna miss some phones, so I smuggled some out, and Duc sold them to somebody. I never knew who he sold them to. Me and Duc split the money.

"One of guys in the warehouse saw me carrying some phones out one night and finked on me. I was convicted in a court-martial and spent six months in the stockade. Then I was sent home with a dishonorable discharge. The wife and kid are still in 'Nam. There was no way I could get them out after the court-martial. That's just the way it is. Sometimes you win, sometimes you lose."

It didn't seem to bother Jack that he'd stolen from his government while in a war zone nor that he had gone to the stockade for his crime. And leaving his Vietnamese wife and child had been no harder than leaving a piece of furniture behind.

Jack tossed his cups from the fries and Coke into a trash can, and we continued our walk. The sky was an azure blue with marshmallow-shaped clouds that moved eastward while cries from seagulls mixed with the drone of human conversation, high-pitched squeals of small children, and the dinging bells of pinball machines in arcades. It was a perfect day, and I thought I might try to get in a couple of hours taking pictures for Pyramid Photos before getting in some floor waxing at The Sands. Then, just in front of us, two families came off the beach and stepped onto the boardwalk. One of the wives wore a yellow beach cover with a garish pattern of large red flowers. She had a beach bag of towels and toys slung over her left shoulder and a four-year-old little girl in tow holding her right hand. The other wife wore a large straw sun hat and a solid white beach cover. She held onto the hands of two small boys, who looked between the ages of four and six. The smaller boy carried a blue plastic toy sand bucket in the hand that was not attached to his mother. One of the men wore a white T-shirt over a blue bathing suit and carried a large green bag of beach paraphernalia. The other man wore a dark green bathing suit with a two-inch wide vertical stripe down the side. He was just over six feet tall with a lean body that suggested he did something to keep himself in good physical shape. He was shirtless and carried a little girl who may have been eighteen months old. They were talking to each other, the children were yelling, and they were not watching where they were walking. I stopped and yielded to the group, but Jack did not. Instead he deliberately walked into the shirtless man who carried the child. The man never saw Jack and stumbled to catch his balance.

"Excuse me," said the shirtless man.

"You need to watch where you're going, and you'd better put a shirt on," Jack said.

"What?"

"I said you'd better get a shirt on, buddy. It's against the law. You have to wear a shirt when you're on the boardwalk."

Mr. Shirtless stepped forward, towering over Jack, and with a clenched jaw said, "Who the fuck are you?"

At this the baby in Mr. Shirtless' arms began to cry, and the two wives started shouting.

"Leave him alone, Danny!"

"Just ignore the creep."

"The guy's an asshole," said the other man to Danny Shirtless.

"George, watch your language in front of the boys."

Jack, with his chest puffed out and his jaw thrust forward, calmly stood in the middle of the firestorm staring down Danny Shirtless, continuing to fuel the fire.

"I'm just telling you it's the law. You're breaking the law. And besides that, you need to watch where you walk."

With the last comment, Danny's face took on the countenance of a furnace about to explode. A bulging blood vessel created a blue vertical border dividing his forehead. His face turned the color of molten lava, his eyes bulged, and he bared his teeth like an attacking hyena. Mrs. Danny let go of the little girl's hand and jumped between Danny and Jack. The children were crying, and strangers on the boardwalk stopped and stared at us. I grabbed Jack by the arm, pulling him away. Jack turned his back on the chaos he had created and looked at me with a self-satisfied smirk. The city did have an ordinance requiring a cover when walking on the boardwalk, but this was not about Jack's respect for the law. Neither Jack nor I said anything for the next two blocks until I said, "I gotta split, Jack. I'm going to take some photos and make a few bucks."

"I'll call you," Jack said as he waved goodbye.

Chapter 16

May 20, 1964
Drinking and Smoking

I T WAS ELEVEN-THIRTY at night when I walked into the lobby of the Majestica Atlantica through the boardwalk entrance. The place felt old but was appointed with rich, plush carpet that looked Oriental, large comfortable chairs and sofas, and floor-to-ceiling windows that in the daylight offered views of the boardwalk and the ocean. Jack had changed out of his bellhop uniform and was leaning into the front desk, talking to his relief. We left through the lower side entrance that went into the parking lot and crossed the lot to the liquor store. Jack picked up a fifth of Bacardi and a couple of Cokes.

"Jack, I can't help pay for that."

"Don't worry, Delaney. I've got it."

At the register, he asked for two packs of Camels and laid out a ten to cover the $8.37 bill. We left the liquor store and walked to the beach, Jack carrying the Bacardi and I the Cokes. Once on the beach, we crossed the cool sand, going in the direction of the pier. The sight of the pier reminded me of Wendy and our first dance there just a few nights ago. I remembered my vow of early in the day—her name would not be mentioned to Jack tonight. We sat down on the soft sand in the shadow of the pier and short of the high tide mark, opened two Cokes, and poured out a few ounces from each can before adding the rum. Swirling the mixture in the can and taking my first sip of the evening, I wondered if the expectation was to finish the fifth that night.

"Smoke?" Jack offered me a Camel from his pack.

"No, thanks. I don't smoke."

"Never?"

"Not really. When I was six or seven, some of the older kids in the orphanage would..."

"Orphanage! What are you talking about?"

"Nothing to tell, Jack. I was raised in an orphanage. That's it, end of story."

"Go ahead. These older kids..."

"So these kids would snitch cigarettes from a corner market, and we'd all smoke them in the woods. But we were so young and stupid we didn't know what we were doing. More often than not, we would blow through the cigarette instead of drawing the smoke in. When we did try to inhale, we would nearly choke to death. It was pathetic. Anyway, when kids started smoking in high school, they seemed to be doing it to show off or be one of the cool kids, but I felt like I'd already done it, so there was no need to do it again. I just never felt any pressure from my friends. Some did, some didn't—it was no big deal either way."

"Here, try one of my Camels."

"No."

"Come on."

After some coaxing from Jack, I relented and put the Camel to my lips while Jack sparked his Zippo and gave fire to the cigarette. I drew in the smoke and exhaled.

"You didn't inhale."

"No, I don't know how."

"It's just like taking a breath. Watch," Jack said and then proceeded to demonstrate. He blew smoke rings on his exhale to show off. "Just like that. It's easy."

I tried it several times, and each time was the same: a burning pain in my lungs followed by choking coughs as my body rejected the noxious fumes. We sat talking and drinking. We talked about James Bond, Jack Kerouac, going to Miami, to New Orleans for Mardi Gras, and then on to California. We talked about which one of us would be Sal Paradise and which would be Dean Moriarty. Jack thought it appropriate that he would be Sal until I reminded him that Sal was Kerouac's alter ego, and if anyone was going to write about our journey, it would have to be me since he couldn't type. We'd had enough to drink by this time, so Jack was malleable to the idea after the logic was put to him—the logic of someone who was now slurring his words.

Jack moved the conversation to his recent conquest of Louise. He was disappointed that she had had to cancel that night's date, but she promised to make it up the next time. He then went into unnecessary details of their sex life. The sex talk led to a discussion of Misty and Sylvia. With both of us under the influence of alcohol, Jack got me to admit my affections for Misty.

"Of course, I'd like to bang her. Who the hell wouldn't?" Besides slurring my words, I was loud. What causes a drunk to start talking louder than necessary?

"I've always preferred big tits," said Jack. "I'd love to get my face between Sylvia's big titties."

"Jack, I think you'd love to put your face on any woman's titties and probably put your face anywhere on their bodies."

"Ya know what? You're right."

We were quiet for a while, both of us playing out fantasies in our minds. At least I was, and I had little doubt about what was on Jack's mind. Then Jack spoke, and his fantasy wasn't quite what I had thought.

"Ya know, I think we're gettin' really close to gettin' those two to work with us. Just a little more time and they should be convinced that we can help them make more money than they can make alone."

"Jack, what do you want to be a pimp for?"

"The money! The money, of course! Not to mention the no-strings-attached sex. If we can hook up with them, we'll be in Fat City."

"What are you talking about? You're making a ton of cash with your bellhop gig. Excuse me, I mean, as the bellhop captain. It's legal, it's safe, and you won't get arrested carrying suitcases to people's rooms."

"My cash doesn't exactly come from carrying suitcases, Delaney."

"What? What do you mean?"

"After I take people to their rooms, carry their bags, tolerate their snotty-nosed brats, and get a twenty-five cent tip, I watch for them to leave. If they're dressed in street clothes, it means they're going to eat or shop, which means they got their cash with them. But if they're in bathing suits and carrying a bottle of Coppertone, they're going to the beach. And that means they've left cash behind. People are here for vacation, Delaney, and they bring a lot of cash with them. But nobody wants to take a bunch of cash to the beach. They don't want the worry. So they leave it in the room. That's when I go back with the master key. It's usually not hard to find. Ninety percent of the time it's in the top dresser drawer. Very original. What I take depends on how much they have. The key is to take a small amount so that they won't miss it. Like a five or ten—on rare occasions a twenty. I consider it my bonus tip for putting up with their shit."

Now my head was spinning, and not just from the rum and Coke. I needed to go to my room, go to sleep, and forget tonight had ever happened, but I wondered if I could make it without falling flat on my face or passing out. The sound of crashing waves slowly got my attention. The waves were breaking in a rapid rhythm—not a romantic sound like you hear in movies, but the ominous crashing sound of an impending storm.

Chapter 17

May 22, 1964
Meeting the Coworkers

THE FLOOR WAXING was finally finished. Except for the one day of surfing on Tuesday and hanging out the previous day on the beach with Wendy, my routine was starting to get the best of me—hustling photos for Pyramid during the mornings and early afternoons, followed by waxing until eight or nine in the evening, and then drinking with Jack, sometimes in the company of Misty and Sylvia. At least now in the evenings with the physical demands of the waxing complete, the sedentary job of desk clerk allowed for some rest. One thing about the routine of waxing and buffing the long dark corridors of The Sands was that it sparked extended periods of introspection, with regrets for past mistakes and thoughts of a future at season's end. My hope of returning to school and getting my degree—but without the scholarship—meant I needed money. Working two jobs helped, but I still worried about having enough money after Labor Day to go back. Thoughts of what Jack told me kept crawling around in my mind. With my job, I had the same opportunity, but stealing was something I'd never done and never wanted to do. Jack made it sound like easy money, but it just wasn't for me.

As I headed out for breakfast, I saw Mr. Closterman in the lobby talking to a short, thin elderly man who wore a white short-sleeve shirt buttoned at the collar, a bolo tie with a bronze star, black dress pants, and shiny black shoes with thick soles.

"Delaney, let me introduce you to your coworker. This is Sam Sparks, the day shift desk clerk."

Sam was balding on top with short white hair around the sides. He extended a hand with short stubby fingers and large knuckles with dark brown age spots. I shook his hand. His grip was firm and strong and belied his frail looks. His stooped shoulders seemed to say he had spent a lifetime looking down to see something that wasn't there. He wore reading glasses—the kind that had only a bottom half for a lens—and smiled with his eyes.

"I won't be too much of a bother to you," he said. "I'll only be spending a couple of nights a week in the room. I live an hour west of here in Salisbury with my wife. I like sleeping in my own bed as much as I can, but I hate getting up at five in the morning to get here before my shift starts."

"I know what you mean." I laughed, but from a lifetime of living in a dormitory—first at the orphanage and then at Georgetown—I didn't really know what it meant to have my own bed or my own room. "I'm sure there will be many nights that I'll just be going to bed at five."

"Only the young can do that."

Mr. Closterman continued to discuss protocol with Sam, and I headed out the door knowing that Sam would be a good roommate, even if it was only a couple days a week.

Low-hanging gray clouds and gusty breezes made it a poor day for photos on the beach. I turned my camera in early and headed back to The Sands to get ready for my first official evening at the desk. Sam was behind the desk in the lobby trying to look busy.

"Hey, Sam, we have any check-ins yet?"

"I checked in two girls and a couple about an hour ago. We've got three other reservations that we're still waiting on. You may have to check them in during your shift."

"OK. I'll be down as soon as I shower and change."

"Take your time. I'm not going anywhere. Oh, by the way, our night clerk is here. I think he's still up in the room."

I opened the door to our room without knocking and found the night shift guy lying on the bed reading a copy of *The Sporting News*. He was wearing a button-down collared shirt with white, gray, and light blue stripes with the shirttail out, khaki shorts, and boat shoes without socks. His feet were on the bedspread. It was hard to judge his height as he lay there, but he seemed long and lean.

"Hi," he said, lowering the paper.

"Hi. So you must be the night shift guy?"

"Yeah."

"I'm Tom Delaney. Just call me Delaney."

He nodded.

"And you are...?"

"Jerry."

"Jerry...what?

"Morton," he said as his eyes went back to *The Sporting News*.

Jerry Morton looked like he had stepped out of a Beach Boys album cover with his clothes, an olive complexion that tanned easily, and trimmed sandy brown hair with streaks of yellow that were created with lemon juice. His too-cool attitude and arrogance turned off any charm his wardrobe and looks gave him. He was someone who would be tolerated, but that was about all.

"Where you from, Morton?"

"Baltimore."

"You go to school?"

"Yeah."

"Maryland?"

"No, Towson State."

"You here with friends?"

"Fraternity brothers."

I grew tired of interrogating Morton for information he obviously felt no need to share himself. I showered and changed with little additional interaction with him. Sam's warmth and charm were the polar opposite to Morton's indifference.

Chapter 18

May 24, 1964
This Beer's Not Bad

"**I**T SOUNDS LIKE you raped her," I said.

"No, man, it wasn't rape. I didn't force her," said Jerry.

Jack stepped onto the porch carrying a six-pack of Iron City beer and picked up the thread of our conversation. Jerry had just relieved me, and we were sitting on the front porch of The Sands. It was a Sunday night, and most of the guests had cleared out. There was no one in the lobby, and he and I were the only ones on the porch until Jack arrived. He was filling me in on his latest conquest.

"Who raped who?" Jack asked as he popped the cap off a bottle of beer and handed it to me.

"Jerry, this is my friend Jack. Go ahead and tell him how you raped this girl." I knew from the start I wouldn't like this guy, and he was proving first impressions are meaningful.

"Nobody got raped."

I watched Jack as he popped a cap off the second beer, put the bottle to his lips, tilted his head back, and drained half the bottle.

"Jerry, tell Jack what you just told me."

"OK, Jack, here's the deal. I met this chick Friday night, couple hours before I started my shift. We spent a couple hours together, and I could tell she liked me. She's down here with some youth church group from Falls Church or someplace like that. We hung out together all day Saturday, and we were makin' out real hot and heavy, but I wasn't getting any. It wasn't like she was teasing me, you know, just that her roommates or a chaperone or someone was always around. Well, they were leaving this morning, and I wasn't gonna let her get outta town without giving me some ass. You know? So when I got off my shift this morning, I beat feet to her hotel. Everyone was packed, checkin' out, and loading the bus. I got her in her room by herself and told her I wouldn't let her out until she let me fuck her. Well, not exactly in those words, but you know....She thought I was kidding. The bus was loaded, everyone was waiting, and the phone kept ringing. I told her, 'Honey, you're holding up the bus. Nobody's going home until we do the deed.' Finally, she gave it up when she realized I wasn't letting her leave until we did it. So Jack, you see, it wasn't rape. I didn't hurt her or tie her up or anything like that."

Jack finished his beer, stared at Jerry, was silent for a few moments, and then said, "Don't pay any attention to Delaney."

At that moment, the switchboard phone rang, and Jerry ran inside to answer it.

"This dude's a real skuzz, Delaney." Then Jack gave me an evil smile, unzipped his pants, and pissed in the half empty bottle he had had been drinking. He picked up the cap and wedged it back on the bottle. Jerry was inside for several minutes, and when he finished with the call, he came back outside and joined us again.

"See, Delaney? Told ya." Jerry smiled with the pride of vindication as he sat down in one of the Adirondack chairs.

"Well, Jerry, I guess you just found the secret of how to romance women," I said.

"Jerry, can you chug?" Jack asked.

"Yeah, you bet I can chug."

"Wanna have a chugging contest?"

"Sure."

"Don't put any money on it, Jerry. I've seen Jack chug. He's fast."

"No betting, Jerry. This is just for pride and braggin' rights."

"OK, Jack, I'm game."

Jack opened a new beer and handed it to me. He reopened the bottle he pissed in and handed it to Jerry, then opened a new one for himself. "OK, on three. One, two, three," Jack said, and with that we started draining our bottles.

Jack finished in a flash and then belched. Jerry finished three or four seconds after Jack, and I stopped after chugging only half my bottle. Jack had the biggest shit-eating grin on his face that I'd ever seen.

"Told you he was fast, Jerry."

"Man, Delaney, you didn't even empty your bottle."

"Among other things, I guess I'm just not a chugger."

"This beer's not too bad," Jerry said.

Jack opened the remaining beer and said, "Come on, Delaney, there's something I want to show you." We walked off the porch into the parking lot and up to a 1960 turquoise Corvette. Jack opened the Vette's door and climbed behind the wheel, and my jaw dropped.

"Man, bitchin' set of wheels. What's the deal?"

"Shut up. Just get in and I'll tell ya," Jack said as he fired up the engine.

I climbed in, and Jack pulled out as I was closing my door. He drove out of the parking lot and turned north.

"Gawd, this is a beautiful car. Whose is it?"

"Belongs to one of the hotel guests."

His raised eyebrows and sideward glance gave me a very bad feeling as if worms were crawling in my stomach.

"So does the guest know you're driving it?"

"No."

"Shit."

"Don't worry."

"Right, don't worry...until we get arrested for car theft."

"We're not stealing the car. We're just going for a ride."

"That's not how he'll report it."

"He's not going to report anything. He got so drunk in the hotel bar tonight that I had to escort him to his room. He's passed out in bed right now, dead to the world."

"How did you get the key?"

"The hotel requires the guests to do valet parking. The keys are kept in a cabinet by the parking lot exit. So after I got off my shift and changed, I just walked down to the cabinet, took the key, and here we are. That simple."

By this time we were nearing Thirty-Seventh Street, and I could see the white square turret of the Castle in the Sand Hotel. Just like the time Wendy and I drove by, memories of blisters and questions of "what if?" entered my mind. We passed Fortieth Street, and after that there was nothing but desolate sand dunes and darkness.

"Where are we going?"

"Rehoboth."

"Why?"

"Just to see it."

We didn't talk for a long time after that; there was nothing to say. My mind was busy going through how I would explain my presence in the stolen car to the cops when they arrested us. We were passing street signs with 100s written on them when Jack said, "What the hell is that?" He was pointing east toward the ocean to a block of lights on a high-rise building that lit up the night sky.

"Oh, man, that's Robby Roberts' Sea Circus Hotel." I almost mentioned passing the place with Wendy but remembered my vow before uttering a word.

"Who's Robby Roberts?"

"Big shot from D.C. Actually, I think he had some position in the White House, but I don't know the specifics. I remember two years ago reading about the grand opening of this place in the *Washington Post*. It was a really big deal. Lyndon Johnson and Lady Bird were here and just about the entire Senate and nearly every congressman. It was a big deal. *Life* magazine did a big exposé on Roberts last November just before Kennedy was shot. There was some kind of fraud or tax evasion—can't remember the details. Doubt that LBJ has been here since he became president—probably been too busy with Vietnam and civil rights."

Shortly after that, we crossed the state line and were in Delaware.

"You know what we oughta do after Labor Day?" Jack asked.

"Are you going to bring up Miami again?"

"Yep, head to Miami."

"And do what?"

"Same thing we're doin' here—work on the beach at a hotel or bar or something like that. Unless of course we get Sylvia and Misty to go with us. Then we won't need to get real jobs. We can stay in Miami until February and then go to New Orleans."

"Why New Orleans?"

"Mardi Gras!"

"Yeah, that's right. I forgot. And then what?"

"Well, it's a great party. If the girls are with us, we can work their asses off and make a ton of dough. After that, we can take it a day at time. Maybe work our way to California. We could be just like Sal and Dean. We'll write that book we talked about the other night. I'll dictate it, and you type it." We both laughed, but I knew he was serious about the road trip to Miami and New Orleans. He couldn't stop talking about it.

The Platters sang "Twilight Time" on the Vette's radio as we passed by the little motels and beach houses of Fenwick Island and Bethany Beach. We rolled into Rehoboth Beach as the lights seemed to be going out.

"Not much action here, is there?" Jack said.

"Nope."

I hoped we could get back to Ocean City, and I would be safely in my bed at The Sands without getting arrested for this pointless joy ride.

Driving south, we hit a stretch of road with dunes on the left and tall marsh grass to the right. I looked up at the black, moonless sky that was filled with stars and listened as Roy Orbison sang "Blue Bayou" on the Vette's radio.

Chapter 19

May 26, 1964
Assateague Island

"WHERE TO TODAY?" I asked, hopping into Wendy's Jeep.

"Thought I'd introduce you to Assateague. There's a full moon, so the tide will be extra high. It'll be fun."

"Great."

The short way to Assateague is to just swim across the inlet to the northernmost part of Assateague Island, but that would be crazy, and what would we do with her surfboard? Wendy drove across the Ocean City Bridge, turned left on Stephen Decatur Highway, and continued south until the highway ended at another bridge that took us onto the island. At that point the paved road ended, and Wendy continued south on a clearly marked dirt road. We passed small campgrounds with camper trailers and tents. Because of the dunes, we caught only occasional glimpses of the ocean. We were a world away from Ocean City. I felt relaxed—no Jack and no hustling on the beach—just the sound of waves, the smell of salt air, and dune grass swaying in the wind. It seemed like we had driven a long way, but it was probably only a couple of miles because Wendy could go only about twenty miles an hour on the rough road. When the road ended, Wendy shifted the Jeep into four-wheel mode and continued driving. We were now on the beach between the dunes and the ocean. When we finally stopped, there was no one in sight. I got Wendy's surfboard and carried it to the water's edge.

"Are you ready to show me what you remember from your first lesson?"

"I'll try."

"Go for it, gremmie. Show me what you got."

I paddled out and managed to wipe out on my first wave, but I did better on the next one, riding all the way to shore. After that, we took turns with the board, and I started getting better, more confident, and I stood with better balance. Then Wendy said, "This is getting boring. Let's do some tandem."

"What's tandem?"

"We're both on the board together. Come on, I'll show you."

"Wendy, you're crazy. I can barely stay on the board by myself."

"Come on, loosen up. This will be fun."

We did a little dry land practice, and then into the water we went. Wendy lay on the board in front of me, my upper body between her legs. We synchronized our paddling and bounced over a couple of incoming breakers. We turned the board and waited for a good wave.

"OK, here comes the one we'll catch. Start paddling and do what I say." Wendy was captain of this surfboard.

"Get ready...now, up!"

We jumped up almost simultaneously. Wendy stepped back, and I put my hands on her hips and felt her press her back against my chest. I didn't expect it. I lost my balance, and we both fell backwards into the water. She surfaced, laughing.

"Close. We'll do it again. This time, remember to hold me close like we're dancing. Don't be afraid of me."

The next time out, I knew what to expect. We were up and riding, Wendy pressing her wet back against my chest as I held her hips in my hands. The wind lashed strands of her wet hair against my face. We laughed, hopping off the board in knee-deep water with surf foaming around our legs.

"Oh, yeah, this is a lot more fun," I said.

"Told you so."

We continued tandem surfing until the wind and tide changed and the surf dropped. We were both exhausted in a good way. Wendy got beach towels out of the Jeep, and I put the surfboard in the back. She finished spreading the towels on the sand when I took her hand and turned her around to face me. As I did, she put both her arms around my neck, and we kissed. Her lips tasted of salt water, and her body was cool to the touch from the ocean. It was a moment I never wanted to end. We lay on the towels, allowing the sun to dry our bodies. Occasionally kissing, touching, and talking of nothing, we were alone in our own world. The sky was a dark blue with occasional white puffs of cottonlike clouds. We watched killdeer scurry across sand uncovered by the outgoing tide while gulls floated above, motionless in the air against an offshore breeze. The only sounds were the rustle of the dune grass, the cries of the gulls, and the collapsing of the surf.

"Delaney, tell me about your parents?"

"Mm. I don't know who my parents are."

"What do you mean?"

"Just that. I never knew my parents. I was raised in a Catholic orphanage. I never lived in a house, a house with a family. Just institutions—the orphanage first, then dormitories at Georgetown."

"Well...how did you ever afford Georgetown?"

"Full scholarship. I was the model child in the orphanage: an 'A' student, an altar boy..."

"You weren't in the choir?"

"I tried, but they said I couldn't carry a tune. Sound familiar?"

"Yeah, sounds like the choir director knew her stuff."

"Anyway, I was smart enough to jump through all the hoops, impress the nuns and priests, and snag a scholarship."

"You were never adopted?"

"No. Too ugly, I guess."

"An ugly duckling, maybe. You're sure not ugly now. What happened with the scholarship at Georgetown?"

"Let's save that talk for another time. I need to get to work."

We got up to get in the Jeep and leave when we saw them. The wild ponies, more than a dozen of them, were grazing on the sparse dune grass. I looked at Wendy, and her eyes sparkled with delight. She looked at me and smiled.

As Wendy drove, we didn't talk. Instead we just took in the raw, natural beauty of Assateague. When we got to the main highway, my mind drifted to thoughts of the times we'd been together—dancing at the pier ballroom, surfing at the watch tower, hanging out in Ocean City, and today. I wished we could be together every day, but I couldn't bring myself to tell her that.

"Delaney, I'd really like you to meet my dad. I know you two would like each other. I've already told him a little bit about you."

"Oh, yeah?" She said nothing to my response.

When we reached The Sands' parking lot, we kissed goodbye. I went to my room and showered off the sand and salt water, got dressed, and then relieved Sam at the front desk. A few minutes later, Mr. Closterman came out of his office, and as he walked by me, he said, "What are you smiling about?"

"Just thinking about how lucky I am, that's all."

Chapter 20

May 28, 1964
Riding on a Little Honda

THE RINGING PHONE woke me from a sound sleep, and I stumbled over to pick it up.

"Hello."

"*Bon jour*, Monsieur Delaney."

"Wendy, you're becoming my daily wake-up call."

"What are you doing today?"

"Going surfing with you, my dear."

"So presumptuous. Not today, anyway. The wind and tides aren't right."

"Oh....Well, what are you going to do?"

"Mmm, thought maybe I'd spend the day with you, just fool around Ocean City, not do anything special."

"OK, I'll tell you what. Come on up, and I'll spend the day entertaining you. I'll give you my grand tour of Ocean City."

"Delaney, are you forgetting that I've lived in this area all my life and have spent more time in Ocean City than you ever will?"

"Just go with the flow, will you? Pick me up in an hour at the corner."

"OK, see you in an hour. *Au revoir.*"

"Wait! Have you eaten breakfast yet?"

"No."

"Good. Don't. We'll start the day with me taking you to breakfast."

I could see the red Jeep two blocks away and Wendy's blond hair blowing with the wind. No ponytail today. She parked and got out. I greeted her with a quick kiss on her lips and said, "*Bonjour* to you, my French-speaking cutie. The United Nations will be so happy to see you when you get there."

"Well, before I go to New York and the UN, you to need feed me and honor your promise to entertain me today. That surfing lesson was not free. Today is payback. What are we going to do? And it better be something more than laying on the beach." Despite her protest of the idea of going to the beach, she was dressed for it with a blue one-piece covered with an unbuttoned white blouse and Levi's cutoffs.

"What we're going to do is a secret. First, though, we'll have breakfast. Then we have to go to Pyramid Photos. I need to get my pay from last week. Then it's on to the Delaney Ocean City Tour."

We took my usual table near the back, and Harriet came our way with a pot of coffee in her hand.

"Mornin', Delaney. Coffee? Who's your friend?"

"Wendy, Harriet. Harriet, Wendy."

"Where's your buddy Jack?"

"Either sleeping or working. Not my day to watch him."

Wendy ordered eggs Benedict, and I went for the pancakes. After Harriet left, Wendy leaned into the table with a stern look and asked in a low voice, "How does Harriet know so much about you and your friend?"

"We've eaten here a lot, that's all. I swear."

"Who is Jack?"

"Just a friend, someone I met after coming to Ocean City. He's the bell captain at the Majestica Atlantica. Other than you, he's the only friend I have in town."

"Why haven't I met him?"

"Just conflicting schedules. When you've been here, he's been working or something. But hey, why would I want him around when I'm with you?" She smiled at my response.

Harriet brought our order and refilled the coffee. I watched as Wendy buttered her toast, then cut into the eggs Benedict. She delicately lifted a small bite of egg to her mouth with her fork, which she held with her left hand. Her little finger swung wide of her hand like an outrigger of a canoe. She ate in a refined feminine manner that contradicted her surfing style. We finished our meal without any more interrogation, paid the bill, and got in the Jeep.

I opened the door and entered the Pyramid Photos office with Wendy tugging on my shirttail and trailing behind me.

"Morning, Mr. Devorak. I'm just stopping in for my pay. I won't be able to work today."

Mr. Devorak turned to face us and said, "Good morning to you, Mr. Delaney." Then looking over my shoulder, he spotted Wendy and said, "And who is your pretty friend?" As usual, his voice boomed and threatened to shatter eardrums.

"Wendy, this is my boss, Mr. Devorak. Mr. Devorak, this is my friend Wendy."

"Wendy, Wendy, you're so pretty, you could be a model. How did a beautiful girl like you end up with this guy?"

Wendy blushed. I blushed.

"He asked me to dance, Mr. Devorak, and that's how I ended up with him."

"She's also taught me how to surf, Mr. D."

"Really? You're a surfer, too?"

Wendy smiled and clasped her hands behind her back like a little girl.

"Wendy, have you ever done any modeling?"

"No."

"Hey, I have an idea. Why don't you and Delaney take one of the cameras and go up on the beach. Have him take some shots of you in a couple of poses." Coming from Mr. D, it was more of a demand than a question. "Delaney's pretty good with the camera. If they look as good as I think they will, I'll blow them up and use them in the store for promotional purposes. And I'll give you a Pyramid photo for free. How's that?"

"Come on, Wendy. Let's do it. It'll be fun."

"Was this part of your surprise?"

"No, I'm really as surprised as you."

"OK, I'll do it."

"Great. Do you have your surfboard? That would be a great prop," said Mr. D.

"No, we're not surfing today."

"Mm. No problem," said Mr. D. "I'll call Bobby Clinton at Bobby's Surf Shop and get him to lend us one for the photo shoot. Shouldn't be a problem as long as you don't actually surf with it."

Mr. Devorak made the call, and Wendy blushed again as she overheard him telling Bobby about his beautiful new model.

The door to Bobby's was open. We walked in, and before we could say a word, Bobby said to Wendy, "Hey, I'll bet George Devorak sent you here." As he reached to shake her hand, Bobby turned out to be the same bleached blond guy whom I saw there the last time. The only difference this time was his solid black baggies and a salmon-colored Hawaiian shirt with images of surfers riding big waves. There was a hint of white zinc oxide on his lips and nose. I couldn't figure out why he needed zinc oxide while he was inside the store. He continued to hold Wendy's hand long after she said her name and acknowledged that Mr. D had sent us. She finally pulled her hand away. After a few minutes of chitchat, he gave Wendy a board and we made our way to the beach.

"That was uncomfortable," I said. "I can't recall ever being treated like a statue before. He never even looked at me. I think he's in love with you."

"Not jealous, are you?"

"It's not about you. It's about me. I don't like being ignored."

"Aw. Baby's feelings get hurt?"

"Don't do that. Come on. Get me in a happy mood so I can take some good pictures of you. Stop smirking and start smiling. Let's do the first one with you holding the board vertically with the ocean in the background."

Wendy was a natural. Usually when I posed tourists, they got into stiff awkward positions and made the shot look like nothing more than a home snapshot. I had to move them around a couple of times to get something that looked professional. But not with Wendy—each of her stills captured her natural athletic grace. I burned an entire roll of film on her and thought that Mr. D would have a hard time picking out the best one.

When the roll was finished, we returned the surfboard, but this time I made Wendy stay outside while I took the board in and politely thanked Bobby. When I came out of the surf shop, Wendy was laughing. Then she wrapped her arm around mine as we went back to Pyramid Photos to turn the camera in to Mr. Devorak.

"I don't think you'll have any trouble finding a good shot to use. The problem will be which one to use. They all look great," I said.

"I'm sure that's true, Delaney, but it won't be because you're such a great photographer. You just had a great subject."

"That I won't deny," I replied as Wendy blushed.

"Come back and see your poster, sweetheart. It'll be in the window," Mr. D said as we left.

"Now the real fun starts," I said as we got into Wendy's Jeep. We went to Island Scooter Rental and rented a Honda Super Cub. Wendy climbed on the back of the little red Honda and wrapped her arms around my waist. Her fingers clutched my stomach, and a couple of her fingernails dug lightly into my abdomen. Her breath on the back of my neck sent chills down my spine. We rode out of the lot, and as I banked into a turn, I felt her pull closer. We stayed on the bay side for a while exploring the back streets, then headed to Island Fun Land, where we played a round of miniature golf. Wendy won. Then it was back on the Honda. I drove south to the inlet and parked. We sat on the rocks, watching the powerboats—professional fishermen coming in, sport fishermen and head boats filled with tourists going out.

"You know I let you win miniature golf," I said

"Yeah, right. You've never played any kind of golf before, have you?"

"No, never had the opportunity."

"I'm hungry," Wendy said.

"Me, too. How 'bout pizza?"

We got back on the Honda, drove to Third Street, and parked. We walked to the boardwalk and sat at the counter in Ponzetti's. We ordered slices of pizza, pepperoni for me and cheese for Wendy, and we both had Cokes. As we were eating, I heard Jack's voice say, "Look who's here."

Jack sat down on a stool on the other side of Wendy and said, "Ah, a thorn between two roses. You must be Wendy." Smoke from his cigarette drifted in her face.

"Wendy, this is my friend Jack."

"Hi, Jack," Wendy said as she waved the smoke away from her face.

We finished our pizza and drinks, and then the three of us went next door to play a game of Skee-Ball. After that we walked on the boardwalk. It was then that we saw two young colored couples walk across the boardwalk and onto the beach. They carried a cooler, towels, and beach chairs, and except for the color of their skin looked like any other pair of friends planning to have a day of fun at the beach.

"Why do niggers come to the beach?" said Jack.

Wendy's eyes flared as she stepped in front of Jack and said, "That's ignorant!"

"What? It's a legitimate question. They've already got a tan."

"No, Jack, what you called them is ignorant. They're Negroes or colored. And they have as much right to be here as we do."

I took Wendy by the arm and pulled her away from Jack. "Come on, Wendy. The scooter is parked over here. We gotta go, Jack. See you later."

As Wendy and I walked away, Jack gave a shoulder shrug, his hands palms up, and a puzzled expression tacitly saying, "What's wrong?" My cold stare said, "Dumbshit."

On the way back to the Honda, Wendy asked, "Is he really your friend?"

"Yeah. Why?"

"He's not like you. He's not very nice. I just can't see you two having anything in common."

Chapter 21

June 10, 1964
Two Choices

THE RINGING PHONE woke me, but Jerry answered it. Thinking it would be Wendy, I got out of bed and walked over to him, expecting him to hand me the receiver.

"Yes...yes...he's awake. Right now? OK, we'll be right down."

"Who was that?"

"Mr. Closterman. He wants to see both of us in his office right away."

Jerry had a sour look on his face, like he was about to throw up. I slipped on a pair of shorts and a T-shirt, and we both headed for the stairs. When we entered the lobby, Sam saw us and quickly looked away. He didn't say good morning or acknowledge us in any way. I didn't know what was wrong, but whatever it was, it wasn't good.

"Close the door. Can either of you guess what this is about?" said Mr. Closterman when we arrived to his office.

"No, sir," we replied in unison.

"Delaney, when you took over for Sam yesterday, did you balance the cash drawer?"

"Yeah. Everything was OK. It balanced."

"Morton, did you balance the cash drawer when you relieved Delaney?"

"No, sir. I should have, but I didn't."

"Why not?"

"It's always the same. It always balances. I just thought it was a waste of time."

"When Sam balanced the cash drawer this morning, he came up twenty dollars short. Can either of you explain that?"

"No." Again, the response was in unison.

"Well, it seems to me like someone helped himself to twenty bucks from the cash drawer. Would one of you like to admit to taking it?"

"I didn't take the money, Mr. Closterman," I said first and looked to Jerry, expecting him to admit to the theft. His eyes were blinking like a girl flirting with a lifeguard.

"I didn't take it either, sir."

"Well, one of you took the money. Unfortunately, I don't know which, and the one who took it isn't man enough to admit it. Since that's the case, I'm afraid I have to fire both of you."

I looked at Jerry, expecting him to confess to the theft and at least save my job since he couldn't save his. He just stood staring at Mr. Closterman, blinking. He swallowed hard and said, "Yes, sir."

"I'll go with you to your room and stay while you pack up your things. Then I'll escort you out of the hotel. I don't want to see either of you in here again."

It was fortunate that Mr. Closterman stayed with us as we packed. If he had not been there, I probably would have beaten the shit out of Morton and pushed him out the window. As soon as we were out the door, Morton took off in the direction of Philadelphia, probably to get with his fraternity friends. I went to the boardwalk, found a bench, and sat down to count my friends. Wendy. What could she do? Nothing. Jack. What could he do? It was hard to say. That was it: Wendy and Jack. I got up and walked in the direction of the Majestica Atlantica.

"What are you doing with that suitcase in your hand?" said Jack.

"I thought I'd check in and get you to carry it up to my room in your monkey suit." Jack gave me a puzzled look. "Come here," I said, and we moved away from the front desk. "I just got fired."

"What? Why?"

"Morton stole twenty bucks from the cash drawer last night. Closterman couldn't prove who took it. It had to be one of us, and since he didn't know which one, he fired us both."

"That's bullshit. What're you going to do?"

"I don't know, Jack. That's why I'm here."

Just then a dinging sound came from the front desk. A family had just checked in, and Jack needed to take their luggage to their room. He told me to take a seat in the lobby and he'd be right back. I picked out a comfortable wingback chair and sat down. The chair was close to the registration desk but positioned so that my back was to the desk. A few minutes after sitting down, a colored family walked into the lobby, passed me, and went to the registration desk. The family was exceptionally well dressed for the beach. The man wore a navy pinstripe suit with a white button-down collared shirt and a red necktie. The woman was in a cream-colored dress with a wide black belt cinched at her waist, a wide-brimmed straw hat with a veil, and gloves—white gloves. The two children, a boy about twelve years old and a girl a couple years younger, mimicked their parents' attire. I heard the man say they were there to check in and had a reservation under the name of Robinson. The desk clerk stuttered and said there must be a mistake. This exchange went on for a couple minutes until Robinson asked to speak to the manager.

"What seems to be the problem?"

The voice sounded familiar, but I didn't want to turn around. I scanned the lobby and noticed a mirrored column a few feet away. Adjusting my position, I was able to see the reflection of the Robinsons and the manager. The manager was Charlie

MacGuffin. I held my breath and hoped he wouldn't see me. Most of my visits here to meet Jack were after eleven at night, and it was unlikely MacGuffin was ever here at that late hour.

"Two weeks ago, I made a reservation for one week in adjoining rooms for my family, and now your clerk is telling me there is no reservation."

"Well, then, there is no reservation."

"I made the reservation."

"Are you sure you're in the right hotel?"

"This is the Majestica Atlantica, isn't it?"

"Yes, but we don't have your reservation."

"Would you be good enough to look? Maybe your clerk made a mistake."

"There's no point in looking. He's very competent. I'm certain there has been no mistake on our part."

"I would like to speak to someone above you, sir."

"There's no one above me. You're talking to the top man."

"You're the owner?"

"I'm Charles MacGuffin, and I'm proud to say this hotel has been in my family for forty years."

"Do you have any rooms available?"

"No. Sold out."

"What about for tomorrow?"

"Nope. Sold out for the whole week."

"You won't rent us a room because we're colored, isn't that right, Mr. MacGuffin?"

"Well, you could put it that way."

"I suppose you have colored people cleaning your rooms and working in your kitchen in the hotel, but you won't let a colored person stay in one of the rooms, right?"

"If you're interested in one of those jobs, I can get you an application, but I can't guarantee employment. I'd have to check your references."

"I'm a physician, Mr. MacGuffin."

"Oh, well, we already have a house physician."

"I don't need a job, Mr. MacGuffin. I need a room." He turned to his wife, saying, "Come, Sarah. We'll find better accommodations." The family marched out the door, holding their heads high, showing a dignity and class that I knew MacGuffin was incapable of possessing.

"Morning, Mr. MacGuffin," said Jack.

"Morning, John E. Walker. Having a good day?"

"Off to a good start so far."

"Good. Keep it up, boy."

I heard MacGuffin walking away and looked around. I got Jack's attention and held my index finger over my lips to signal him to be quiet. He looked around and walked over to me.

"What is it?"

"I didn't know Charlie MacGuffin was your boss."

"How do you know Mr. MacGuffin?"

"Never mind. It's a long story. I'm going to see if I can get a bed at Millie's."

"No, I got another idea. Give me your suitcase. You still have your job at Pyramid Photos?"

"Yeah."

"Well, go take some photos and meet me in front of the hotel at four."

Chapter 22

June 10, 1964
Evening
Damsels in Distress

ALLING WENDY AND explaining what had happened was difficult.

"What are you going to do?"

"I've got to find a place to stay and get another job."

"Any ideas?"

"I can probably get a room at Millie's. That's a rooming house I stayed in the first couple of nights in town. But for a job, I don't know. I still have the Pyramid job, but I need more money than that pays. Look, don't come to town tomorrow. Let me get settled, and I'll call you."

"Are you sure? It's no problem for me. I'm not doing anything anyway."

"No. Let me concentrate on this for now. I need to get settled."

"I want you to meet my dad."

"Well...this isn't a good time."

"I don't mean today or tomorrow. Do you know what Monday is?

"No."

"It's Monday, June 15. Care to guess?"

"Wendy, please."

"It will be our one-month anniversary. I've been telling Mom and Dad about you, and now Dad wants to meet you. Can we do it next Tuesday? It would be an anniversary present for me. Wouldn't cost you anything."

"OK."

"Promise?"

"I promise."

I picked up my camera at Pyramid Photos and tried working the beach, but my attitude wasn't great, and it reflected on my photo sales. It seemed as if no one wanted to pose for me. By the time Jack met me, I was pretty depressed. We walked along the boardwalk discussing my problems for a couple of hours, and I started smoking his Camels. My first problem was where to sleep. Jack's idea was for me to sleep in one of the empty rooms at the Majestica Atlantica. Only half the rooms had been rented for the week. MacGuffin's story to the Robinson family was bullshit, but the Robinsons knew that. Part of me didn't like the idea. What if I got caught? I could be arrested for trespassing. Another part of me delighted in the idea of pissing on Charlie MacGuffin without him knowing it. Jack pretty much convinced me to give it a try. After eleven o'clock, the only person on duty was the bellhop, and since Jack was the boss of the bellhops, he could get me into one of the empty rooms for the night. I had to get out of the room early in case there was an early check-in. It wasn't a long-term solution, but it could work for a couple of nights. The second problem was finding another evening job, ideally one that came with a room. Jack couldn't help me with that. He had tried to get me to take a bellhop job with him before Memorial Day, but even if I wanted to now, all the spots were filled. I was just as glad for that. The idea of taking orders from Charlie MacGuffin was repulsive.

We finally ended up at Cowabunga's, where we concluded that at least for tonight, I'd sleep on one of Charlie MacGuffin's fine beds. We sat at our usual barstools.

"Let's get a six-pack to go. We can finish it on the beach and then get you a bed. Butch's gonna close soon," said Jack.

"Good by me."

"Hey, Butch. Give us a six-pack of National to go. Some Boh to go," Jack said.

"Hey, Goldie. Get a six of Boh outta the cooler for these guys," Butch shouted to Goldie.

I paid Butch. He had his back to the bar as he rang the sale up on the cash register. Goldie set the six-pack on the bar in front of Jack with a thud.

"Hey, goddamn it. What the fuck you doing? Don't go shakin' up my beers like that, you motherfucker," said Jack.

Butch spun around and was between Goldie and Jack in a flash.

"Hey, hey, cool it, Jack. Don't talk to my help that way. You got a problem, you bring it to me. Understand?"

"He's fuckin' with me, Butch. Last week he tried to take a half-finished beer from me."

"You hear me Jack? You got a problem, you come to me. Now take your six-pack and go."

Goldie was staring straight at Jack, seething hatred with unblinking eyes. I picked up the six-pack and nudged Jack off his stool. We headed for the door. As we went out, I looked over my shoulder and could see Butch talking to Goldie. He was pointing his finger at Goldie, and it didn't look like he was saying nice things to him. Then I saw Misty sitting in a booth by herself. We hadn't seen her come in, and if she'd seen us at the bar, she made no effort to say anything. She wasn't looking in our direction, and I wasn't sure if she had heard the commotion at the bar or not. The music was loud. She probably didn't know we were there—or maybe she did and just ignored us.

"Jack, why do you have it in for the poor kid? He's never done anything to you."

This time Jack ignored me. We didn't talk much after that. We walked south on St. Louis to Somerset Avenue and then turned left toward the beach. Passing an alley, we heard a cry. "Give me my money, you bastard."

"Fuck you, bitch."

We stopped and looked down the poorly lit alley and could tell from the profile of her ponytail that the woman was Sylvia. She grabbed the man's arm as he was turning to walk away from her. He turned and pushed her to the ground. Jack walked into the alley. The man was walking toward Jack but looking back at Sylvia lying on the ground when Jack put his hand on the man's chest and stopped him.

"Hey, get outta my way," the man said.

"No, no, not so fast. What's the problem here?"

"What's your bag, dude? This ain't none of your fuckin' business, buddy. Outta my way."

"I think you're wrong, *buddy*. I think it *is* my business."

The guy was at least three inches taller than Jack and kept getting closer to him, trying to intimidate him. I knew this would be the tall man's mistake.

"He won't pay me, Jack—and he hit me," Sylvia said.

"You need to pay the lady, *buddy*."

"What are you, her pimp? Well fu..."

Jack sprung like a cobra, head-butting the guy's nose. The guy, dazed, stumbled backward, putting his hands to his face as Jack followed with a high roundhouse right that landed flush on the tall guy's temple. He fell to the ground like a trap door had opened. Jack kicked him in the head one time.

"Shit, Jack, don't kill the guy," I said, pulling him back.

Sylvia pounced on her fallen friend like a hungry lioness and went for his hip pocket. She pulled out his wallet, took all the cash in it, and tossed the wallet aside. Then she pulled off his watch.

"Come on. We gotta get outta here *now*," I said.

"I gotta go to Misty." Sylvia was sobbing, and in the semi-darkness I could see swelling around her left eye.

"We'll get Misty, but we gotta get away from this area. Delaney, you go back to Cowabunga's for Misty. I'll take Sylvia, and we'll meet under the pier. Give me the beer, and you run back for Misty. Don't come back this way."

I gave Jack the beer and took off running. I got to Cowabunga's as the crowd was thinning out for closing. I stepped through the door and looked to where Misty had been sitting. She was staring at me. Upon eye contact, she immediately grabbed her purse and ran straight for me.

"What happened to Sylvia?"

"How did you know?"

"I just know. Where the hell is she? What happened?"

"She and Jack are at the pier. I'll tell you on the way."

We took Talbot Street straight to the boardwalk, then onto the beach and ran along the shoreline to the pier. Jack was standing with a cigarette in one hand and his beer in the other. Sylvia was sitting cross-legged, holding her face in her hands and crying. Misty dropped to her knees and hugged Sylvia, saying, "Oh, baby, baby, are you OK?"

Sylvia embraced Misty, sobbing, "I'm sorry, Misty."

"It's OK, baby, it's OK. It's not your fault. You'll be OK."

Jack and I gave each other puzzled looks.

"Where's the beer?" I was breathing heavy from the running, my adrenaline still surging from Jack's fight.

"Over by that piling."

I popped open one of the Bohs and asked, "Do you think you killed that guy?"

With a shrug, he said, "I doubt it."

I carried the beers to Sylvia and Misty. "Here, Sylvia, you need one of these." She pressed the cool can against her swollen eye, then took a long drink.

"Misty?"

"Not now. Later, maybe. Sylvia, what's that in your hand?"

"Oh, this? It's the asshole's watch. I took it after Jack kicked his ass."

"Let me see." Misty took the watch and looked at it in the light shining from the pier. "Just a cheap-ass Timex." Then she threw it in the ocean.

The drama had died down by the time the four of us got into our second beers. Misty was still in a consoling mode, stroking Sylvia's hair and rubbing her arm and shoulder.

"Misty, you know tonight just proves what I was tellin' you last week," said Jack. "You need me and Delaney. If we had partnered up, this wouldn't have happened. How many times have you been stiffed already? How many times have you been roughed up? I wouldn't let this happen. And here's another thing. How many parties have you two done, huh? There's big bucks in that. Bet you haven't done one since you've been in OC."

"What the fuck do you know about our business, big mouth?" Misty said.

"I know enough. Let's just say I was in Saigon for a coupl'a years."

I doubted Jack had anything to do with prostitution in Saigon other than being a customer. Black market? Yes. Prostitution? Probably not.

"What's this about parties? How can you get them and we can't?"

Oh, Christ, Misty was actually thinking about this arrangement.

"That's where Delaney comes in."

Really, this is where I come in?

"Delaney's 'Joe College.' He's got tons of fraternity contacts. You get four, eight, ten guys at twenty-five bucks each. Do that a coupl'a nights a week for the rest of the summer, well, you do the math."

Oh, yeah, I'm "Joe College" with all these frat boy contacts. I hate fraternities. What the hell was he doing?

"You can approach a single guy or sit at a bar somewhere by yourself, which is what you're doing now, and hope somebody approaches you. Maybe you score that night, maybe you don't. You two could never go up to a guy and say something like, 'Hey

there, want a coupl'a girls for a party with your friends tonight?'"
Jack said this in falsetto, then added, "First of all you don't know
who to approach. Second, there's the issue of getting your money
from everyone in the room. And third, ain't no one gonna hurt
you when we're around. I'm tellin' ya, the four of us partner up,
we'll be in Fat City."

I started thinking maybe Jack had run some prostitutes in
Saigon. At least he had thought this thing out. I'd have gone for
it if I had been them.

"Delaney, is that true? You can line up parties for Sylvia and
me?"

"Sure. Give me a smoke, Jack."

"Could you get us a party before next weekend?"

Shit. That bitch. What a hard-ass. She was doing the math.
Jack was lighting my cigarette, and I could see his shit-ass grin
from the light of his Zippo. I took my time with the first puff
and held the smoke, still unable to inhale, before blowing it out
and answering, "Sure."

"You can? Really?"

I took another drag on the cigarette before answering, "Yes,
really, I can."

Misty and Jack continued their banter about the partnership. I was getting tired, and there was no more beer.

"Hey, it's time to call it a night. It's late, and we're outta beer."

"Wait a minute," Misty said. She fished through her purse
and announced, "Ta da!" while holding up a fifth of Gibson
vodka.

Oh, shit, an all-nighter, I thought to myself. It never ceased to
amaze me what you could find in a woman's purse. Misty took
the cap off and took the first swig, followed by Sylvia, Jack, and
then me. By the time the bottle was finished, it was almost daylight. As I stood at the shoreline, my thoughts went to Wendy
and how we had met just above where I was standing.

The surf of the cold Atlantic shocked my bare feet. I looked
for the sunrise, but low dark clouds blanketed the eastern
horizon. Morning came in a gray light that matched my mood. A

horseshoe crab washed ashore, and I couldn't tell if it was alive or dead. I stared at the large brown and green oval, the creature's spiky tail almost as long as my own bare foot. How could this animal—not even a crab but called one—have survived for 400 million years without changing? It lay on its back, its underbelly of yellowish flangelike body parts exposed and unmoving. I watched another wave roll the beast upright. It was dead.

Chapter 23

June 11, 1964
Dealing with Misty

MISTY REFUSED TO make a decision on the beach. She said she wanted to "study the matter" and suggested we meet for a late breakfast at Melvin's.

Jack and I went to the hotel where he woke up a bellhop named Jeff and told him to get dressed. Jeff would have to take Jack's seven to three shift. The room these guys shared was a pit—it was no surprise, knowing MacGuffin ran the place. After Jeff left, we showered, shaved, and changed clothes. We sat on the bunk, killing time and smoking cigarettes. I was in that mysterious zone between still having a buzz from the alcohol and not yet having a hangover.

"Jack, I can't be part of this."

"Why?"

"Wendy."

"What's she got to do with it?"

"Everything, man. You know how I feel about her."

"Look, think about it. This can solve all your problems. First, you'll make a helluva lot more money with this than working in a hotel or slinging dishes. And it solves your other problem about where to sleep. We're gonna move in with them."

"What?"

"We have to. We'll be partners with them."

"Jack, I can't do that and keep seeing Wendy."

"Sure you can. She doesn't need to know anything about it."

"That's ridiculous. How can I keep that from her?"

"Has she ever been to your room at The Sands?"

"No."

"OK, see? No need for her to know where you're sleeping."

"I've already told her I'm not at The Sands anymore. She knows I got fired. I told her I'd call her once I got another job and a room."

"No problem. Tell her you're working with me at the Majestica, but she can't call you there because they have a strict rule: employees can't receive calls. You'll have to call her."

We started walking to Melvin's as my head moved closer to the hangover zone. I didn't like Jack's plan, and I knew it risked destroying my relationship with Wendy, but there was logic to it. It would solve my money problem, and I didn't feel as if I'd be committing a crime. True, what we would be doing would be against the law, but where was the victim? It was a transaction between two willing people, an exchange of cash for a service. Money or possessions weren't being stolen; nobody was getting beat up or hurt. The worst thing would be lying to Wendy. I didn't like that, but I couldn't see any other choices.

We arrived at Melvin's, and Misty and Sylvia were already sitting at a four-top. Like Jack and I, they looked like they hadn't slept, and Sylvia's eye was starting to show a bruise. Harriet came and poured coffee into my cup, then Jack's. She was her typical gum-chewing self and offered no warm morning greeting. Instead she gave a stern look and cast sideward glances at Sylvia and Misty. She probably thought I was responsible for Sylvia's eye. We gave Harriet our breakfast orders, and then Misty leaned forward and spoke in a low voice.

"OK, I studied the star charts, and they showed favorable indications. We'll go with the partnership, but the only way I see it working is if the four of us live together." Jack flashed me a look and smiled. "I've already paid in advance for the place Sylvia and I are in now, so you guys will have to move in with us. We'll split income and expenses evenly, twenty-five percent each among the four of us. Doesn't matter who gets the jobs or who gets laid how many times. It's all equal. Same with expenses. We eat together, and we drink together. It'll all come out of the same pocket."

"Sounds like communism," I said.

"Actually, it's more like a commune," Misty said.

"There's a difference?"

"Of course there is. I'll also control the money."

"Wait a minute," I said. "I'm the one with the accounting background. I'll handle the money." What was I doing? My mind was saying one thing while my mouth was saying something else. The money was nice, but we could all get arrested, and how would I do this and date Wendy? She'd never go for this kind of arrangement if she knew about it. And in spite of what Jack said, she'd be bound to find out. My mind was flipping back and forth. I wanted to get up and leave, but I couldn't. And I didn't.

"What would you do? Keep a written record of the money coming in and going out? Like that?" Misty asked.

"Yeah, Misty, something like that," I replied. "Technically it would be journal entries documenting income and expenses, making sure it all balances out equally in the end."

"You know how to do that?"

"Yeah, that's what I studied in college."

"OK, Sylvia and I are good with that. Jack, OK?"

"Sure, he's the brain. He can do it."

"Delaney, how soon can you get a party for Sylvia and me?"

Harriet delivered our breakfast as Misty finished her question. I buttered my toast while my mind raced for a response.

Then it hit me. If I could find that asshole Jerry and his frat friends, they would probably go for it. At least it could be a start.

"I'll find something out before the end of the day."

"OK, fine. You and Jack should move in sometime today."

And that was it. The deal was sealed. I felt like a leaf floating downstream with no will of my own, just following the current. What was I going to do about Wendy?

Chapter 24

June 11, 1964
Moving In

J ACK TOLD MISTY we'd be at their place in less than an hour. He just had to go to the hotel, get his things, and quit. True to his word, we were knocking on their door in forty-five minutes. The room they rented was on the first floor of a boarding house on Dayton Lane, which is two blocks long between First and Third Streets, three blocks from the bay. The shabby building looked like Millie's and the dozens of other rooming houses for seasonal workers. We walked down a dark hallway past a pay phone mounted on the left wall and found door number five on the right. Jack knocked twice and opened the door before there was an answer.

The single room was twelve by twelve with two double beds that Jack and I would share with Misty and Sylvia. Who slept in whose bed with whom had yet to be determined. Both beds were painted-over metal with worn cotton chenille bedspreads. The walls were painted a pale green, the floors a dark hardwood with no covering. There were no pictures on the walls save a black and white poster of what looked like a complicated pie chart with strange symbols. The ceiling light was not turned on in favor of a lamp on the dresser that gave the room a sepia glow. A clock radio sat on the dresser with the lamp and an array of jewelry. There were no closets, only a dresser with a mirror and an armoire. Two windows, one with a fan, faced the back wall of the building next door.

"The dresser and armoire are full. You guys will have to live out of your suitcases," Sylvia said.

She opened the armoire, and I saw a large collection of black or black and white muumuus that were obviously Misty's. Neither Jack nor I had a problem with the suitcase arrangement; we had few possessions compared to Misty and Sylvia. However, the small bathroom was another story. The fixtures and the black and white tile had a pre-World War II look, along with a slight mildew odor. I was not accustomed to living with women, and the sight of underwear hanging from the shower curtain and tub would take some getting used to. Coordinating the bathroom use would take some sorting out.

Sylvia and I sat on one bed while Misty sat on the other. Jack sat in the only chair in the room. He pulled four cans of National Boh out of one of the two six-packs he had bought on the way over. We were starting early.

"Well, let's get to know each other," Misty said. "Delaney, let's start with you. I can't remember ever hearing your first name. What is it? I only know you as Delaney. That's not your first name, is it?"

"No, my name's Tom."

"Ah, Thomas. I see. What's your birth date?"

I then went on to give her a short biography, including my curse of being born on Groundhog Day. Next was Sylvia's turn.

"My last name is Peters, and I grew up in Dundalk. It's a rough part of Baltimore. My dad was a stevedore, and my mom, the bitch, worked as a hotel maid. I have an older brother and sister and two younger brothers. I dropped out of school in the eleventh grade and left home. I got some lousy jobs, shampoo girl, I cleaned offices, did some waitressing. After a couple of years and guys comin' on to me, I realized I could make money havin' sex with guys, so I tried it and liked it. I figured I was gonna have sex anyway; might as well make money doin' it."

Jack was next and told them everything that I pretty much knew except he left out the part about a wife and child in Vietnam and the dishonorable discharge. He brought up Jack Kerouac again and how we were going to Miami and then New Orleans and possibly LA after that.

"Jack, that pitch is playing like a broken record. How about giving it up?" Misty said.

"It's my dream," said Jack.

He shrugged his shoulders, looking wide-eyed as though everyone should understand.

Then it was the mysterious Misty's turn.

"My last name is Vail, spelled with an 'a' instead of an 'e.'"

"Wait," I interrupted. "Your name is 'Misty Vail,' and we also have 'John E. Walker.' Come on, this is too much to believe."

"I will never lie to you, Thomas Delaney," said Misty.

"Please, you don't need to call me Thomas—or Tom."

"Very well," said Misty. "So as I was saying, unlike my friend Sylvia, I was an only child, raised in the middle-class Baltimore suburb of Towson. I was an honors student at Towson High School and graduated in 1956. Then I entered the University of Baltimore and subsequently earned a Bachelor of Science degree in psychology. I have more than a passing interest in astrology and consider myself an accomplished astrologist. I entered my current profession of healer in my sophomore year of college."

"What? Whaddya mean 'healer'?" asked Jack.

"The service Sylvia and I perform heals people—men and women—heals them of stress, tension, bruised egos, low self-esteem. We allow them to be their real selves, to release their innermost desires and demons. What we do is allow them to achieve satisfaction—and that is true healing."

"OK, I get that part," Jack said. "But what about this psychology bit? Are you able to read our minds, get in our heads? What's that about?"

"Not exactly, but knowing your names and dates of birth and combining psychology with astrology, I can tell an awfully lot about each of you. Using this natal chart on the wall to start, I can give you an idea about your future."

"What's this shit about our names?" I asked.

"Well, Mr. Delaney, since you asked, I'll start with you. You don't like using your first name because of negative connotations. You're passive, a voyeur, a 'peeping Tom,' if you will."

"Oh, bullshit."

"And our friend here, Mr. John E. Walker—how can he ever be anything but an alcoholic? And then of course we have Miss Peters. Need I say anything more about the relationship between her surname and her current occupation?"

Sylvia turned her head away, her eyes glancing downward. In the low light, I couldn't tell if she was turning red or not. She held her beer with two hands between her knees, her posture a portrait of shame, while Jack tilted his head back and drained his can of National, then released a belch followed by a grin.

"You don't care who you hurt, do you?" I said to Misty.

"What? Sylvia? Or you? Does the truth hurt? I've not said anything out of malice. I've merely answered your question, Delaney." As Misty spoke, she hunched her shoulders and splayed her fingers with open palms as though she were performing a magic trick and showing that she had hidden nothing in her hands. But it was not her hands that worried me. "Is it not true that you sit there in Cowabunga's as an observer, not an actor or player—but rather you act like part of the audience? This is you. You *are* a voyeur. And as for Jack, he sits in his chair with a smiling acknowledgment. He will not deny his destiny. And Sylvia? Is your concern for her? I have not hurt her. She knows I love her and protect her."

"Well, you weren't there last night when I beat the shit out of her client for not paying her and roughing her up."

"She knows. I told her not to go with him. I foresaw the danger."

"What do mean you 'foresaw the danger'?" I asked.

"It's true," Sylvia said. "She told me not to go with the bastard, that there'd be trouble."

"Yesterday was a new moon," said Misty. "That is a time when evil is most likely to happen. The darkness of a new moon allows for evil to appear under the cover of the shadows. I told Sylvia that it wouldn't be wise to challenge the stars."

"So you can tell the future?" Jack asked.

"Through the stars and charts, I can foresee a kind of future. I didn't know exactly what would happen last night, but I knew something bad was likely to happen."

"How?" Jack and I asked.

"It goes back to our names being our destiny. I am able to see the future through a 'misty veil.' I sought out astrology for this purpose and trained myself to read the stars. I've learned to understand and interpret personalities as well as forecast future events. You, Delaney, are under the Aquarius sun sign. Your issues do not so much have to do with being born on Groundhog Day as just being born within a specific thirty-day window of time. As a result of being born when you were, you are now carried in many diverse directions, and you attract unusual people as well as unexpected opportunities. Very much like the situation you find yourself in now."

"Yeah, you're right. I have attracted some unusual people."

"Before I agreed to this partnership with you and Jack, I consulted my star chart and Sylvia's star chart and determined that it would be a profitable arrangement for us."

"So are you going to tell Delaney and me our futures?" Jack asked.

"In due time, in due time, be assured that I will. For now, I know you are a Scorpio. You have determination and willpower, but you are stubborn and vengeful. It will take time to study your charts, but study them I will, for my own welfare if not for yours."

Jack hung out with the girls while I spent the rest of the day doing photos on the beach and keeping an eye out for Morton. He and his frat friends hung out on the beach around Ninth Street, so I stayed in that area most of the day, but he was nowhere to be seen. After turning in my camera, I went to the room. Jack had just finished showering; both Sylvia and Misty were already showered and dressed. They told me they'd spent the day on the beach while I worked and looked for Morton.

"Did you find him?" Misty asked.

"No, not yet."

"So you haven't lined up the party you promised. Did you find any other clients for us while you were on the beach?"

"Tomorrow's Friday. I know where he and his friends hang out. I'll find him tomorrow and go from there."

"So," Misty said, "you just walked around taking photos of pretty girls and moms and dads and their kiddies. What happened to all this talk last night? Where are all these dates you were going to line up? Was it all bullshit?"

It became clear my job was to line up customers for the girls. Misty wasn't going to let me off the hook. Jack looked away from me and lit a cigarette. I hadn't thought about approaching guys on the beach while working Pyramid photos. Apparently it was an unstated expectation. I went to the bathroom to shower and avoid further conflict. After I showered and changed clothes, we all went to the boardwalk. The mood lightened as we went from one arcade to another, tossing darts at balloons, picking up floating ducks, and playing Skee-Ball in futile attempts to win stuffed animals. We ate boardwalk food—burgers, hot dogs, fries, cotton candy, and frozen custard—and wandered until nightfall. It was as though we were all trying to put off the inevitable. Ultimately we would have to return to the twelve-by-twelve room with two beds.

When we got back to our room, Sylvia opened a fifth of Smirnoff vodka and poured a healthy portion into four plastic cups while Misty lit a couple of candles and some incense. Misty then turned out the overhead light. Shadows danced on the walls as the girls began to peel off their clothes to reveal two beautiful but different bodies—Misty slim and small-breasted, Sylvia full-bodied with magnificent curves. Sylvia came to me, and my mouth went as dry as beach sand. Misty pulled Jack into her bed. Sylvia and I played with each other's bodies, enjoying ourselves. Noises from Jack and Misty were mildly distracting, but Sylvia would always get my attention back when it waned. We lay cuddling each other while pangs of guilt washed over me as I thought of Wendy. But then Misty climbed into the bed with me, and Sylvia went to Jack. Eventually exhaustion overcame the smell of sweat and sex, and the four of us fell into a deep sleep.

Chapter 25

June 12, 1964
Getting Clients

WAKING UP WAS different, not unlike those times when you wake up and don't remember where you are. I knew where I was, but it was not like any other time or place. There was someone in my bed. It was Misty. She was breathing and moving and pulling the cover from me. The morning light was unusual, another angle of the sun. Its rays filtered through a different window shade. The air was heavy with smells of stale cigarette smoke and sex. Under that layer were softer feminine smells of perfumes, hair sprays, nail polish, and soap. And then there was the close scent of Misty. Her back was to me, her hair a fan of silky black threads across her pillow, her exposed shoulder with flawless skin as pale as the sheet that fell from it. I had to call Wendy.

"Do you two have any change in your purses?" I'd showered and dressed and was heading out to take photos and search for Morton, but I needed to call Wendy from the pay phone in the hall. I was scrounging loose change off the dresser. Jack was in the bathroom.

"What do you want change for?" Sylvia asked.

"I need to call my girlfriend."

"Girlfriend! What are you talking about, girlfriend?" Misty asked.

"Oh my gawd," said Sylvia.

"Well, Delaney, I hope you're calling her to tell her you're breaking up."

"No, Misty. I'm not going to break up with her."

"Break up with who?" Jack asked as he came out of the bathroom.

"Delaney's got a girlfriend," Sylvia said as she replaced Jack in the bathroom.

"Talkin' about Wendy, huh?"

Misty got out of bed and put on an oversized T-shirt to cover her nude body.

"You can't be on the hook with someone now. How do you think you'll keep it going with the girl while you're living here? I thought you were smart."

I'd already said too much. The instant the word "girlfriend" rolled off my tongue, I knew it was a mistake. I left with some coins and decided against making the call from the pay phone in the hall. Instead I picked up my camera at Pyramid Photos and found a phone on the boardwalk. Wendy meant a lot to me. I envied the life she lived and wished to be part of it. Jack's suggestion was to live in two different worlds. I needed the money and wanted Wendy. It was worth a try to get both.

"Wendy, it's me."

"Where are you? Are you OK?"

"I'm fine. Everything's going to be OK. Jack got me a job at the Majestica Atlantica. The job comes with a room." There was pause, and I knew she was thinking about Jack. She didn't like him after their first and only meeting.

"Jack...gee, you're lucky. Is it a desk clerk or bellhop job?"

"No, ah...it's, ah...housekeeping, maintenance, stuff like that. Fixing faucets and replacing light bulbs. It's another night job, so I can still do photos during the day." I hated lying to her and was glad it was over the phone. She would have known it was a lie if she saw my face. "Hey, I have an idea. Why don't you come up on Tuesday? We'll have breakfast, and I'll entertain you for a change."

"What about tomorrow or Sunday?"

"No, that wouldn't be good. They want me to put in some extra time while I'm learning my duties, and if I get to do any photo work, it'll be real busy. By the way, you can't call me at the hotel. They've got a strict rule on employees receiving phone calls. Crazy. Let's plan to meet at Melvin's around eight-thirty, OK? On Tuesday?"

"Can I bring you down to Princess Anne to meet Dad? I told you he wants to meet you. I can get him to take us to lunch."

"Yeah, right. OK, that'll be good. It'll be a break getting away from Ocean City."

"Alright. Delaney, are you OK? You sound kinda funny."

"Yeah, I'm...great. Just great. See you Tuesday."

I said goodbye, hung up the phone, and then headed to Ninth and the boardwalk, keeping an eye out for Morton. I worked the beach in the area for photos and would swing by the boardwalk every fifteen to twenty minutes to see if Morton and his buddies had shown up. Around one o'clock, I spotted his lanky figure at the counter of the Alaska Stand. He was walking away from the counter, licking on a chocolate soft ice cream cone as I approached him. He was with four friends and saw me coming.

"Don't fuck with me, Delaney, or I'll pound the shit out of you." They formed a semicircle around me as if they were expecting some bare-knuckle fight to break out and they'd have front row seats. I gave the group the best fake smile I could muster.

"Don't worry," I said. "I'm not pissed at you anymore. Getting fired may have been the best thing to happen to me. My new job pays a lot better, and it's a helluva lot more fun."

"Oh yeah? Well, good for you. Now outta my way," said Morton.

"Wait, I think you and your friends will want to hear this. I'm...ah, let's say a talent agent. And I can supply you with some very attractive talent if you and your boys here want to party."

"What are you talking about?"

"I think you get my drift...girls, chicks, man, to party with. A guaranteed score."

"Knowing you, Delaney, they're probably pigs."

"I'll let you see the merchandise. You'll like them."

"Are they here? Where are they?"

"They're busy right now. Where are you working? I'll bring them around tonight."

"Bullshit. How do I know it's not some trick? You'll bring your buddy Jack and try to kick my ass."

"Hey, Morton, I'm not stupid. I do that and then you and your friends track me down, pound me, and do something stupid like take my camera. I'm no fool. I don't want to start a war. Tell ya what—you don't trust me, bring a couple friends."

"Yeah, Morton. I'll go with you," said the biggest guy in the group. He looked like the type who thrills at mixing it up with his fists. Morton was thinking about it. His eyes went up and down my body as if it were some sort of sign that would tell him what to do. The muscles of his jaw were working as he clenched his teeth.

"OK, I work right there," he said, pointing to a hotel on the other side of Ninth. "I go on duty at eleven."

"Look for us sometime after midnight."

After my encounter with Morton and his frat buddies, I felt more confident about approaching potential clients. On the beach, I spotted a man who looked to be in his mid-thirties and alone. That was unusual. I approached him pitching a Pyramid photo and found out he was salesman making calls on customers on the shore. He had decided to play tourist for a day. I eased the conversation into evening entertainment. He started to get a little hostile, thinking I was queer, but after convincing him that I could provide female company for him, his attitude changed.

"Yeah, I got a nice friend, blond with a ponytail and a knock-out body."

"What's her face look like?"

"She's pretty. Look, tell you what. I'll bring her by your room tonight about ten o'clock. You like her, you pay me twenty-five bucks, and she stays. You don't like her, no problem. We leave."

He agreed, said he was staying at the Jolly Roger, and gave me his room number. That was it. I'd lined up two dates for the girls, and the thought crept into my mind that now it was official—I'd entered the criminal world of prostitution. I was a criminal. A pimp.

Chapter 26

June 13, 1964
Introductions

MY STOMACH DID a flip as the Ocean City police car drove by. The two cops gave me a hard look but kept going. I was hanging out at the entrance to the Jolly Roger Hotel, waiting for Sylvia to finish with the salesman whom I'd lined up for her. It was twelve-twenty in the morning when she walked out the lobby door.

"Everything go OK? You were in there for over two hours."

"Yeah. He seemed like a pretty nice guy. Wanted to talk a lot, though. I think he was mostly lonely. He really liked my ponytail, said I reminded him of his high school sweetheart. He wished I'd had bobby socks, saddle shoes, and a pleated skirt."

"Hmmm. Maybe I should start taking orders....Ah, yes, sir, how would you like the lady to dress for the evening...before she takes her clothes off, that is?"

"Hey, now, there's an idea. We'll have to talk to Misty about that. Anyway, I woulda made things happen faster if we had more to do tonight, but I figured no need to rush him." She was smoking a cigarette and gesturing wildly with her arms. It looked like she was trying to flag a cab.

"I told Jack we'd meet him and Misty at Ninth and the board-walk," I said. "Morton's working at a hotel there. He's probably going to have a muscle-bound friend with him, maybe a couple of them. He's a little spooked with me over getting us both fired. He's afraid I'll do something to get even. I'll introduce you two to Jerry and his friend, or friends, and get a place and time for the party."

When we were a block away from Ninth, I spotted Misty and Jack. I had no trouble identifying them by their silhouettes—Misty with her odd haircut and muumuu and pumpkin-headed Jack. Two little red dots told me they were smoking.

"How'd it go tonight?" Misty asked.

"Good," said Sylvia.

"Couple of cops drove by while I was waiting and gave me dirty looks."

"They won't bother you. They might get on our asses if we walk around with our tits hanging out, looking like we're selling it, but if we're clothed decently, they won't do anything unless there's a complaint. Key is to keep it hassle free," said Misty.

"Let's go see my friend Mr. Morton and let him see the mer-chandise."

It was after one when we got to the hotel. I told Misty, Sylvia, and Jack to wait on the porch, that I'd bring Jerry out to them. Jerry and Mr. Muscles were sitting in chairs in the empty lobby when I walked in. They stood up when they saw me.

"Hey, Delaney," Jerry said.

"Shh. Not so loud. I don't want the entire hotel to know I'm here. Come on outside. I want you to meet the girls."

As soon as we stepped onto the porch, Misty and Sylvia seemed to float to Jerry and Mr. Muscles, drawn like metal flakes to a magnet. They pressed their bodies against the guys, cooing and aahing, stroking their hair and faces. I heard Sylvia say the word "muscles." Jack was about to have a hernia trying to hold back his laugh. Jerry was in a trance. It was possible he could have come in his pants right there. Mr. Muscles was puffing out his chest, putting tension in his biceps and forearms to pop his veins and show off his muscles.

"OK, OK, enough. Back off, girls. Jerry and I need to talk business. What's the deal, Jerry?"

"Yeah, Delaney, the boys are up for it. You know. Tomorrow night at eight. A couple of the guys have a small apartment on the bay side." Jerry, excited, spoke fast while his friend grinned and nodded.

"How many?"

"Five for now, but there might be six."

"That's no problem, Jerry, but remember, it's twenty-five bucks a *person*. Jack will do a head count and collect the money before the girls do anything. And do yourself a favor: don't hide anyone in a closet."

Jerry and I went inside to get the address for the party.

"Sure, sure, Delaney." Then Jerry, in a raised whisper, said, "Thanks, dude. This is *sooo cool*, you know. I really owe you, man."

Somehow everyone managed to hold in their laughter until we reached the boardwalk. We were all smiling, but then Sylvia started to giggle, and then we all exploded with laughter.

"You two gave Morton a hard-on without even taking your clothes off," Jack said.

"I thought for sure he was gonna come right there," Sylvia said, shaking her head and spreading her arms wide.

"If his friends are as easy as he is, it should be a fast one-fifty," said Misty, then added, "Delaney, maybe you should try to get a second party for later. We're liable to be done with these guys by nine."

We laughed, but Misty looked at me and said, "Seriously."

"You realize that twenty-five bucks is half a week's pay for this guy."

"Don't worry. He'll get his money's worth. Besides, we're worth it," said Misty.

Chapter 27

June 16, 1964
Visiting Princess Anne

A s I was standing in front of Melvin's and waiting for Wendy, it occurred to me that the weekend proved Jack right about our ability, or more correctly my ability, to get the girls into party work. In addition to Morton's little group of friends, I was able to line up two other parties as well as a Sunday matinee with two guys from D.C. Once I was over the initial fear of approaching guys, it became easy—very easy. We were going to make a lot of money this summer—that is, if I could handle the hours. My days started at ten with picking up my camera from Pyramid Photos, hustling photos for Pyramid and dates for the girls on the beach, taking the girls to their dates, waiting for them to finish, then back to the room by two or three in the morning. The days were long. But now I had to face Wendy for the first time since moving in with the girls and taking on my new illegal activities. I just hoped I could pull it off.

Wendy wanted me to meet her father, and I didn't mind at all. I liked the direction our relationship was going. She'd been driving up from Princess Anne on Tuesday and Thursday mornings, days that she wasn't working for her father. I wouldn't see her on weekends because those were really busy days working the beach for photos. But on the days we were together, we'd have breakfast together, and if we didn't go surfing, then she'd follow me as I took Pyramid photos. Sometimes she'd even help by posing with guys. It was a plan that worked really well for sales. The guys would buy the photo, then go home and lie to their friends about a beach romance. Mr. D marveled at the strategy, and my sales numbers were always in the top three.

As Wendy drove, we didn't talk. She acted like she had something on her mind, and I was certain it had do with my story about Jack getting me a job, a job that didn't exist. Thoughts of Misty came into my mind and confused me. What would make me think of her now? Maybe it was just the thought of leaving the mess in Ocean City behind me. Maybe it was the thought that Wendy deserved someone better than I. Finally, Wendy broke the silence.

"I'll be leaving for a family vacation Friday."

"Friday? This coming Friday?"

"Yeah. I didn't tell you sooner because I thought maybe I could get out of it."

"Where are you going?"

"To Deep Creek Lake in Western Maryland. We've gone there every Fourth of July as far back I can remember."

"Why don't you stay here? I thought everyone went to the beach for the Fourth."

"Well, when you live near a beach, you don't want to go someplace that you can go to every day. You want to go someplace different."

"Oh, so you have to vacation in the mountains if you live at a beach, but if you live in the mountains, you have to vacation at a beach."

"Right, something like that."

"I wish you didn't have to go. I'm going to miss you."

"I'll miss you, too."

We rode into Princess Anne in her Jeep with the top down. The town seemed like most small towns on Maryland's Eastern Shore—some might say picturesque. On the outskirts were mainly two-story frame houses on flat farmland. Living in town offered old, large, two- and three-story homes on city-sized lots. No commercial building stood more than three stories tall, and most stores and businesses sat in shopping plazas. There was no sense of a town center, no village square setting, just intersecting streets. Wendy showed me the courthouse as we drove by, a Georgian style, red brick and limestone building that could easily have been the town center, but instead it seemed to simply occupy one corner of the intersection. Nevertheless, it occupied that corner in grand style.

"What keeps this town going?"

"Not much. Mostly farming, and then there's the college, Maryland State. It's a Negro college. I guess there are almost as many students as there are residents in town,"

Wendy pulled the Jeep to the curb in front of a two-story white clapboard building with black shutters. The building looked like it had been a house at one time but was now converted to an office building. Gold letters on a large bay window proclaimed, "William A. Morrison, Attorney at Law."

We walked into the law office. Wendy smiled at the secretary and said, "Hi, Renee. This is my friend Tom Delaney. Delaney, Renee. Renee's my real boss when I'm working."

"Hi, Tom. Nice to meet you. You both may go in. Mr. Morrison is expecting you."

"So this is the mysterious Mr. Delaney that I've been hearing so much about," said Mr. Morrison.

He was on his feet as we entered his windowless office. He walked from behind his desk and shook my hand with a firm grip, making eye contact that seemed to be searching my soul for faults. He released my hand and greeted his daughter with a hug and a kiss. We sat and chatted, mostly a get-to-know-each-other chat but not threatening, not the interrogation that one might expect to receive from a father who was an attorney. It felt as casual as meeting someone at a party or a bar. My eyes scanned the room while we talked. His office was comfortable without being ostentatious. Law books lined two of the walls. The wall behind Mr. Morrison's desk was filled with certificates, degrees, and photographs. In each of the photos, Mr. Morrison was shaking hands with someone or receiving a plaque or award. I recognized only a few of the people in the photos. There was one with Governor Tawes, another with President Kennedy, one with Attorney General Bobby Kennedy, and another with Martin Luther King. Any potential sense of intimidation this gallery might have imposed was defused by Mr. Morrison's warmth and sincerity.

"Let's eat, kids." With that, the three of us stood up, and Mr. Morrison put on the jacket of his seersucker suit. "How's Fred's Fryers sound to you, Wendy?"

"Sure. You like fried chicken, don't you, Delaney?"

The plate glass window of Fred's Fryers said they specialized in fried chicken, fried fish, and fried oysters. It occurred to me that they would sell just about anything that could be breaded and dropped into a deep fryer. As soon as we stepped in the door, the smell of fried food hit my nose, and my mouth began to water as I heard the sizzle of meat and fat hit the grease in the fryers.

"Welcome, Mr. Morrison," said a large man with a mustache in a white short-sleeve shirt and a red bow tie with white dots. He was standing behind the cash register at the door.

"Afternoon, Fred. Brought you a new customer today. You want to be sure to impress the young man."

Fred gave me a big toothy smile as we walked past his counter. The tabletops were red Formica, the chairs and booths red- and cream-colored vinyl. Eight tables set as four-tops were in the center of the restaurant. Four booths lined one wall while a counter had stools for eight. Ceiling fans the size of airplane propellers, covered with grime, slowly rotated overhead. Half the tables were occupied, as were two of the booths. Three men sat at the counter. Mr. Morrison selected a booth, and Wendy and I sat beside each other with our backs to the window, her father opposite us. We all ordered the fried chicken special, which included mashed potatoes with chicken gravy and green beans. The green beans were especially good, cooked country style in bacon until they were almost too soft to stab with a fork.

We were nearly finished eating when I noticed that Mr. Morrison seemed distracted. Wendy was chatting, but he had been silent and unengaged as he kept looking toward the window. I looked around to see what was holding his attention and saw a group of a dozen or more young colored people gathering at the front of the restaurant. A well-dressed man and woman from the group walked through the restaurant door. They were dressed like they were going to church, the young man in a suit that looked too heavy for the hot day, with a thin black tie and horn-rimmed glasses. The woman wore a pillbox-style hat with a veil and a full-length white dress. Fred no longer had his toothy smile. He walked from behind his counter and stepped in front of the couple.

"We don't serve Negroes here."

"Excuse me, sir, but we have a right to be served," said the young man.

His voice was so soft I could barely hear his words.

A hush fell over the restaurant, the only sound the sizzle of the fryers. People stopped chewing their food. Everyone in the room stared at the three people. Outside, the group of black faces watched through the plate glass window.

Fred leaned into the face of the young colored man, pointed to a framed sign on the wall behind the cash register, and said, "Can you read? I'll read it for you in case you can't. It says, 'We reserve the right to refuse service to anyone.'"

With that, the couple turned and rejoined the group. I couldn't hear them talking but could only guess at what was being said. Everyone knew what had happened.

In what seemed like seconds, signs that read, "Freedom Now," "We Deserve to Be Served," and "We Demand Equal Rights" appeared in the hands of members of the group. They spread out, formed a wide oval, and began walking the oval, holding up their signs. Everyone in the restaurant heard Fred call the police.

"Well, kids, I guess our pleasant little lunch is over. Wendy, I want you to take Tom back to Ocean City now. I'm going to be pretty busy the rest of the day."

"OK, Daddy."

While paying the bill at the cash register, Mr. Morrison said to Fred, "Why don't you just give in? There's legislation pending in Congress right now that will require you to serve everyone, regardless of color."

"It's not a law yet, Bill. I have my rights, too, and right now I have the right to refuse service to anyone I please."

"Yeah, well, that'll change as soon as LBJ signs the civil rights legislation."

"You know, Bill, you haven't exactly helped matters any. If you hadn't filed that lawsuit against the National States' Rights Party back in '56, we wouldn't be in this kinda fix now."

"You mean the restraining order that stopped that white supremacist group from holding a second racist rally in the middle of town? If those bigots had gotten their way, the streets would have been flowing with blood. It's just a good thing I got it stopped, Fred. You don't know what could've happened. Why, this restaurant could have been burned to the ground. What I did was for your benefit as much as everyone else's."

Mr. Morrison took his change, and as we started out the door, we heard the words "nigger lover." The three of us turned to see who said it, but everyone's head was turned. We had no idea who the coward was who made the comment, only that it was a male voice. I suddenly felt like vomiting. The situation reminded me of the hatred Charlie MacGuffin exhibited, a hatred that I couldn't understand. I would have bought a meal and taken it out to the couple, but of course they weren't hungry for Fred's greasy chicken; they hungered for respect. That was their right, and it was what they deserved.

We stepped out of Fred's Fryers into the middle of the demonstrators just as cop cars, sirens screaming and lights flashing, pulled to the curb. Mr. Morrison looked to Wendy and said, "Get on down the road now, honey. Take Tom back to Ocean City, and tell your momma I may be late getting home tonight."

We walked away quickly, looking back briefly to see Wendy's father talking to one of the cops.

When Wendy pulled into the Majestica Atlantica's parking lot, I saw Misty and Sylvia sitting on a bench near the hotel entrance. What the hell were they doing here? When the Jeep stopped, I leaned over and kissed Wendy goodbye and then watched her drive away. When Wendy was out of sight, I turned. Misty and Sylvia stood up and walked toward me. The bitches had been waiting for me.

CHAPTER 28

June 18, 1964
A Peaceful March

MY STOMACH WAS queasy as Wendy drove onto the Maryland State campus. Wendy wanted us to participate in a peaceful protest demonstration over the arrest of the picketers at Fred's Fryers. What we were doing would have been unimaginable to me just a month ago, but after what I'd seen at Fred's, I knew I had to be part of it. Wendy said it would be nothing more than a peaceful march through town, and then we could go to her house for lunch before going back to Ocean City. Wendy parked the Jeep, and we joined a crowd of several hundred people in the parking lot. They were mostly colored students from the college. There appeared to be a couple dozen older colored people, a few who looked like ministers, and a handful of white people. Many held protest signs like the ones at the restaurant. A leader called for everyone to form a circle around him, and then he gave the crowd instructions. He emphasized that this was a peaceful march. Should bystanders call us names or throw rocks, we were to ignore them. Under no circumstances were we to retaliate. The leader then invited one of the ministers to seek the Lord's blessing for the march.

The minister began praying, and he prayed for a very long time. He asked God to bless the march, and then he asked God to bless certain people. He named names, a lot of names. Then he asked God to bless their enemies, and then he proceeded to name them. I didn't know any of the names, but there were a lot of them also. The longer he prayed, the more tension I felt. I began to get an idea that this march might not be as peaceful as Wendy had promised.

The blessing finally ended, and in the name of Jesus, the march began. The leader, along with the ministers and a couple of others, walked in the front, arm in arm. Everyone else followed in rows with arms locked as a sign of unity. Wendy and I locked arms together and worked our way into the crowd. A young colored man with a mustache and goatee took Wendy's other arm, while a young, round-faced colored woman took my other arm.

"Are you a student here?" I asked.

"Yes, and I want to thank you for coming out today for the cause. It's very brave of you."

Very brave of me? What did she mean? I looked at Wendy and smiled, suppressing the fear that was building in my gut. Wendy's expression was one of joyful anticipation, the same expression I first saw from her on a surfboard. It gave me courage. The crowd started to move, and we found ourselves close to the middle of the pack of people. We marched off the campus and onto Broad Street. The sense of doom left me, replaced by a feeling of doing something important. We were righting an inequity, correcting a wrong, changing the world. It felt good. I held my head high and stuck out my chest as we marched in solidarity.

We turned the corner at Somerset Avenue, and our leaders were stopped at the intersection of Prince William Street. Craning my neck, I could see that a line of state troopers and firemen had stopped our march. There seemed to be a peaceful discussion with our leader, but I couldn't hear what was being said. Then everything changed so fast, I couldn't tell what had happened. Fire hoses were turned on, dogs were barking, people were screaming. It was chaos. In an instant, the crowd in front of us disappeared, and a force of water hit Wendy and me like a stinging club. Then we were lying on the wet pavement, water hitting us like bees. I tried to cover Wendy with my body. I looked up when the fire hoses subsided and saw police dogs attacking the leading marchers. Police were swinging billy clubs.

"Wendy, are you OK? Can you get up?"

"Yeah, I think so."

"Come on. We gotta get outta here—fast."

The crowd scattered except for those at the front who were taking a beating. Wendy and I ran back to Broad Street and around the corner before stopping.

"You OK, Delaney?"

"I think so, except for my head. It took that first blast from the fire hose. I'm just glad I turned my head in time and it didn't hit my eyes. You've got an abrasion on your forehead. You OK?"

"Yeah," she said, looked down at her legs. "I skinned my knee, too, but I've had worse getting pounded by the surf. I'm OK. I guess the march is over."

"That's an understatement."

"Come on, let's go to my house and get out of these wet clothes."

I wasn't sure that was the best idea but couldn't think of a better one at the time. Wendy steered the Jeep through some backstreets, avoiding the mayhem on Somerset. She parked on the street in front of a three-story, white frame colonial with black shutters, two dormers on the third floor, and a wraparound porch. Azaleas and boxwoods lined the front yard, while tall maple trees stood guard on the sides of the house.

"Let's go around this way to the kitchen. We're too wet to go in the front door," Wendy said as she led the way on the porch to the kitchen door.

"Missy Wendy...what have you done?"

A heavyset colored woman raised both hands to the side of her face with her eyes wide and her mouth forming a big O.

"Nothing, Miss Barbara. We're just wet."

"Your forehead's skinned up. What'd you do to yo'self? Who's this?"

"This is my friend Tom Delaney. Tom, this is Miss Barbara."

"You both look like two cats got throwed into the washtub."

"Hi, Miss Barbara," I said.

"What's all the commotion?...Wendy, what happened to you?" It was Wendy's mother.

"Mom, it's nothing."

"I'll get some towels and dry 'em off, Mrs. Morrison."

"What happened, Wendy?" Mrs. Morrison held Wendy's chin while examining the forehead abrasion. "How'd you get this scrape on your head? That's not something from surfing. Why are you two wet? Who are you, young man?"

"Mom, this is Tom Delaney..."

"Oh, yes, the famous Mr. Delaney that I've heard so much about."

"How do you do, Mrs. Morrison?"

I didn't like the way things were going. Miss Barbara appeared with the towels, handing me one and then wrapping one around Wendy's shoulders.

"We went to march with the protesters and..." began Wendy.

"You what?" interrupted her mother.

"Oh, Missy Wendy, shouldn't oughta done that," said Miss Barbara.

"No, Wendy you shouldn't have," agreed Mrs. Morrison. "What part in this did you play, Mr. Delaney?"

"It's not his fault, Mom. I talked him into it. And it was the right thing to do. Everyone should have a right to eat in any public restaurant without getting arrested." Tears welled in Wendy's eyes as she spoke.

"I'm not arguing with you. I'll get some dry clothes for you and something for Mr. Delaney. Miss Barbara, put some lunch together for these children."

Mrs. Morrison returned with clothes for Wendy and a bath-robe for me. I changed in the laundry room off of the kitchen. Miss Barbara put my clothes in the dryer. I was sitting at the kitchen table when Wendy came in wearing jeans and a short-sleeve white blouse with a towel wrapped around her wet hair.

We were eating BLT sandwiches and drinking iced tea when I heard the front door close, followed by the sound of heavy footsteps in the hallway. Mr. Morrison walked into the kitchen, gave us both a wry smile, and then pulled out a chair, spun it around, and straddled it, resting his arms on the back of it. *This can't be good,* I thought.

"What were you two thinking?"

"Daddy, don't blame Tom. It's my fault. I wanted to do this, and I convinced him to go with me. It was the right thing to do, Daddy. You've taught me that." Her lip quivered, and I was sure she was about to cry.

"The cause is right, but there's a way to go about it. A process, a legal process. Honey, I don't want you to get hurt."

"I didn't get hurt. I've had worse surfing."

"No, you don't understand. Look at me. This is very serious, what you're doing, what you did today. In Mississippi, people are being murdered for less. White people and black people are being beaten to death, shot, and killed...murdered by bigots in gangs and hiding behind sheets with masks. Change is coming—and soon. The Civil Rights Act is about to pass, and as soon as President Johnson signs it into law, it means there will be federal power to enforce equality."

He got up and walked over to Wendy. Gently pulling her from the chair and embracing her, he said, "Things will change for the better, honey, and I love you...for the way you are."

"I love you, too, Daddy." Tears streamed down her cheeks.

He looked down at me, smiling, and said, "That robe looks a little big for you, son."

I looked up and said, "Mr. Morrison, I don't think I'll ever fit into your clothes, and certainly not your shoes."

CHAPTER 29

June 25, 1964
Wendy's Last Day

THE SOUND OF a door closing woke me up. Then I heard the sound of a heavy stream of water from the bathroom, and I knew that Jack was up and urinating. The time on the clock radio said 7:40. It was time to get up, dress, and meet Wendy. It was her last day before going on the family vacation to Deep Creek Lake. We wouldn't see each other for more than a week. It had been difficult since moving in with Misty and Sylvia, but it was the way it had to be. I needed the money, and the money was good. Jack was right; in less than two weeks, the cash was rolling in, and it looked like we were headed to Fat City. I'd gotten good at seeing opportunities, and my pitch had become smooth. Hundred-dollar nights were not uncommon, and even with my twenty-five percent share, I was still making five times what I had made at The Sands. Everything would be fine as long as Wendy didn't find out.

"Morning, sleepyhead," Jack said.

"What are you doing up at this hour?"

"Had to piss."

Jack lit a Camel, then sat on the bed, jostling Sylvia.

"Please shut up and go back to bed." Sylvia's face was buried in her pillow, and her words were barely understandable.

"I've got to shower, shave, and get going," I said.

"Oh, yeah, this is your date with Wendy day. What do you two do when you're not surfing, anyway?" Jack said.

"I don't want to tell you people anything. You're all too unpredictable. I couldn't believe these two showed up last week to watch Wendy drop me off. That really pissed me off, goddamn it."

"Shh. Please, there are people trying to sleep. Don't you know what time we got to bed last night?" said Misty.

"Yes, Misty, I was in bed with you. I know what time it was."

After showering, I looked in the mirror to shave. Dark circles were forming under my eyes after only four hours of sleep. I wondered if I could keep up this pace the rest of the summer. Back in the room, Misty had propped herself up in bed and was smoking a cigarette.

"You know, Delaney, this is all a waste of time, this thing with Wendy. I've worked on your chart, and love and romance are not in it. This thing with her is going to come to a bad end."

"Chart?"

"Your birth chart and sun sign."

"Look, the only thing that's going to wreck my 'thing with Wendy,' as you put it, is *you*."

"I'll never say anything to her, nor will Jack or Sylvia. We won't have to. The stars will do their work. It's destiny, and I'll never interfere with that."

It was 8:20 when Wendy arrived at Melvin's. Harriet came by to pour the coffee and take our order. She was really sweet to Wendy but kept giving me disapproving looks. Twice a week she would see me with Wendy, and the other five days I would be with Jack and the girls. I had a feeling Harriet knew what the girls did to make money. God only knows what she thought I was trying to do with innocent Wendy.

"What are you going to do while I'm gone?" Wendy asked.

"Hopefully make some money taking Pyramid photos."

"Money, is that all you can think about?"

"No. I think about you a lot, but when you don't have much money, you do tend to think about it. You gotta understand, Wendy; I don't have anyone to help me financially. If I'm going back to school, I'll have to pay my own way."

We had finished eating, and I was looking at the check when Wendy said, "There's your friend Jack with two girls."

My heart skipped a beat. I looked around and saw the three of them sitting at a table across the room. They smiled at us and waved. They were like the three witches of Macbeth, and that was not a good thought considering the witches' prophecies of the inevitable. I smiled, but it was more of a grimace, and waved.

"Who are those girls?"

"Friends of his."

"Do you know them?"

"Barely."

I paid the bill at the register, and we left without any further acknowledgement of their presence. We walked to the inlet jetty, and on the way I made sure we walked past her poster at Pyramid Photos.

"You came here on purpose." She blushed and punched my arm.

We got to the jetty, went halfway out on the rocks, and sat down. An occasional wake or surge of surf would hit the rocks below and shower us with a spray of cold seawater.

"What do you do at Deep Creek Lake?" I asked.

"Mostly boating and water-skiing."

"No surfing, I guess."

"There's also a state park, and sometimes we'll go hiking there."

"Where do you stay?"

"Dad rents a cabin. It's really pretty. It's so different there. Lots of hills. Maybe you could even call them mountains. In the winter, people ski there."

We climbed down from the jetty and onto the beach, took our shoes off, and walked along the shoreline. The tide had gone out, and the cool, wet sand massaged the soles of our bare feet as we walked. We reached the pier, walking under it into the cool shadows, and watched the waves break against the pilings and split apart in white foam. I thought of the night we met and stood on this same pier: the Beach Boys, the Beatles, the scent of peaches in her hair. Then I remembered the night Jack proposed our arrangement with Misty in this same spot, and I pushed the thought from my mind.

"Wendy," I whispered. When she turned to look at me, I held her face in both my hands and kissed her, deep and long, then spread my fingers wide and ran them through her golden hair.

"Wow. What brought that on?"

"I'm really going to miss you. I wish you didn't have to go with your parents."

"Me, too, but it's probably the last time I'll ever go on vacation with my family. There's no way I can get out of it." She was holding my right hand in both of her hands and was pulling it down. "I have an idea. When you start to miss me, just go look at my poster." She started to giggle. "And then you can kiss the poster."

I laughed at the thought of Mr. Devorak's reaction.

We went back onto the boardwalk, stopped at Fisher's, and bought a box of popcorn before sitting on a bench. In a few minutes, a pigeon landed at Wendy's feet. She reached to take the box of popcorn from me.

"What are you doing?"

"I just want to give this poor fellow some popcorn. He's hungry."

"No, don't."

"Why?"

"He'll tell his friends, and before you know it..."

"Don't be silly."

Then she threw a couple of pieces of popcorn at the stupid pigeon. Within seconds, two more pigeons landed next to the first one, and one aggressive fellow landed on our bench next to Wendy. She tossed a handful of popcorn to the ground, and the birds scrambled for their share or more. That action brought another half dozen. Before I knew it, pigeons had surrounded us. I was having visions of Rod Taylor and Tippi Hedren running for their lives in the movie *The Birds*.

"Dump the popcorn. Let's get outta here," I said, grabbing her hand. She turned the box upside down, and we ran down the boardwalk. After running about twenty feet, we looked back at the pigeons feasting on our popcorn.

"Those bastards," I said.

"They were just hungry."

We spent the day like that, just wandering along the boardwalk or the beach, enjoying the day and our time together. Sometimes we just sat on a bench and watched people. Wendy liked to guess which couples were married and which ones were dating.

"OK, see that couple? They're married."

"How can you tell?"

"They're not holding hands. She's talking, and he's looking at the T-shirt shop. But that couple behind them—they're dating."

"You know that because why?"

"They *are* holding hands, and see? They're looking at each other as they talk."

I laughed. She was so cute in so many ways. We never knew if she was right or not because we didn't have the nerve to ask the couples. In the afternoon, we had burgers and fries and shared a vanilla shake at the Alaska Stand at Wicomico. After that, we found the Jeep, kissed goodbye, and held each other as though we feared it would be the last time.

"I hate it when you drive off in your Jeep. I just want to be in it with you."

"I know. I feel lonely when you're not with me."

She got in the Jeep, and we kissed one more time before she started it up and drove away. I stood watching until the Jeep disappeared.

Chapter 30

June 29, 1964
The Poster

I RUBBED MY SLEEPY eyes, climbed out of bed, and made my way to the bathroom. Living in an orphanage and a college dormitory had prepared me for a lot of things; however, it did not prepare me for living with two women. We'd been living together for over two weeks, but I still hadn't adjusted to the bathroom conditions. My toiletries consisted of five things: a razor, shaving cream, deodorant, toothpaste, and a toothbrush. Looking at Misty and Sylvia's bathroom made me think I had wandered into a drugstore. What could they possibly do with all this stuff? I could understand two bottles of perfume, but the other stuff? There was something called concealer. Maybe Misty used it in some astrology practice. Something for foundations, mascara, eyebrow pencils, blush, and maybe a dozen tubes of lipstick. There was more than two of everything. I could understand Misty having hers and Sylvia hers, but they had enough for a half dozen women to have one each. There were jars of cold cream and moisturizers, several brands of shampoos and hair conditioners, baby oil, alcohol, cotton balls, Q-tips, and sanitary pads. There were six or seven bottles of nail polish and a couple bottles of nail polish remover. Then there were tools: a couple of types of small scissors, popsicle-like sticks covered with sandpaper, nail files, and other pointy things. The bathtub was an old-fashioned type with feet and a shower curtain that wrapped around. Hanging from the shower curtain rod were underwear, bras, and a couple other girly things. I wondered if it would be easier to just go to the public restroom on the boardwalk to shave and brush my teeth.

When I came out of the bathroom after shaving, Jack was sitting on the edge of the bed in his skivvies, sleepy-eyed and smoking one of Misty's Parliaments. The girls were awake but stretched out on their beds like cats.

"I have to swing by Pyramid Photos to get my pay from last week, then see if I can line up another party for the girls. Jack, you wanna come with me?"

"Sure." He got up and slipped on some shorts while his cigarette hung from his lips. "See ya later, girls."

"You want to meet for lunch?" Misty asked.

"Yeah, good idea," I said.

"How 'bout Thrasher's?" said Misty.

"Let's do Ponzetti's," said Jack.

"OK, cool. See you guys there around one," said Misty.

As Jack and I walked down Philadelphia, I looked at him and smiled, saying, "What's the matter? Afraid to face Louise?"

"It's not that I'm afraid to face her; it's more a question of why. We don't owe each other anything. We had a couple of tumbles in the sack, and that was it."

"All over for the girl who would do anything for you. So what's that mean? Thrasher's french fries are off your diet from now on?"

"No, I'll just get my fries at a different time of day."

I had forgotten about Wendy's poster and saw it as we approached Pyramid Photos. Waves of guilt flowed over me again, my ears felt hot, and my mouth went dry.

"Hey, there's a familiar face. Damn, she's a fox. As good as she looks on that poster, she looks even better in person. Forget about my Louise. What are you doin' about Wendy?"

"Ah, Jack...man, I don't know. You talked me into this mess."

"Yeah, and if I hadn't, you'd be panhandling on the boardwalk and sleeping on the beach."

"She's at Deep Creek Lake with her family this week. I don't have to deal with it until she gets back next week. I don't know what I'm going to do. I don't want to lose her."

"Have ya fucked her yet?"

"Jack...don't go there, man."

"OK, that answers that question—you haven't. That makes it easier. Just drop her and move on. I mean, we got a really good thing goin' here with Misty and Sylvia."

"Hey, Delaney, where's that beautiful girlfriend of yours?" asked Mr. D.

"Vacationing with her parents at Deep Creek Lake."

"She's a keeper, young man. Here for your paycheck and camera, I guess?"

"Thanks, Mr. D. See you this afternoon."

On the way to the boardwalk, one of Pyramid's photographers was walking toward us.

"Hey, Gordon, on your way to report for work and get your camera?"

"Yeah. I see you're off to an early start."

"Gordon, this is my friend Jack."

"Hi, Jack."

"Ah...Jack's got a, ah...unique sort of job. He can fix you and your buddies up with some chicks. The kind of chicks that you're guaranteed to score with, if you know what I mean."

"Hookers?" he asked, looking to Jack.

Jack stared back with raised eyebrows, his lower lip protruding, and nodded.

"How much?"

"Twenty-five bucks a guy," Jack said.

He thought for a moment and said, "OK. I've got three room-mates. I think they all might go for it. They've been getting kinda horny lately."

I got his address and told him to expect a visit between nine and ten that night. It made me think—maybe Morton and his friends were ready for an encore. If I could line them up, I'd be two for two for the day, and it could be a $200 night.

Jack hung with me while I did the photo routine. We found Morton at his usual hangout on Ninth Street, and my hunch was right. He and his boys were ready to go again. When we got to Ponzetti's, Misty and Sylvia were sitting in a booth. I sat down next to Misty, smiled at her, and said, "Good news, Misty. I got two parties for you tonight."

"Two?"

"Yeah. This could be a $200 night."

"It's about time you started to produce, Delaney."

"Misty, I'm gonna work your ass off."

Chapter 31

June 30, 1964
The Number 5

"ARE YOU GOING to the Landromat?" Misty asked.

"What does it look like?" I said, stuffing my dirty clothes into a pillowcase.

"Mind if I go with you?"

"Sure, come along."

Misty went to the bathroom, dabbed herself with perfume, and then gathered her clothes together. We walked the three blocks to the Landromat. As we walked, I asked, "Why'd you put perfume on just to go to the Landromat?"

"Do you like it?"

"I don't know. I haven't really smelled it."

Misty stopped, pulled me toward her, tilted her head, and flipped her hair back so I could smell her bare neck.

"Like it?"

"Yeah, but I can't tell any specific fragrance."

"You're not supposed to. It's a complex fragrance that doesn't allow one fragrance to overpower another. It's supposed to smell like a woman."

"Didn't you smell like a woman to begin with?"

"Don't be stupid."

"What's it called?"

"It's Chanel No. 5. Marilyn Monroe once said that the only thing she wore in bed were a few drops of Chanel No. 5. That's appropriate for me considering my profession, don't you think?"

"Mmm."

"Also, the number five is a good number. The ancients believed the number represented man in perfect balance with the universe."

"Mmm, I'm not sure I understand that, but five is also a Fibonacci number."

"That's a new one for me. What's a Fibo...whatchamacallit?"

"Fibonacci. He was an Italian mathematician. He basically succeeded in replacing Roman numerals with the Arabic numerals we use today. Five is part of a sequence. The sequence is obtained by adding two numbers together, then adding the last number to the sum: one plus two equals three, then add two plus three equals five, and so forth."

"What does it mean?"

"I don't know. Probably nothing."

When we got there, I dumped the contents of my pillowcase into a washer.

"What are you doing?" Misty asked.

"What?"

"You're putting your whites in with your colors. You can't do that. Your whites will fade."

"I always do it this way. It saves me a quarter."

"Yeah, well, that's why your whites look gray. Here, let me put your whites with mine, and my colors with yours. It'll still save you a quarter, and your whites will look better."

"Uh...I don't know. It, ah...it just doesn't seem right, maybe too intimate."

Misty stopped mixing our whites and colors, leaned into my face, and said in a harsh whisper, "Washing our clothes in the same washer is not 'intimate.' What we've been doing in bed at night is 'intimate.'"

Misty continued the sorting and took over the laundry project. I walked outside and sat on the bench in front of the Landromat. A few minutes later, Misty joined me. She pulled a box of Parliaments out of her purse and lit one.

"Cigarette?"

"No thanks."

"You have some hang-ups, don't you? You're really way too uptight."

"Misty, most *normal* people have hang-ups."

"So you're saying I'm not *normal*? You're probably right. At least, I don't consider myself normal. Exceptional, maybe, but definitely not normal."

I looked at her and smiled. "Different, definitely. I'm not so sure about exceptional."

She laughed. It was the first time I had ever heard her laugh. It was deep, throaty, and genuine.

Misty continued to smoke her cigarette, and we were both quiet for a while until she broke the silence. "What is it about what we're doing that bothers you? You've gotten off to a good start setting up parties. You took over keeping track of the money. You're, like, copacetic with it but not completely. It's the sex, isn't it?"

"Yeah, I guess so. The rest of it is just business. I got used to approaching people and selling a service working the photo gig. But the rest of it, I don't know...just seems wrong. Blame it on my Catholic upbringing. The Church does a good job of making you feel guilty of just about everything. How'd you get into this, anyway? You're smart, educated. You don't have to do this."

"No one has to do it, Delaney. I'm in this for the same reason you are: the money. And don't kid yourself—you are *intimately* involved. If you define prostitution as using your sex for personal gain, I guess you could say my first time was in college.

I was struggling in a statistics class, and I started flirting with my professor. He flirted back, and next thing you know, we're having an affair, and my grades are improving. I got an A, but I still struggle today with the difference between mean, mode, and median. Don't get me wrong—I was a book buster. I got good grades. After I graduated, the only job offers I got were for secretary or file clerk. I took a job as a cocktail waitress to pay the bills until I could find something appropriate to my education. I made more in tips than I would have as a secretary. Besides, I'm not a fast typist. Pissed me off. I knew guys who didn't do as well as me in school, and they were getting good-paying jobs.

"In the cocktail waitress job, I had to wear this skimpy costume with fishnet hose and show a lot of cleavage, which...I don't have much of. It was a cocktail lounge in a big hotel in downtown Baltimore. The customers were businessmen in suits and ties. Every night, I was getting groped or propositioned. One night, this decent-looking guy in his thirties propositioned me. I thought, 'Hell, I can see myself in bed with him without getting paid for it, so why not?' So I said yes and went to his room after my shift. After that, I said yes more often.

"There were always one or two women, dressed real sexy, who would come to the lounge by themselves, tip the bartender, and leave with one of the guests. The women were obviously local. The same ones would be in a couple times a week. The guys—some you might never see again; others might be back every couple of weeks. I started thinking about these women. They weren't getting groped and didn't have to put up with bullshit from drunken customers. I thought, 'Hey, if they can do it, so can I.' So I quit my waitress job and started visiting the cocktail lounges in the big hotels, and I was making a very nice living."

"How did you meet Sylvia?"

"I've known Sylvia only since January. We met at a New Year's Eve party. We were both paid to be there. That next morning, we shared a cab. I invited her to my place for breakfast, and we've been together ever since.

"Sylvia is a totally different person than me. Different background, education, everything. She'll tell you she's in prostitution for the money, but it's deeper than that. Sylvia can't remember a time in her life when she didn't have sex. As far back as she can remember, she was having sex with her older brother. That continued until she was thirteen or fourteen. Then when her brother quit having sex with her, she started having sex with boys at school. The rest of what she told you the other night is true."

"The other night...after Sylvia got hurt...the way you two reacted, it wasn't what I would have expected. It was almost like you were mothering her."

"Yeah, well, I guess I tend to do that with her. She's very fragile. She has low self-esteem and great mood swings. If I were a practicing psychologist, I'd say she suffered from manic-depressive reaction. She needs help—professional help. I do what I can for her, but she's a mess and a half."

We went in to check on the laundry. The wash was done. Misty gathered the clothes from the washing machine and put them together in one of the dryers.

She looked at me and smiled, saying, "Now we can mix the whites and colors together. We can also put boy clothes with girl clothes together."

"Very funny."

Chapter 32

July 9, 1964
An Inauspicious Day

A LOUD CRASH OF thunder awoke us. The morning light painted the room a dark gray, and it was cold. The clock radio said 10:20. I got out of bed, walked to the dresser, and turned on the radio, hoping for a weather report. Instead I heard the middle of Jimmy Jones' "Handy Man." It was Thursday, and Wendy had returned from Deep Creek on Sunday, but it hadn't occurred to me to call her since she had returned. I should have but didn't, and I didn't know why. Fourth of July weekend had been huge for us. The girls were busy day and night, Friday through Sunday, with clients. I had my best days of the season with Pyramid Photos, but it was pocket change compared to what the girls raked in. It didn't matter; the photo gig was just a front for scouting business for the girls. And it was working.

Sylvia got up, went into the bathroom, and closed the door. Jack stretched and yawned while Misty buried her face in a pillow. It was raining hard. A cold front had changed the temperature. I turned off the window fan and opened the blinds. Rain can be refreshing, cleansing. Grass is greener, and trees, weighted down with moisture, fluff out their branches. But rain is not refreshing at a beach. There is little grass and no trees. It's depressing. It's boring. You can't go to the beach when it's raining, especially if there's lightning. There's nothing to do at the beach when it rains. Lightning flashed, then a few seconds later there was a crack of thunder.

By eleven, we were all dressed and headed for Melvin's, only a block from our room. We had no umbrellas or rain gear, so we ran. Water dripped off us like a broken faucet. Most of the breakfast crowd, if there was any, had left, and it was too early for the lunch crowd. While we were looking at the menu, Misty said, "We ought not to take any jobs tonight. It's an inauspicious day."

"Well, if this rain keeps up, it'll be hard to line up anything," I said. "Nobody will be on the beach. If guys aren't in their rooms, they'll be in bars and drunk before 5:30."

"It's not because of the weather. Today's a new moon. It's a period of darkness, and bad things tend to happen during a new moon. Let's just hang out tonight. Be low-key. We need a night off, anyway. It's been a busy two weeks, and this past weekend was a killer. We don't have to work every night."

"What's this new moon business?" I asked. "I thought it was a full moon when everyone went crazy, women had babies, were-wolves came out, and the tide got real high."

"I don't know about the werewolves, but some of that is true," said Misty. "The full moon is a time of illumination, light, good spirits. That's why more babies are born during a full moon. It's a good thing. It's the opposite of the new moon phase. The darkness of the new moon invites mischief. For evil spirits, it's their time to come out and play."

"Do you have any examples?" I asked.

Misty cast her eyes to the ceiling in a thoughtful pose. "Well, the most recent new moon was the night Sylvia got beat up and you guys found her. Oh, yeah, the new moon before that was the first time I met you, Delaney. Remember that night on the boardwalk? Did anything bad happen to you that day?"

My first day in Ocean City was the day Georgetown expelled me, but there was no way I'd ever admit that to Misty. It had to be a coincidence, nothing more.

"Yeah, Misty, now that you mention it...something bad did happen to me that day. That was the same day I met you and Jack. Double trouble, I guess."

Harriet started accepting us as a regular foursome and was gradually getting friendlier, maybe because we were leaving large tips. She had just finished pouring our coffee when I heard the door close. I looked over my shoulder and saw Wendy in a yellow rain slicker looking at me. Rainwater running off her slicker pooled at her feet. She lowered the raincoat's hood. Her blond hair was damp but still beautiful. As she walked toward me, I stood up.

"Hi, Wendy," said Jack.

Ignoring him, she said to me, "What happened? Why haven't you called me? Where are you working? I went to the Majestica, and no one there knew your name. They'd never heard of you."

"Let's talk outside." I took her hand, but she pulled it away as we walked to the door.

Thunder continued rumbling, and rain fell from the low clouds, filling the gutters in the street. We stood under the restaurant's awning, and I shivered in the cold dampness as Wendy looked up at me, her eyes shifting between anger and bewilderment.

"Those women with you and Jack, we saw them with Jack before I left. Why are you with them? Did you sleep with one of them last night? Is that why you're here having breakfast with them?"

"Well...I don't know. I guess the easiest...yes, Jack and I spent the night with them."

"Delaney, why? I thought we had something special. I missed you so much. Why are you doing this to me?"

"It's hard to explain, but it's not what you think."

"Not what I think? Not what I think? What am I supposed to think? You just admitted you slept with one of those women."

"It's really more of a business deal."

"What? What? Oh, oh, you are *such* a disappointment." Her eyes were welling up.

"I can't really..."

"Oh, forget it. Forget everything," she said as she pushed past me and ran, splashing across the street to her Jeep. She climbed in and started the engine. The wheels spun in the rain-filled street before gaining traction. She drove off, and I knew I'd never see her again. I stepped out from the awning to the curb, watching until she disappeared from view. The rain beat down on me until lightning struck something nearby. The booming thunder startled me, and I went back inside Melvin's.

"We ordered for you while you were having your conversation," Jack said.

"I'm not hungry."

Sylvia sat across from me in a rare speechless moment, staring at me with wide eyes. Harriet stood near the back of the restaurant like a statue, holding the coffee pot. I had become the unwilling center of attention when all I really wanted was to find a place to be alone and cry.

"I said it was an inauspicious day."

I couldn't tell if Misty was being sympathetic or sarcastic. My eyes looked into my cold cup of coffee as if the answer could be found there.

Chapter 33

July 10, 1964
Lauren Bacall

THIS MORNING, I'M paying the price for trying to wash away my sorrows with alcohol, as the expression goes. After the scene at Melvin's, I punished myself by walking on the boardwalk in the rain, hoping lightning would strike me and put me out of my misery—an appropriate retribution for hurting Wendy. I was depressed, angry, and hateful. When I bought a fifth of vodka and paid for it with a soaking wet ten-dollar bill, the clerk was pissed. He wanted to know how he was supposed to dry the bill. I felt like hitting him with the vodka bottle. Instead I told him to stick the ten up his ass. Back at the room, I drank from the bottle until I passed out. Misty, Sylvia, and Jack wisely left me alone. At that moment, I hated them and felt they were to blame. My thoughts were of Wendy, her father, her family, and their home, and how I'd so much wanted to be part of that family. In drunken fantasies, I imagined undoing the damage and winning Wendy back. With the soberness of morning and the pain of a hangover came the realization that it was not possible. There would be no undoing. Instead I tried to think of a way to break free of this unholy union with my three Macbeth witches.

While I shaved, my hand trembled from the effects of the previous night's binge, and the trembling made me wonder if I could hold the camera steady today. Then the dry heaves hit me. I cleaned up and popped some aspirin with a glass of water, hoping it would stay down.

"You OK?" Jack asked.

I ignored him and walked out of the room. At the corner market, I got a cup of coffee and a package of Twinkies. I found a bench to sit on to eat, hoping my breakfast wouldn't come up later. My unsteady hand caused the hot coffee to splash onto my bare leg. That was it—time to walk over to Pyramid and pick up my camera.

"You look like shit, Delaney."

"Thanks, Mr. D. That's exactly what I feel like."

I revived some as the morning progressed, and by midday, I was able to eat a burger with fries. A vanilla milkshake from Kohr's settled my stomach, and everything was better in the afternoon. It was getting close to four, and with over thirty Pyramid photo shots, it was turning into a great day. I just did photo work—no soliciting, or more accurately, no pimping. It was time for me to get back to the office to turn in the camera, log, and film. I still didn't have a plan to break away from Jack and the girls, and I didn't know what to do about the night. I didn't want to go back to the room. As I was making my way to the boardwalk, I heard a female voice say, "Don't you want to take my picture?"

To my right, a woman sat upright on the sand with her arms wrapped around her legs. Her shoulder-length brown hair was parted on the left and swept across her forehead with a large curl close to her right eye. Her hair had remarkable body in spite of the humid air. Her large sunglasses hid her eyes, making it hard to tag her age, but I could tell she was mature, something like the mid-forties.

"Excuse me?"

"I asked if you wanted to take my picture."

The words came from deep in her throat and had a huskiness that reminded me of Lauren Bacall. In fact, everything about her reminded me of Lauren Bacall.

"Yeah...yes, of course."

I assumed my professional Pyramid photographer mode and took charge of posing her, having her move into different positions while trying shots at different angles. She wore a black one-piece that flattered her body, and her legs looked great.

As I was finishing up the paperwork, recording her real name (which was not Lauren Bacall) and logging in the film numbers, I heard her say, "Would you like to stop by my room for a cocktail when you finish working?"

"Ah...yeah, I would."

"Write down my room number. It's 223 at the Safari Motel."

"Great. I know where that is. I used to work around the corner."

"Do you like martinis? I can make you a martini."

At the mention of martini, a queasiness came over me, but I soldiered on. "As a matter of fact, I do like martinis. Vodka, dry, with a twist, shaken, not stirred."

"I'll give it to you any way you want it."

"OK, see you at seven."

She never responded. She just rolled over on her stomach. Gawd, was she cool.

After turning in the Pyramid Photo camera and log, I had three hours to kill. I was determined not to go back to the room tonight and figured spending the night with the Lauren Bacall lookalike would take care of that, at least for tonight. There was still no viable game plan for me to get out on my own, but I was sure I'd figure something out. Eventually.

I knocked lightly. She opened the door holding a vodka martini with a twist in a hotel glass, wearing a silk navy robe that displayed her ample cleavage. The robe stopped at mid-thigh, revealing her gorgeous legs. She smiled without showing her teeth, her eyebrows raised. I stepped into the room as she handed me the martini and closed the door. She kissed me on the cheek, then softly on my lips. I smelled vanilla and powder.

"You smell good. What are you wearing?" I asked.

"Shalimar. You smell of salt air, ocean, and suntan lotion."

"Yeah, well, Coppertone has become my aftershave."

We kissed again, this time deeply. We broke, and as I was taking my first sip of the martini, she began to pull down my pants. We frolicked and played for hours. When I was having sex with her, I imagined she really was Lauren Bacall, and that made me forget about Wendy, Misty, Sylvia, and Jack. It was after one in the morning when she turned on the bedside lamp and lit a Benson & Hedges. She offered me one, and I took it. She lit it for me with a gold Ronson lighter and then said, "You'll need to leave as soon as you finish your cigarette."

"Don't you want me to spend the night?"

"Gawd, no. I don't want you to see me in the morning. It will spoil the illusion."

For the first time, I noticed her gray-green eyes, the makeup that hid the bags under her eyes, and her crow's feet, and I understood what she meant.

It had been fun and some foolish wishful thinking, but now I felt defeated, with no other option than to return to the room with Misty, Sylvia, and Jack. I stubbed out the cigarette in the ashtray, dressed, and walked to the door while she stayed in bed, a cigarette in one hand and martini in the other. We smiled at each other, and then I left her.

It took a few moments before my eyes adjusted to the dark room. Jack was breathing heavy, spooning with Sylvia, his arm over her shoulder, while Misty, with her back to me, appeared to be sleeping in our bed. I slipped out of my clothes and slid into bed with Misty, my back to hers, hoping not to wake her. Some time went by before I realized Misty wasn't asleep. We lay in bed together, both of us pretending to sleep, both of us wondering what was going on in the other's head. Neither of us spoke.

Chapter 34

July 11, 1964
Music Trivia

I FELT LIKE THE porcupine in the room. Nobody wanted to talk to me, let alone get close. We took turns in the bathroom and dressed, barely speaking to one another, and when we did, it was in hushed tones as if we were in a library or funeral home. With the somber faces, it was more like a funeral home. Even our march to Melvin's reminded me of people in the movie *Teenage Zombies*. Expressionless, we plodded along the streets of Ocean City. However, coffee, a meal, and the presence of other people seemed to stimulate everyone, including myself. After breakfast, the four of us went to the boardwalk and walked in the direction of the pier. Another cold front had moved in, and locals talked of this being the coldest July on record. Wind blew out of the northeast, and we hunched our shoulders as if that would protect us from the cool air and occasional squall. Ugly low clouds raced inland, and the ocean was filled with gray agitation, like a washing machine. Hardly anyone was on the beach, and the only people out and about were families with children suffering from cabin fever. There were lines at the Skee-Ball vendors, and the arcades were packed with kids pouring nickels into pinball machines. Nobody was buying ice cream or snow cones.

Jack said, "This is Nowheresville. Nothing's gonna happen until this weather breaks. Let's get some more vodka, beer, and cigs and go back to the room."

I was still zombielike and didn't care what we did or where we went. No one else said anything, so we all just turned and walked toward the liquor store.

When we got back to the room, Misty turned on the clock radio. Bill Haley's ancient "Rock Around the Clock" was playing.

"My God," said Sylvia, throwing her hands over her head. "That song's gotta be at least ten years old. Doesn't this station play anything new?"

"Don't have a conniption fit. It's only music," said Jack. "Hey, here's a question. Who first recorded 'Shake, Rattle and Roll'? Don't get confused on this. Bill Haley recorded it, too, but not first."

"Big Joe Turner," responded Misty.

"Wow, Misty, that was good," said Sylvia.

"OK, now here's a newer one. who sang 'Funny'?" Misty asked.

"Oh, that's hard," said Sylvia

"Peggy Lee," Jack answered.

"Not even close. Delaney, are you in this? Come on, try a guess."

"Chuck Berry," I said.

"That's worse than Peggy Lee. Here's a clue: it's a woman."

"Tammi Terrell."

"Better, but wrong."

"Alright, Miss Smarty-pants, who is it?" Jack asked.

"Maxine Brown. Maybe that was too hard."

"OK, OK, I got one. Who sang 'Heartbreak Hotel'?" Sylvia asked.

"Sylvia, honey, you don't want to ask an Elvis song in any trivia game."

"Why, Misty?"

"Sweetheart, everyone knows all of Elvis's songs."

"Isn't that the purpose of the game, to get the right answer?"

Jack looked away, his shoulders shaking as he stifled a laugh. Misty offered a warm smile and rubbed Sylvia's shoulder, saying, "You're right. That's the purpose of the game."

Jack straightened up. "Who sang 'He'll Have to Go'?"

Sylvia jumped off the bed, hopping up and down like a twelve-year-old. "I know, I know! Bill Reeves! No, no, Jim Reeves. I heard that song every night in the hillbilly bars in Dundalk."

It went on like that for a couple of hours, and I started to get out of my blue mood. These people weren't the problem. They were my friends, my only friends. Nothing that happened with Wendy was their fault. Around two o'clock, we could see that the sun was shining. We went outside and back to the boardwalk. The weather had changed. Gone was the cool air, replaced by a sultry presence. People were everywhere now. It was as though someone had opened a humanity gate and every human being flooded out. It was time to go to work. There were men who that needed to be entertained and satisfied, and I needed to find them because Misty and Sylvia were the answer.

Chapter 35

July 13, 1964
Misty in the Morning

I FELT MISTY LEAVE our bed. A reflection of natural light on the wall told me morning had come and that it must have been after eight. Despite the hum of the window fan, the room was growing warm. Hearing the blinds being raised, I rolled over and looked to the window. Hundreds of tiny specks of dust rose and floated to greet a sun that gave Misty's alabaster skin an orange glow. With a fixed gaze, she stared out the window, looking at nothing but the back of another boarding house. In the morning light, her natural beauty was revealed without the eye shadow, without the eyeliner, without the flaming red lipstick. A beam of light reflected off her coal black hair that lay naturally without combing. A strong jawline and prominent cheekbones provided an enduring foundation. Watching her at the window, I realized for the first time that she was a beautiful woman, beautiful in a different way from Wendy. Wendy was a bud beginning to bloom, Misty in full flower, one with an excited naïveté for the unknown future, the other with the wisdom of experience.

Misty looked at me. "You're awake. Get dressed. Let's go for a walk."

I put on my cutoffs and a T-shirt. Misty slipped on a muumuu and picked up a box of Parliaments, matches, and her broad-brimmed straw hat. As we walked out the door, I looked back at Sylvia and Jack. Sylvia's leg twitched, and Jack's heavy breathing bordered on a snore. They were both in a deep morning sleep, the kind that is deepest and soundest just before waking.

When we reached the corner of First Street, Misty stopped and lit a match. Sheltering the flame with her cupped hands, she put the match to her Parliament and inhaled deeply. She gave me a serious look and started walking toward the beach. Then she started to talk.

"I tend to believe, as do many others, that the beginning of the Age of Aquarius was July 16, 1945. I believe this for essentially two reasons. First, it is a provable astronomical fact that the sun passed into the sign of Aquarius during this period. Second, this is the date the first atomic test bomb was exploded. This event signaled a significant change in the power of the universe. Man could now destroy himself and the planet. Never before did that possibility exist."

"So what?" I said. "What does it mean? The sun being in one place, a constellation in another, the moon somewhere else... does it really have anything to do with us?"

"Delaney, think about what happens when change occurs. Nobody likes change. Change is bad for someone but maybe good for someone else. I'll educate you. Each astrological age follows a precession of the equinoxes which occurs approximately every 2,150 years. The last one was when the Age of Aries passed to the Age of Pisces. This ended a two-thousand year Egyptian Empire and marked the beginning of the Christian Empire."

We had reached the boardwalk and were walking south in the direction of the pier. I chuckled. "The precession of the equinoxes—wow, that's something I want to see."

"So what is happening to us?" Misty continued. "We're at the cusp of this change, and already we can see disasters building. After ending World War II, we went to war in Korea. Then we came very close to nuclear annihilation two years ago during the Cuban Missile Crisis. Then our president was assassinated. Now we're again entering a war in Vietnam. Why? People won't stand for it again. Their children are being sent off to God knows where to die for God knows what."

I was grateful this conversation was taking place at this early hour, for there were few people on the boardwalk who would overhear it. When we reached the pier, Misty turned, and we walked out toward the end of it. There were a few people fishing, taking advantage of a rising tide. I tried to get her off the subject with some levity. "Why do you have a clock radio?"

"Last summer, Martin Luther King led over two thousand people on a march in Washington. It was peaceful, but race relations in this country will not remain peaceful."

"I mean, it doesn't make any sense—you sleep until you wake up. You never set the alarm for a wake-up."

"As long as Negroes are treated as second-class citizens and denied equal rights, there will be protests, and eventually the protests will turn violent. As long as there are people who think they can change things by murdering the president of the United States, there will be people who think by murdering someone like Martin Luther King, they can stop this movement. There will be more assassinations and rebellion. Families will be torn apart—father against son, daughter against mother. Like Bob Dylan's song, 'The Times They Are a-Changin,' our times are changing—and it won't be pretty."

"That's nice." When Misty mentioned equal rights, my mind flashed back to the march in Princess Anne, and I didn't hear anything she said after that. My head was filled with a jumble of thoughts—thoughts of Wendy, her father, Fred at the restaurant, the picketers, the prayer before the march, the Negro woman locking arms with me, the police dogs, the fire hoses, people falling and crying, and the maid at Wendy's home.

"This is important, Delaney."

We were at the end of the pier. There was nothing but the Atlantic to our east, and it felt like we were standing at the edge of the Earth. The west wind stiffened and moved a lock of raven hair across her face. I felt like I wanted to kiss her. She took both of my hands in hers and continued. "I don't want to see you hurt, but I can't help you if you won't listen to me." Her pleading eyes showed her worry, and for the first time, I realized she really cared about me.

"Go on."

"I've studied your complete chart, and you need to be very careful. You probably shouldn't have come to Ocean City this summer."

"Why?"

"Well, for starters, your Venus-Pluto-Neptune configuration is not good for romantic relationships. It's set up for a potential loss, and we both know that has already happened. You were in love with Wendy, and from what you told me about her, she was probably in love with you. You see how that ended."

"Misty, it's easy to look in the past and say some planet alignment mumbo jumbo caused it all." With the mention of Wendy, my desire to kiss Misty fled.

"I'm only saying, if I had worked your chart before you met Wendy, I could have told you it wasn't going to work out before it happened."

"I don't want to talk about Wendy."

"OK, forget about Wendy."

"Yeah, easy for you to say."

"You need to know about your future, and I'm going to tell you it doesn't look good financially."

"Oh, really? Well, can you explain why I now have more money than I've had in my entire life?"

"Uranus is in the second house, and that is a concern because it means unexpected financial losses. Libra is in the second house cusp, and that means the loss will be due to a partnership."

I laughed as I said with raised eyebrows, "*Your anus* is going to experience financial losses?"

"No, yours."

Misty let go of my hands and undid her zodiac necklace. She began working on one of the symbols. "Delaney, I don't really believe in lucky charms, but I want you to have this." She removed the water bearer symbol from the necklace. "This is the symbol for Aquarius. The fact that your birth sign is in the middle of the Aquarius sign means all the negative aspects of the Age of Aquarius will have the greatest impact on you. This isn't going to protect you."

"You mean like a Saint Christopher medal?"

"Whatever that means. It won't protect you, but you should keep it to remind you of pitfalls to come so you can take steps to protect yourself."

She looked at me as she handed me the Aquarius symbol. I looked deep into her eyes, touched by her sincerity. I felt the Aquarius in my hand, and then it wasn't. I looked down as it hit the decking of the pier, saw it bounce a few inches in the air and disappear in a gap between the boards. Misty gasped. The water bearer was in the ocean.

"Oh, Delaney...Aquarius has fallen." Tears streamed down her cheeks.

Chapter 36

July 15, 1964
The Latest from the Beach Boys

SYLVIA WAS SITTING cross-legged on her bed with curlers in her hair, applying an orange-looking nail polish to her fingernails while Jack sat in the chair blowing smoke rings. With great concentration, Misty was flipping pages of astrology charts and sun signs, scribbling on a sheet of paper. She finished, stared at her result for a moment, then shuffled the papers together and looked at Jack.

"OK, Jack, here's your horoscope for today. Give it everything you've got, and opportunity will flow like an incoming tide. Extra effort will pay big dividends. Be flexible and ready to make adjustments. What seems obvious at first may not be."

"Don't worry, Misty. I'll give it everything I've got," he said, taking a drag from his Camel and blowing another smoke ring.

"You're such an ass. You don't appreciate the work I put into this."

An argument was brewing. I closed my eyes and laid my head down on the pillow, trying to listen to Buddy Holly finish singing "Peggy Sue" on the clock radio. The DJ introduced the next song by saying, "Continuing with today's theme of songs with girl's names in the title, here is the latest from the Beach Boys." He didn't offer the name of the song. It started with Brian Wilson plucking five lonely notes on his bass, followed by Dennis Wilson's drum intro. Then everything went wrong for me. Their vocals began with their great signature harmony by asking, "Wendy, Wendy, what went wrong?"

"Goddamn it, turn that thing off," I shouted, and before anyone moved, I jumped up and turned the radio off. A full minute went by without anyone saying a word until Sylvia timidly broke the silence.

"I thought you liked the Beach Boys."

She looked at me with the wide-eyed innocence of a child, and for a change, I began to feel sorry for her rather than myself.

"Maybe I should have worked on your chart first," said Misty. "It probably would have said something like don't listen to the radio today."

"Misty, you bitch." I started laughing. "You fucking bitch."

She started to laugh with me and stood up as I walked to her. We embraced and laughed until tears streamed down our checks. My sides started to hurt from laughing so hard.

"What's so funny?" Sylvia asked.

"Ignore them. They're both crazy," Jack said.

"I have to laugh. It's better than crying," I said to Sylvia.

"But you are crying," she replied.

Misty fell onto the bed and rolled over, laughing hysterically. Sylvia's facial expression said that she was completely perplexed. I sat on the bed next to her and put my arm around her as she held her hands away from me so as not to smear her nail polish.

"You're right, Sylvia. I'm crying, but it's a good crying. Thank you, Sylvia, for everything," I said as I hugged her.

"Well, you're welcome, I guess."

"Come on, everybody, get dressed," said Jack. "We gotta get out on the beach and catch some rays before everyone in the room loses their minds and goes crazy."

His comment changed the mood. We all followed his advice and headed out for the activity of the boardwalk, the sunshine, and the fresh air.

Chapter 37

July 15, 1964
The Lifeguards

MISTY AND I were an improbable pair walking on the beach—me with my camera and wearing my Pyramid Photos T-shirt and Ray-Bans, Misty with a straw hat, Foster Grants, and her muumuu. We walked the hot sands in our bare feet, looking for Pyramid photo customers and prospective clients for the evening, but all we saw on the beach were families and couples. I was doing OK with photos, but nothing was happening for the girls.

Looking at me, Misty said, "We've never tried the lifeguards."

"You've got to be kidding."

"No, I'm not. I'm serious. How many do you suppose there are?"

"Misty, think about it. These guys have their pick of girls every day. They show off their muscles all day long, have great tans, and are the heroes of the beach. They don't have to pay for sex."

"Delaney, Delaney, you're so naïve. You'll never understand."

As we walked between sun worshipers, dodged beach balls, and stepped over children's sand buckets, Misty made a forty-five-degree change in direction. Her path aimed straight for a lifeguard chair. She turned to me with a big smile, saying, "Wait here."

I obeyed, watching from about twenty-five feet away. The lifeguard sat like a naked bronze king on a throne consisting of a large red wooden chair about six feet above the beach, surveying his subjects as they frolicked in the surf, occasionally summoning a floater who ventured too far out to sea to return to the safety of the shore. Misty took her straw hat off and looked up as a breeze danced through her raven hair. Her lips moved. The lifeguard looked down. He talked to her and she talked to him, but the wind captured their words and took them away from me. Unexpectedly, he climbed down from his red wooden throne. Misty took off her sunglasses, his eyes locked on hers, and their pantomime continued. Misty held her hat and glasses high on her chest. Then she let her left hand, holding her hat and glasses, drop as she stepped forward. Her right hand disappeared behind the hat, and the lifeguard jumped back with a startled look, then a smile as he stepped toward Misty. They both laughed as she raised her right hand and placed it on his chest, where it lingered. Their heads were nodding, and their smiles grew bigger as Misty put her hat and glasses on. As she walked away, he offered a wave, and she wiggled her index finger at him with a limp wrist.

We turned our backs on the lifeguard chair, and as we walked away, I looked straight ahead. "What just happened?"

Her chin held high with pride and confidence, she answered, "I've got a date with a lifeguard tonight."

"That wasn't what I meant."

Stifling a laugh, she said, "What? What do you mean?"

"I mean, did you grab his crotch?"

"Did you see me grab his crotch?"

"No. Your hat was in the way."

When we got back to the room, Sylvia and Jack were sitting cross-legged on the bed playing pinochle, and the radio was playing Clyde McPhatter's "Lover Please."

"Got Sylvia a job tonight with two guys at the Majestica Atlantica," said Jack. "That deal I worked out with my replacement seems to be working."

"That's nice, but you should have seen Misty groping a lifeguard."

Sylvia let out a shriek, followed by, "No, Misty, what did you do?"

"You're groping lifeguards now?" asked Jack.

Grinning from ear to ear, Misty responded, "Hey, what can I say? It worked. I got a date tonight, and it could open the door to a whole bunch more business. Like I said to Delaney, how many lifeguards are there here? Has to be more than a hundred. It's a whole new group of customers."

"Misty, you never said, but I assume this is a paid date."

"Yes, Delaney, it's a paid date. What do ya think I am? I worked the price out right there."

"I just don't get it. Why? These guys can have almost any girl on the beach."

"Delaney, there's no such thing as a sure thing unless there's money involved. I'm telling you, some nights these guys score, some nights they just get pissed off because some babe gets her kicks teasing them."

"So what's the story on groping the lifeguard?" asked Jack.

"Oh, you're not going to believe it," I said. "You had to be there. I'll let her tell you."

The lifeguard lived in a shotgun-style house on Eighth Street between St. Louis and Philadelphia. It was just after nine when we knocked on the door. The sandy-haired lifeguard opened it with a smile, then stepped back with a surprised look when he saw me. He looked at Misty and said, "Hey, honey, you're lookin' mighty fine tonight. You bring a friend?"

"Ah, I'm the money guy. You pay me the twenty-five bucks, and then she goes in."

"Oh, yeah, right. Just a minute."

He closed the door, and I said, "I don't like this. There are other guys in there. Let's bug out."

"Don't be chicken. This is a great opportunity. I can handle it."

The door opened, and the sandy-haired lifeguard said, "Here ya go, daddy-o. Two tens and a five. Now get lost. Come on in, honey."

With confidence, Misty stepped over the threshold, and the door slammed behind her. I walked to the corner of Philadelphia and with my hands in my pockets watched traffic go by. An hour passed and no Misty. Something was wrong. I went back to the house. The sound of ugly male laughter pierced the door as I pounded it with my fist. I opened the door and walked in, the sandy-haired lifeguard in white jockey shorts coming toward me.

"What the fuck you doin' comin' in here?" he shouted.

"Where's Misty?"

I saw another muscular figure in underwear come out of a room behind Sandy Hair.

"MISTY!"

Sandy Hair's fist surprised me. There was a crunching sound on my nose and a coppery taste in my mouth. My eyes blurred from the pain, and I cupped both hands over my face. Then a hard blow to the left side of my rib cage took my breath away, and my knees buckled. I was on my back when two guys picked my feet up and dragged me out the door. A third grabbed my left arm, and together they slung me off the porch. My head hit the concrete, and I saw one bright star. The hard landing on the sidewalk left me breathless again. I heard a loud crash, and then the sound of breaking glass came from the house.

"Leave me the fuck alone!" Misty screamed.

There was a thump followed by "Ow!"

"Get outta here, bitch!"

"Fuck you, fuck you, you fucking bastards!"

I was on my hands and knees when Misty came to my side and helped me stand. I was pretty groggy but realized she was naked and holding her dress in front of herself. Lights were starting to come on, and shades were opening in houses of the previously quiet street. A door slammed.

"Put your dress on. I'll be OK. What happened in there?"

She pulled her muumuu over her head. She had no underwear on and no sandals.

"Where are your sandals?"

"Don't worry about my sandals. You must not be in too bad shape if you noticed I don't have my sandals. Your nose is bleeding. Take off your shirt." She took my shirt and pushed it against my nose as we walked onto Philadelphia Avenue.

"Ow, that hurts."

"Tilt your head back."

"What happened?"

"After Harold—that's the asshole's name, Harold—after he finished, he wouldn't let me leave until his roommates had a turn. They held me down. I'll probably be bruised tomorrow. When you burst in, Harold and two of the others ran out of the room to get you. The fourth guy had just dropped his pants for his turn. I gave him a hard shove, and he went down with his pants around his ankles. I pushed a dresser over, and it landed on top of the bastard. My dress was on the nightstand, and I grabbed it and the lamp at the same time. Just pulled the damn lamp right out of the outlet. When I got in the hallway, the other three were tossing you off the porch. They were looking at you, so I was able to whack Harold on the back of the head with his lamp. Bastard will have a headache tomorrow."

"Yeah, so will I."

Chapter 38

July 16, 1964
Playing with Fire

It was after midnight when Sylvia finished with her clients at the Majestica. She and Jack walked into the room together and saw me lying on the bed, Misty holding a wet washcloth to my head and cotton balls stuffed up my nose. My bloody T-shirt was on the floor. Sylvia's mouth gaped.

"What the hell happened?" Jack asked.

Sylvia's eyes welled up with tears as she heard about Misty's gang rape. Jack's eyes were cold with a hard stare. There didn't seem to be any reaction when they heard about my getting beaten up.

When Misty and I finished our tale, Jack said, "Come on, let's get outta here. Too depressing, you all feelin' sorry for yourselves. Let's go for a walk on the beach."

"Jack, I just want to lay here."

"No, Delaney, you gotta get up, keep moving. You might have a concussion. Come on, everybody. Let's go."

Jack picked up some plastic cups and the Smirnoff and marshaled us out to the beach. We walked along the cool, wet sand left behind by the outgoing tide. My side hurt, breathing hurt, and my head hurt, but Jack was right. I felt better moving, and the cool night air was like a salve.

"Where do they live, Misty?" Jack asked.

"Why?"

"Just curious."

"Bullshit, Jack. I know you. What are you thinking? You can't go there and beat up four guys if that's what you've got in your head."

"Sylvia, stay here with Delaney. Misty and I are takin' a walk. Don't drink all the vodka. Save some for us. We'll be right back."

We were around Fifth Street when they left us on the beach. We walked to where the sand was dry. Sylvia sat down, and I used her thigh for a pillow. We were both quiet for a long time, and then I heard Sylvia crying.

"What's wrong?"

"Nothing. Nothing's ever wrong."

"Why are you crying?"

"No reason. You don't have to have a reason to cry."

Whatever was wrong, she didn't want to talk about it, and all I wanted was for my pain to go away. We went back into our mute mode, and some time passed before Sylvia spoke.

"I think I see Misty coming."

"She by herself?"

"Looks like it."

I sat up. What the hell was Jack up to now? When Misty reached us, I asked, "What'd you do?"

"Jack wanted me to take him to the house. I couldn't talk him out of it. We got there and stood across the street looking at it. All the lights were out—looked like everybody was sleeping. He told me to wait, and then he walked around the house, came back, and made me leave. I don't know what the crazy son of a bitch is doing."

Misty sat down beside me, lit a cigarette, and then looked at Sylvia and said, "Pour me a half cup of vodka." I held the cup while Sylvia poured and passed it to Misty after helping myself to a healthy gulp. The vodka's burn felt good going down, and I knew that with a little more time, the alcohol would bury my pain. When Misty started her first sip, we heard sirens. Looking toward the boardwalk, we saw an orange glow and billowing smoke in the dark sky several blocks away.

"That's close to the lifeguard's place," Misty said.

"You don't think...aw, shit!" I said. "Is that him coming now? It is."

"Come on, let's get outta here," Misty said as Sylvia and I stood up.

We started south toward the pier as Jack caught up with us.

"Jack, don't tell me you set the goddamn place on fire," said Misty.

"I didn't do it. Looked like their heating oil tank had a leak and somebody accidently dropped a cigarette, and next thing you know...poof!"

"You dumb fuck! What if somebody dies in that fire? Even if no one dies, it's still arson. That's serious jail time. Cops won't be looking for you—they'll be after Delaney and me. Neighbors know there was a fight there tonight, and those asshole life-guards will put it on us. Jack, don't you understand? You've put me outta business."

"Hey, don't flip your wig. Anyway, maybe it's time we get outta Dodge and go to Miami."

"I'm not going to Miami or anywhere else with you!" she screamed. Only the roar of the surf kept her voice from raising the dead.

We settled in under the pier. Stars filled the black sky like a million silver pinpricks. It was very dark. There was no moon, and that made me wonder if we were in a new moon phase. I didn't believe that shit, but Misty sure did. She had said nothing about a new moon, and that seemed like something she would have brought up. As superstitious as she was, surely she wouldn't have gone into that house after I had expressed my doubts. I'd have to ask her, but not now. No one talked for a long time. Misty continued to seethe, Sylvia whimpered and cried, I was depressed and physically in pain, and Jack sat staring at the ocean like it was another typical night. We were at the bottom of the Smirnoff bottle.

"Yeah, I guess maybe you two ought to lay low for awhile. Misty, you could bleach your hair blond. That'd change your looks."

"I'm not bleaching my hair, Jack."

"I've got a wild idea on how we can stay in business and stay in Ocean City until Labor Day," I said. "Haven't worked out the details, but it might work."

"Delaney, either you have a concussion or you're drunk—probably both," Misty said.

"You know about the Sea Circus Hotel?"

"No," said Sylvia and Misty.

"I'll clue you in. Jack, you remember. We drove by it the night we went to Rehoboth."

"That big-ass hotel way past 100th Street?"

"Yeah. The place is filled with high rollers from D.C. Misty, you've worked hotels before. You know the game. And we could probably charge fifty bucks an hour. Those people have money. Hell, the kids here are giving us half their paychecks. We've picked them clean already. And besides, there's no lifeguard service that far north. Misty and I won't have to worry about that asshole Harold spotting us and turning us in for the fire."

A rose-colored dawn crept up on the eastern horizon, and Misty was nodding her head in serious thought. She would make the decision to move our game to the Sea Circus or not. Jack didn't care. He was ready to go to Miami, and Sylvia would do whatever Misty wanted.

"Let's think on it some," said Misty. "We don't need to decide anything right now. I have to check the charts."

"Right. It's getting light. Misty and I need to get out of sight. Jack, you and Sylvia get some breakfast and coffee and bring it back to the room. We'll see you there. We'd be hanging out at the room today anyway even without the fire."

"Why's that?" Jack asked.

"It's gonna rain," I said.

"How do you know, Delaney? Are you a weatherman now?" Misty asked with a smile.

"Red sky in the morning, sailor's warning."

Chapter 39

July 18, 1964
Transportation Resolved

MARVIN GAYE BELTED out "Hitch Hike" as I surveyed my nose in the bathroom mirror. "The purple's turning kind of brown, but it looks better, except it's not straight anymore."

"It looks cute," Misty said. "How's the cut on the back of your head? That's what you should be worried about."

"It's OK. It's scabbing over."

"Let me see."

She came into the bathroom and started spreading the hair on the back of my head to get a look.

"Ow. Don't press it like that," I protested.

"Oh, you baby. That should have had stitches, but no way could we have done anything about it that night. You would have been carted right off to jail for arson."

"You know, you've been a pretty good nurse these last few days. Have you ever thought about doing that?"

"I'm not good at bedpans. I've just been nursing you 'cause you're my hero. You came to my rescue."

"More like *you* came to *my* rescue. Anyway, right now we need to do something about making more bread. I've got to get back to doing photo work and getting clients. Besides, today's Saturday. The beach will be packed with weekenders, and Jack's only been able to use his contact at the Majestica for any business. We've only brought in fifty dollars in the last two nights. I think Jack scares people when he approaches them."

"Stop worrying. It'll pick up. We just have to keep you off the beach and away from any lifeguard who might recognize you."

"I can't stay off the beach," I said. "I've got to get back to working at Pyramid Photos. It's been the best way to get business. Maybe you could put some makeup on my nose."

"What did Jack tell your boss at Pyramid?"

"Just that I'd be out a couple of days, that I'd had an accident. I'll tell Mr. D I got into a bar fight....There's something I want to ask you about the other night, Misty."

"Yeah?"

"Was the other night a new moon?"

"Oh! I know where you're going with this," she said, throwing a towel against the wall. "You wanna know why I didn't see it coming. If I'm such a good goddamned astrologer, why'd I go in that house? Or better yet, why'd I even approach that bastard lifeguard in the first place?"

"Don't get mad." A small blue vein appeared on her temple, and red blotches formed on the ivory skin of her neck. "I just...I don't know. It was just very dark..."

"No, goddamn it! It was not a new moon. New moons come roughly every twenty-nine days. The next one will be August seventh or eighth."

I didn't say anything, and after a few moments Misty calmed down. More collected, she said, "You didn't see a moon the other night because it had already passed. I knew that something might go wrong, that it could be a bad night. I did check my chart, and it warned about new ventures being risky. But just because I know something bad—or even good—might happen, it doesn't mean I'll do the right thing or take the right path. It's like the night Sylvia got beat up. I know how the stars line up and the impact of the moon phase. I just don't know exactly what will happen or if anything will happen. It's just that the conditions are there. Like the weather, it could be cold and cloudy, so it could snow, but it doesn't mean it *will* snow."

"I think I understand. Sorta like looking through a misty veil."

"Oh, shut up," she said softly, wiping her eyes with a tissue.

Jack's heavy footsteps thumped down the hall before he opened the door with Sylvia in tow. "Great news! We're goin' to the Sea Circus tonight."

"Now what have you done?"

"Don't worry, Misty. It's cool. I'll clue ya in. Delaney, remember when we rode to Rehoboth in that Corvette?"

" Damn it, Jack, it's too risky. You must be outta your tree. First arson, now car theft?"

"Car theft? What? What are you talking about?" Misty asked.

"Hey, keep your cool," said Jack. "Just listen, OK? At the Majestica Atlantica, they have valet parking for all the guests. When I was the head bellhop, I had access to all the keys. None of the guests took their cars out after seven o'clock, especially families. George, my replacement, he's been making a few bucks putting us on to clients, so I thought he might want to make more money by letting us use a car."

"NO! I'm not doing it," I said.

"What's involved?" Misty asked.

"He wants ten bucks, double what he gets for finding a client, and...he wants some free merchandise."

"I'll do him," Sylvia said. "He's not very good-looking and a little on the heavy side, but he's real nice."

"I said no. We're not doing this."

It was nine-thirty when Jack and Sylvia pulled up in a black 1960 Ford station wagon. The vote was three to one, and I'd lost.

Misty started laughing and said, "Jack, it looks like a hearse. What were you thinking?"

"Just get in."

"It's a daddy's car," said Sylvia as she went to the back seat. Misty got in with her, and I took the shotgun seat. As I closed the door, Jack shifted the automatic into drive and turned the black beast north on Philadelphia, and we headed to the Sea Circus. Jack kept the car below the speed limit and made slow starts after every red light. My mouth was so dry I wouldn't have been able to spit. My stomach felt as if, once again, worms were crawling in it. The tension was so great that I thought it would break the windshield. It was almost a relief when Jack pulled into the Sea Circus's parking lot and we got out of the car, but I knew the night was just beginning.

The Sea Circus was like nothing else in Ocean City. It had a lavender carpeted lobby with plush chairs and couches and floor-to-ceiling windows covered with gold drapery. A sign for the cocktail lounge pointed down a short flight of stairs. As we started to walk into the lounge, we were stopped at the doorway by a tall, broad-shouldered, heavyset man with a shiny bald head and short gray hair on the sides. He was wearing a tuxedo.

"Excuse me, but I'm afraid that jackets with slacks for gentlemen and dresses or skirts for ladies are required for the cocktail lounge and the restaurant in the evening. Only this lady meets the dress requirement." He gestured with open palm toward Misty in her muumuu.

Jack and I in T-shirts and Bermudas and Sylvia in cutoff jeans and a halter top that flaunted her large breasts didn't cut it. What were we thinking? We looked at each other for a moment as if to try to find which of us we could blame for the fiasco. With universal embarrassment, there was a group shrug of our shoulders, and then we turned and headed toward the exit with heads bowed.

"Ain't that a bite?" Jack said.

"Wait a minute," Misty said before we reached the door. "Let's not make this a total waste. I can get in. I'll take a walk through and eyeball the place. See if it's going to be worth coming back."

"Misty, we don't own any jackets or slacks, and Sylvia doesn't own any skirts or dresses," Jack said.

"No sweat, Jack. There are clothing stores in Ocean City. We can shop, you know. We have plenty of cash, don't we, Delaney? If we can double our fee for a trick, Sylvia and I will pay for the gladrags the first night. Think of it as an investment."

"Yeah, we've got more than enough bread for the threads. It makes sense to at least check it out before we leave. We don't want any more surprises when we come back. We'll wait here in the lobby for you."

Misty grinned at her own brilliance. She shook her head, tossing her hair back, turned, and with her chin up gave that confident stride that implied she knew what she was doing.

"Don't do anything I wouldn't do," said Sylvia. Misty turned and gave a big smile. To no one in particular, she added, "She's got it so together."

As we waited for Misty to come out of the lounge, we saw an endless parade of activity—people, mostly men with gray hair or no hair, getting off the elevators and going into the lounge, or leaving the lounge and going to the elevators. A few of the men were accompanied by women of similar age, but a lot of the men were accompanied by women who could have been their daughters or, in some cases, granddaughters. Ten minutes went by, then twenty.

"What the hell is she doing?" I said.

"Maybe she decided to have a drink," Jack said.

"If she got herself a drink, then I guarantee you she's gonna come outta there with a trick on her arm," Sylvia said.

Two minutes later, Sylvia's prophecy was fulfilled. Misty was walking arm in arm to the elevator with a short, portly man in a white linen suit, white shirt, red tie, and Buddy Holly glasses. His jet-black hair looked like a cheap toupee. Misty never looked at us. Jack and I looked at each other and rolled our eyes while Sylvia sang, "I told you so."

"What now? We have at least an hour to kill," I said.

"We can't get a drink in here. Let's just go outside and walk around," Jack said as he lit a Camel for Sylvia and himself.

When we had first arrived, I was too tense to pay attention to my surroundings. Now more relaxed, I noted the types of cars in the parking lot: Chrysler Imperials, Lincoln Continentals, Cadillac El Dorados, and a half-dozen limousines. The property was the picture of perfection with trimmed grass surrounding blooming flowers, shrubs, and small trees. The giant pool was between the front of the hotel and the road, and there were 75 to 100 well-dressed people drinking, dancing, and talking. A string quartet was playing "Tea for Two."

Jack said, "Not exactly our kind of music."

"I can dig it. It's so romantic," Sylvia said. "I wish I was in there with them."

The musicians took their break. We walked to the beach side of the hotel and through the dunes onto the beach. We watched the white surf break on the black water. Out of boredom, I asked for one of Jack's Camels. He shielded his Zippo from the wind as he put the fire to my cigarette. I smoked half of it and flicked the butt into the surf. Sylvia was shivering.

"I'm getting goose bumps," she said.

Without comment, we turned and went back to the lobby. When Misty stepped out of the elevator, she was beaming. As we walked out the door together, she said, "Yes, this place definitely has possibilities."

Chapter 40

July 20, 1964
Shopping Day

"OLD GUYS, THEY'RE the best," Misty said as she dipped toast in her egg yolk. "They take a little longer, but they're nicer and more generous. And there are a lot of old guys at the Sea Circus. Sylvia, we're going to have a blast. After we finish breakfast, we'll take the guys to Carson's Menswear to help them pick out their clothes, then..."

"Misty, don't you think me and Delaney know how to buy our own threads?"

"That's a good question. Maybe you do, and maybe you don't. We'll see, but it doesn't matter 'cause I'm gonna be there to help you anyway."

"Misty, no need to flip your wig," I said. "I've never seen you like this. You're talkin' a mile a minute."

"I'm just jazzed. There's so much opportunity there! I'm tellin' you, it's cool, and these people are movers and high rollers. There's serious dough to be made."

We left Melvin's after breakfast and went straight to Carson's, where Misty took charge again. She picked out a black double-breasted blazer, pleated gray slacks, a white shirt with red pinstripes, and a solid maroon tie for Jack. For me, her choice was a navy two-button worsted sport coat with flat-front khaki slacks, a blue Oxford button-down shirt, and a canary yellow tie with images of ducks sewn into the fabric. The tally came to $68.72. We were just about to leave when Misty shouted, "Shoes! Shoes! What kind of shoes do you guys have? I've never seen you in anything but sandals and tennis shoes."

Jack and I looked at each other, shook our heads, and sat down to be fitted for docksiders.

"And one more thing," Misty said. "I'm tired of smelling Aqua Velva men. Here, add this to the bill." She picked up a bottle of English Leather and put it on the counter with the rest of our merchandise.

After paying for the shoes, Jack and I were sent back to our room with the purchases while Misty and Sylvia went shopping for their clothes. We were relieved. A couple of hours later, the girls tumbled into the room, giggling as if they were still in grade school.

"That was so much fun," Sylvia said. "We need to do that every day. I feel so good."

"Let us show you what we got," said Misty. "Come on, Sylvia, let's go in the bathroom to change, and then we'll model our dresses for them."

After they scampered into the bathroom and closed the door, Jack looked at me. "Why are they changing in the bathroom? These are two women that we see naked every day."

"They just want to play dress-up."

The door opened with a "ta da" from Misty as Sylvia strutted out wearing a spaghetti strap cream, brown, and black dress that fell a few inches below the knee. The scoop top of the dress offered an ample view of Sylvia's healthy chest. Misty followed with a flourish. "Voila," she said as she modeled a solid red strapless dress that appeared to wrap around her. It had a split starting at her left hip and falling to a point a few inches above her knees where an inverted V was created, dropping the remaining fabric an inch or two below her knees. They both looked stunning.

Jack and Sylvia went to pick up a car from the hotel. A little later, when we heard Jack blow the horn on the ride for that night, Misty was primping in front of the mirror, putting last-minute touches on with her lipstick. The radio was playing "The Way You Look Tonight" by the Lettermen. I turned off the radio, Misty dropped her lipstick into her matching red clutch, and we walked out to the front porch. Sylvia had already moved to the backseat of the surf green 1961 Plymouth Fury coupe. The ride was cherry. The grille had a frowning face and the fins were gone, giving the rear a curvy look. The coupe was a four-on-the-floor with a 413 under the hood. Jack would need to be careful not to burn rubber. Misty went to the backseat with Sylvia, and I took the shotgun seat again.

Tonight we smiled at the man in the tuxedo as he stepped aside, and we entered the cocktail lounge decked out in our new threads. Misty led the way as if she owned the place, and Sylvia followed with eyes as wide as a picture window. Jack turned to me, nodding his head with his usual smirk. The room, dominated with well-dressed middle-aged men, was full of chatter. A broad gray cloud of smoke hung below a ceiling that was covered with black soundproof tile. At the bar, Misty ordered a frozen daiquiri, Sylvia a sloe gin fizz, and Jack and I had vodka martinis with twists.

"I'll work the room on my own," Misty said. "Delaney, take Sylvia and move around the room and find her a trick. You take the lead for her and set it up. Jack, stay where you are, and don't get drunk."

None of us objected—this scene was Misty's neighborhood, her domain. We trusted her judgment. Sylvia seemed grateful as she held my arm and we walked the room. We saw Misty chatting up her friend from last night. He was by himself at a table for two. They smiled at each other, and Misty moved on as they waved goodbye to each other.

"I think he just turned Misty down. He must not have enjoyed last night," I said.

"More likely he's running low on cash," Sylvia said.

We positioned ourselves at the corner of the bar. At one angle, there were two men with half-full glasses of draft beer. They looked like they had been at it for a couple of hours. Their top shirt buttons were undone, and their ties hung loosened below their necks. One was standing, smoking a cigarette, and leaning against the bar. He was tall and bald with a bulbous nose. The man sitting had wispy gray hair. His ears, nose, and lips were large and out of proportion to the rest of his face. Sylvia positioned herself between the men and me. The men had been looking at each other as they talked. The one standing was furthest from Sylvia and took notice of her cleavage. The other continued to talk but soon realized his friend was distracted and not listening. He turned to see the distraction and caught an eyeful of robust flesh. He looked at his friend, and they smiled at each other with raised eyebrows and nodding heads, like little boys being offered cake and ice cream. It was my cue.

"You guys look like you're here for business."

I knew they would respond so that they could keep looking at Sylvia's cleavage as they talked to me.

"Yeah, we're both with trade associations in D.C., and we're here to mingle," said the standing bald man while Mr. Big Lips continued looking at Sylvia's chest. "Of course, in this place, mingling means business. Right, George?"

"Huh? Yeah, right, Paul. Say, what's your name, honey?"

"Sylvia," she said. She smiled, tilted her head, and put her hand on the arm of Mr. Big Lips.

We chatted a few moments. I could tell they wanted to get friendlier. I moved with Sylvia and positioned the two of us between the men. I stood slightly back from Sylvia so that she would have center stage. She kept touching the men, smiling, laughing, and flashing her cleavage at every opportunity. The guys were really warming up to her, and the time was right for a move.

"Sylvia really likes to party," I said. "Would you two like to party with her?"

They both gave quizzical looks at me and then at Sylvia. She was smiling and nodding her head with enthusiasm. "Yeah, just you two and Sylvia...in your room," I said, answering their unasked question.

"How much are you talking about?" The tall bald guy got the picture.

"A hundred total, and she's with you for ninety minutes."

The tall bald man looked at his buddy, smiled, and said, "Deal."

He pulled a gold money clip out of his pocket and counted out five twenties. The happy trio headed in the direction of the elevator. I finished my martini and joined Jack at the other end of the bar.

"That seemed like an easy hundred. Where's Misty?"

"I don't know. Lost sight of her."

"That's not still your first drink, is it?" I asked, eyeing Jack's half-empty martini.

"Second."

"Bartender, another vodka martini with a twist."

We nursed our drinks for about an hour before moving to a table near the door where we could see the girls when they returned. We ordered our third martinis of the night from our waitress when we took the table. It was around eleven-thirty when Sylvia walked through the door, smiling with hips swinging side to side. Jack spotted her first and waved.

"That was a kick," she said as she sat down. "They're are really nice people here. The guys tipped me another twenty. I'm gonna like this place. Where's Misty?"

"Don't know."

I was starting to worry. Sylvia ordered a gin and tonic while Jack and I continued to milk our martinis. Finally, just before midnight, Misty entered the lounge with a stride that reminded me of a thoroughbred racehorse, her head held high and a smile so wide that you would have thought she had just sold the hotel to someone.

"Ah, what a fine night." She flopped in her chair, still grinning.

"Well, where've you been? We were starting to worry. No one saw you leave." Before she could answer my question, our waitress appeared.

"Can I get you anything?" she asked Misty.

"No thanks."

"To answer your question, Delaney, I was with a very nice gentleman. Very nice and generous," she said. She opened her clutch and flashed a hundred dollar bill.

"I made a hundred, too, but I was with two guys," said Sylvia. "There are still a couple of hours before last call. Wanna see if we can do another before the place closes?"

"I don't think we need to," Misty said.

"I agree. We had a very successful first night. Let's not be too obvious. We're still trying to get the lay of the land," I said.

"I'm cool. Let's get the check and cut out," Jack said.

My Windsor knot was still in perfect place, but I was swaying as we walked through the parking lot.

"Jack, we're gonna hafta find something less potent to drink if we're gonna be waitin' in that bar for a couple hours every night. Are you OK to drive?"

Chapter 41

July 21, 1964
Spam

I NOTICED HIM RIGHT away. He watched Misty and Sylvia like a shark watches a seal. We had entered the smoke-filled room just past ten o'clock. The noise level in the Sea Circus's cocktail lounge was at a peak. Someone who sounded like Tony Bennett was singing with the band, but I couldn't hear the lyrics. Our plan was to split up and cruise the room like the previous night. Jack headed to a stool at the end of the bar. I took Sylvia by the arm and walked in the direction of the shark while Misty strolled around the room. The shark was a heavyset man in a white sport coat and black slacks. I was ordering our drinks while he and Sylvia smiled at each other. He focused on her breasts for several seconds before looking at her face again.

"Hiya," tweeted Sylvia.

"Hello, kiddo."

"My name's Sylvia." She was up, all touchy-feely with the shark, and he seemed to like it.

"Hey, that's a pretty name. Mine's Louie, but everybody calls me Spam."

"Spam? You mean like the meat?"

I fought to hold back a laugh, not sure how Spam would react. He was big in a heavy but solid way. His bearlike body said if he got hold of you, you would never get away. His curly black hair had an oily sheen, and tufts of hair sprouted from his ears and nose. He may have been in his late forties or early fifties. His white sport coat was too short in the sleeves and showed off a gold Rolex Oyster on this left arm. He also wore a diamond pinky ring on his left hand. His white shirt was open at the collar, allowing a forest of black and gray chest hair a chance to escape.

"Yeah, like the meat. I'm Louie Spamanado. That's where the Spam comes in, short for Spamanado."

"Oh, that's cute," giggled Sylvia, putting her hand on Spam's shoulder and leaning forward so that he could get another look at her cleavage.

"Looks like she likes you, Spam," I said.

"Who da hell are you?" I detected a hint of garlic.

"Name's Delaney."

I extended my hand and saw it get swallowed up in his giant paw.

"Ha, a mick. I like the Irish. They're spunky. Knock 'em down, and they get right back up."

"Hope you don't wanna knock me down." The whiskey glass in front of him was almost empty, so I said, "Tell ya what. Promise not to knock me down, and I'll buy you another drink. What're you having?"

"Thanks. Glenlivet neat."

I got between Spam and Sylvia after I ordered the Glenlivet and said to Spam, "Like I was saying, she likes you, and I think you like her. I can tell. How would you like to spend some private time with her in your room?"

"You her pimp?" Spam asked in a low voice with a snicker, raising his bushy eyebrows.

"I prefer the term 'manager.'"

"Manager!" He followed the word with a loud boisterous laugh. Sylvia stepped back with a half-smiling, half-frightened look. When the laughter stopped, he said, "Yeah, I like dat... manager. Let me ask you dis, Mick. What about da girl in the red dress dat came in wit' yous. Are yous her manager, too?"

"Yeah, are you interested in her?"

His giant paw grasped my shoulder, and he pulled me forward. Leaning his head close to mine, he said in a loud whisper, "I'm interested in bot'."

"Let me bring her over."

Always bold, Misty extended her hand to Spam, and I watched as it disappeared into his.

"Hiya, sweatheart."

"Hiya, Spam."

"Hey, Spam, the price is a hundred for ninety minutes," I said.

"Tell ya what, Mick. How 'bout five hundred, and I keep them for the night? Girls, yous OK wit' dat?"

"Yeah," said Sylvia.

"Sure," said Misty

"We got a deal, Spam."

He pulled the biggest wad of cash I'd ever seen out of his pants pocket and counted out five bills with Ben Franklin's picture on them.

"Have fun, everybody," I said. "See you in the morning."

I took my martini and found a stool next to Jack.

"We can go home after we finish our martinis if you want."

"Why?"

"Some big Italian guy paid five hundred dollars to have them both spend the night with him." Jack's face smiled so much I thought it would break.

"Ya think the guy's Mafia?"

"Oh, shit! I don't know."

Chapter 42

July 22, 1964
Spam's Proposal

THE RINGING PHONE in the hallway woke me up. The calls were never for us. It was morning, and the sun was shining into the room. I closed my eyes, rolled over, and realized Misty was still at the Sea Circus. The call might be her. I jumped out of bed and went into the hallway in my underwear.

"Hello?"

"Delaney?"

"Misty, how'd it go?"

"Great! Just great! You guys have gotta get back here right away."

"Why? What's wrong?"

"Nothing's wrong. Spam's got a proposition and connections. He can get us hooked in here as regulars and some other stuff. He'll explain it when you get here. Hurry up. Oh, yeah, it's room 213. Got it?"

"Wait, hooked in where?

"Here at the Sea Circus."

"You mean a room?"

"No, not like that. Just get Jack and get your asses down here. Room 213."

"Room 213."

The next sound was a click and a dial tone. When I went back in the room, Jack was propped up in bed smoking a cigarette. The clock radio said it was 9:20.

"What was that about?"

"I don't know. Something about how this Spam guy has some sort of a proposition."

"I thought we were the ones with the propositions."

"Yeah. Oh, shit...we can't take a car from the Majestica at this hour. I guess we're gonna have to hitchhike to the Sea Circus. That's OK for you and me, but how are we getting the girls back?" We looked at each other and then broke up laughing at the image of Misty and Sylvia standing in the road wearing their dresses and thumbing a ride. "I guess we'll cross that bridge when we get to it."

About an hour later, we were knocking on the door to room 213. Sylvia opened the door wearing her tricolored dress. It looked great on her at ten-thirty at night but a little odd at ten-thirty in the morning.

"Delaney! Jack!" she squealed, hopping up and down like a jack-in-the-box.

"Here's something for you." I handed her Misty's small suitcase. "I brought a change of clothes for you both."

"Oh, Delaney, you're so sweet. You think of everything." Then she kissed me on the lips.

She had never done that. Never. Then she kissed Jack on the lips. We looked at each other and shrugged our shoulders. I figured she was drunk. Spam's room was actually a suite, and the three of us were in the living room area when Misty came walking in from what I assumed was the bedroom. She reminded me of Loretta Young, the way she glided into the room in her red evening dress, her arms floating in air as though she were about to embrace someone. It was getting bizarre.

"Look, Misty, Delaney brought our clothes." Sylvia's laugh bordered on hysteria.

"Delaney, Delaney, bless your heart. You think of everything," Misty said. She was laughing as she gave me a big hug, then gave one to Jack. He and I looked at each other again. There was some joke that we weren't in on. Spam followed Misty into the room. He was wearing a pale blue, short-sleeve silk shirt with the top three buttons undone and charcoal slacks.

"Hey, Mick. Morning." Once again my hand disappeared in his paw. "Who's dis brute?"

"This is John E. Walker."

"What? In dat case, I'll have one on da rocks."

"Everyone calls me Jack," he said, extending his hand.

"Nice ta meet ya, Jack. Everyone calls me Spam." He shook Jack's hand and held it a few seconds longer than necessary. Jack winced.

Misty came back to me and held my arm in hers like we were bride and groom leaving the church. She affectionately put her hand on my chest and drew her face close to mine. Her pupils were as wide as a cat's in a dark room. I thought she was going to kiss me.

"Delaney, honey, Spam's got some great ideas on how we can make more money—a lot more. He can get us in tight with the Sea Circus. We'd be regulars and work special parties. Tell him about your idea, Spam."

"Yeah. Sit down, boys. Misty, get us some coffee. You boys want coffee?" We nodded. "T'ree coffees, Misty." As she hustled off to the kitchenette, Spam continued. "We're gonna be adults here, got it? You boys know what cocaine is?"

Now I understood why the girls were acting like squirrels.

"Yeah, I snorted some in 'Nam," Jack said. He never ceased to surprise me.

"I know Sherlock Holmes used it, and it's an illegal drug," I said.

Spam tilted his head, giving me a disgusted look. "Is he a real person? Anyway, 'course it's illegal, but so what? It used ta be legal. Hell, you could buy it everywhere. It was even in Coca-Cola. Did ya know dat? Cocaine in fuckin' Coca-Cola. Dat's what the coca was in the cola! If da government knew what it was doin', dey'd legalize it and tax da hell outta it."

"Delaney, you didn't bring our underwear!" Misty shouted from the bedroom.

"Alcohol useta be illegal, too. Ya know how much da government lost in revenue durin' Prohibition? Billions! Billions! Hell, probably wouldn't been no depression if it hadn't been for Prohibition. Anyway, I'm willin' ta put yous kids into business. You make more money in a week doin' dis than the girls can make on their backs in a month. Whaddaya say?"

"Come on, we gotta do this," Misty said. She and Sylvia had changed clothes, and both were carrying the coffee into the room.

"Sounds good to me," Jack said. I looked at him as if to say, "Who asked you?" Jack continued, "I know a little about coke from 'Nam. Heroin, too. Saw a lot people usin' H in Saigon."

"I don't know, man," I said. "We don't know anything about dealing drugs."

"Ah, Mick, it's easy. I'll teach ya everything ya need ta know."

"Why do you keep calling me Mick?"

"That's what ya are, ain't ya? An Irish Catholic kid?"

"Well, I'd never think of calling you a wop."

Spam bellowed out a hardy and sincere laugh. "Dat's what I am, Mick. Dependin' on how you said it, I wouldn't get pissed. Let's quit dis bullshit and go have breakfast. I'll fill ya in on everything and get da hotel to work wit' da girls."

We walked off the elevator and into the dining room, Misty hanging on Spam's left arm and Sylvia on his right arm. Jack and I walked behind like stepchildren.

"Table for five, Mr. Spamanado?" asked the hostess.

"You bet, sweetheart."

"Yes, sir. Right this way."

As we were being seated, Spam said to the hostess, "Sweetheart, do me a favor and ask Mr. Porter to stop by and see me for a few minutes." He slipped her a bill. I didn't see its value.

"Yes, sir, Mr. Spamanado. I'll do that right away, sir."

"Let me explain it to ya. Mick, here's how ya triple your money quickly. I sell ya a key for 2k. Yous guys got two grand, don't ya?" I nodded. "OK, ya add five ounces of bakin' soda to it, put it in packs of one-sixteenth of an ounce, and sell dat. It's called a sweet sixteen. Now you take dat and..."

"Are you all ready to order?" our waitress interrupted.

"Oh, sure. Go ahead, kids."

As we finished placing our orders, a tall, broad-shouldered man with blond hair and wearing a black pinstripe suit, button-down collared shirt, and solid red tie approached the table.

"You wished to see me, Mr. Spamanado?"

"Ah, Porter, how ya doin'? Dese two ladies are friends of mine, and I want ya ta put 'em on your approved list for da VIP room. You can also use 'em for any special events."

"Yes, sir, it will be a pleasure. Your names, ladies?"

"Sylvia Peters."

"Misty Vail, spelled V-a-i-l."

"Thank you, ladies. When you come to the hotel in the evening, if you would check at the office behind the reception desk, someone will tell you if there are any special events that evening. Also, if you wish to go to the VIP room, it opens at two a.m. Just give your names at the door. Will that be all, Mr. Spamanado?"

"Dat's all, Porter. Good job." Spam winked and gave Porter a thumbs-up gesture. "Where were we?"

"Sweet sixteen," I said.

"Oh, yeah. But wait, before we get back on that subject and I forget, now dat you're in good wit' da hotel, you gotta up your rate to a Benjamin."

"A Benjamin?" Sylvia asked.

"A hundred bucks. Anythin' less, dey t'inks you're a whore off da street."

Sylvia's eyes widened as she looked to Misty and mouthed "a hundred bucks."

"The sweet sixteen," Spam continued, "is one-sixteenth of an ounce, or one an' a half grams if you're doin' da metric system. I get you a key—dat's a kilo, thirty-five ounces. Ya mix it wit' five ounces of baking soda, and ya have forty ounces of product. Put another way, ya have 640 sweet sixteen packs, and ya sell 'em for a dime. That's ten bucks a pack. What ya got?

"Ten times 640, sounds like $6,400."

"Smart kid, Mick. Yous was payin' attention. Ya get a A-plus."

"Where does the 640 come from?" Jack asked.

"Tell 'im, Mick."

"Sorry, Spam, I need a little help with that myself."

"I'll talk slower. Yous got a pack that is one-sixteenth of an ounce, and there are sixteen packs for every ounce, and you're workin' wit' forty ounces. So sixteen times forty is what, Mick? Tell your buddy."

"Ah... 640." My head was spinning, the girls were grinning, Jack looked happy, and Spam was checking his Rolex. The waitress brought our food, and I wasn't sure I'd be able to eat. I felt like I was leading by following. Spam's whole pitch was directed at me as if I was the ultimate decision maker. It looked like everyone was on board and the train was leaving the station. I might as well get on the train, too.

Breakfast was finished, and the agreement had been reached. We were now going to be drug dealers.

"Gimme yous address, and I'll have a delivery from Baltimore late this afternoon. What kinda wheels ya got?"

"Ah...well...we don't exactly have our own car," I said.

Spam gave me a quizzical look, and with a tilted head, asked, "Wha'...whaddaya mean? How'd ya get here?"

Jack explained how he was getting cars from the hotel by way of the bell captain and how we had hitched a ride that morning.

"We weren't sure how we were getting back with the girls," I said.

Misty and Sylvia got sour looks on their faces. They hadn't thought about going back until I mentioned it. Spam looked at Jack and me as if we each had two heads.

"Ya dumbshits, dat's not gonna work. Yous get stopped for somethin' or even someone ass-ends ya, can't prove ya own the car, go ta jail, get searched—nah, not gonna work. Come on, let's go up ta the room. I'll t'ink a' somethin'."

Spam signed for the breakfast bill, and we all marched to the elevator and back to his room. No longer his effusive self, Spam was working on the transportation problem in his mind. We entered his room, and he went straight to his phone and dialed a number. He thrust a paper and pencil at me and said, "Gimme yer address."

"Hey, Tony. Yeah, it's me. Got a coupl'a things I need ya ta do. I need ya ta deliver some product down here. Only a key. I'm collectin' da cash, so yous only need ta deliver da product. OK, and ya need to git a car, a clean car, and deliver that ta the same people. Here's the address, Tony: 27 Dayton Lane. Yeah, in Ocean City. No, da car don't need ta be nothin' special, just clean and not conspicuous, if ya know what I mean. You gonna give the product and the car ta a kid named Mick. No, I won't be here. I'm leavin' today. No, that's it." Then he hung up.

"OK, you'll have a car until Labor Day. Maybe we'll work somethin' out after that, or I just take it back. We'll see. I'll drop ya at you's place on my way outta town."

He went to the bedroom and returned a few minutes later with a small leather satchel. On the way out, he dropped his room key off at the desk, waved to the clerk, and walked out to the parking lot. He opened the driver's door of a 1964 black Lincoln Continental, then opened the rear passenger door that was called a "suicide door" because of its unique rear-opening feature. With both doors open, I felt as if I were looking into Spam's living room with cream-colored leather chairs. I sat in the middle rear between the girls while Jack took shotgun. It was the nicest ride I'd ever been in. We beamed at one another as if we owned the world.

"What yous kids plannin' on doin' after Labor Day? We might be able to keep some kinda business arrangement," said Louie.

"We're goin' to Miami," Jack said.

"Miami? All of ya goin' there?"

"No, Sylvia and I are going back to Baltimore."

"What 'bout you, Mick? You goin' ta Miami?"

"I don't know, Spam. I'd like to finish my degree, take the CPA exam."

"CPA? You mean like that bookkeepin' stuff?"

"Well, it's more than just bookkeeping, but yeah, that stuff."

"Doin' taxes and stuff?"

"Yeah, taxes and stuff."

"Well, we'll keep in touch, Mick. I might need some tax help. And Johnny Walker Scotch, I might be able to help ya in Miami. I got associates down dere. Dey's always on the lookout for talent like you."

"Great!"

When we got to the house, everyone waited outside with Spam while I got the cash. I opened the shoebox we hid in the bottom of the armoire and counted out the two thousand dollars. It was half our money. Spam took the cash without counting it and drove off while the four of us stood on the sidewalk. The girls were waving goodbye and were a little more subdued having come off their high.

"That's the nicest car I've ever been in," said Sylvia. "And he's such a nice man. He didn't have to buy us breakfast like that. He's so sweet."

"Nicest car I've ever been in," I said.

"What's this shit about goin' back to Baltimore?" asked Jack. "And Delaney? CPA? What are you talking about? Man, I thought it was agreed we were all goin' to Miami."

Misty turned and walked toward the door. Without looking at Jack, she said, "I have always told you, Sylvia and I are never going to Miami with you."

As we walked into the room, Jack gave me a pouting look like I was his father who had told him he couldn't have the puppy he had brought home. "Delaney, what's this CPA shit?"

"I don't know, Jack. I really don't. I have a little more than a year to finish my degree at Georgetown, if I can get back in. I hate to walk away from that. I lost the scholarship, but with the money we're making, that doesn't matter. I can pay my own tuition."

Jack lit a Camel and poured two fingers of vodka into a plastic cup. Sylvia collapsed on her bed and closed her eyes. She and Misty had partied most of the night, and I knew they'd be asleep in no time and sleep through the day.

"I'm gonna go for a walk," I said.

"I'll go with ya," Jack said.

We were walking down Philadelphia when a terrible thought hit me.

"Shit, Jack. Do you realize what we just did?"

"Yeah, we're gonna be dealing cocaine."

"No, not just that. We just gave half our cash to a mobster and watched him drive away. How do we know he didn't fake that call or call the guy back and tell him to forget it? I've got a feeling we've just been screwed."

"Nah, that cat's good for it. Haven't ya heard of honor among thieves? While we're out, let's buy the stuff we're gonna need to cut the coke."

We bought the baking soda and other items we needed for cutting and packaging the cocaine. Jack seemed to know what we needed and took care of the buying. It was close to six-thirty, and Jack and I were sitting on the steps in front of the house when a two-tone brown and tan Buick Roadmaster pulled up and parked. A 1960 gray Plymouth Valiant sedan followed it.

"Think that's them?" said Jack. "Man, look at that tuna!"

The fattest man I'd ever seen managed to squeeze himself out of the Buick. His head was a giant round ball that sat on an even bigger round ball of a body. Strands of thin black hair fell across his forehead. His brown suit coat had no chance of being buttoned in the front, and he looked as if he was about to burst out of his clothes any minute. The yellow necktie he wore was knotted several inches below the neckline of his open-collared shirt. The driver of the Valiant was already beside the Roadmaster, waiting for Mr. Big. The two were a comical sight together because of their differences. The Valiant driver was four or five inches shorter than his friend and as skinny as the other was fat. His shiny black hair was combed in an Elvis style, including long sideburns. He wore a black open-collared shirt with a pattern of two connected white diamonds from shoulder to hip on each side of the shirt. His black pants were pegged, and the white socks he wore set off his wingtip shoes. He looked like he had been transported from 1956.

"Yeah, that's them."

Mr. Big waddled around the Buick and came toward us. His arms, unable to drop to his side, hung at an angle that reminded me of a penguin. The 1956 throwback followed but disappeared from sight behind Mr. Big's massive form.

"One of yous Mick?" Mr. Big was breathing hard and sweating from his short walk around the car.

"That's what Spam calls me."

"Here, Vinnie, get da delivery outta da trunk," he said, tossing the Buick's keys to his little friend. "Spam must like yous guys. He ain't never done nuttin' like dis before. I'm Tony." He extended his hand to shake mine. His hand looked like another small ball with short, pudgy fingers protruding. His grip was soft and loose. His large, gentle brown eyes lent serenity to his face. I felt as though I could believe anything Tony said to me.

"I don't know, Tony. I guess that's it. He just likes us."

Vinnie approached with a brown paper bag that looked like it could have contained a loaf of bread. His thin face accentuated a long, pointy nose and close-set eyes, giving him the unfortunate appearance of a weasel.

"Here," Vinnie said, handing the bag to me.

"What about the car?" Jack asked.

"Oh, yeah. Vinnie, give 'im da keys."

Vinnie reached in his pocket and tossed a set of keys to Jack. When Jack saw they were the keys to the Plymouth, he said, "Hey, I thought we were gettin' the Buick."

"Ha! Dat'll be da day. I wouldn't fit in dat Valiant. Come on, Vinnie, git in da car, and let's go over ta Phillips Crab House. I wanna eat somethin' before goin' back to Baltimore." They got in the Roadmaster and drove away.

When we went to our room, Sylvia and Misty were up and about. "Tragedy" by the Fleetwoods was playing on the radio. "Let's get to work," Jack said. "We'll wanna start selling this tonight."

Jack did the blending of the baking soda into the cocaine. He weighted the mixture and I bagged it while the girls watched. Jack seemed to know what he was doing and had no trouble with the recipe. By nine-thirty, we had the coke bagged and were dressed for the night. We were ready to go when Jack said, "Let's sample the product before we go."

"Great idea," said Misty.

She sprinkled some on the dresser, then separated it into four two-inch lines. Using a straw that Jack and I bought earlier, she put her left index finger against her left nostril and the straw to her right one and vacuumed up one of the lines with her nose. Jack did the same thing, then Sylvia. They were giddy.

"Your turn, Delaney," Jack said.

I mimicked their actions, and when the powder hit my nostril, I said, "Wooo, that burns." I rubbed my nose while the others laughed at me. Then my head cleared, and my vision focused. I thought I could hear every board that creaked in the whole building.

"Wow, OK, I'm ready," I said. "Let's go sell some fuckin' cocaine."

"Woo, woo," Sylvia said as we headed for the door.

We climbed into the four-door Valiant. Jack started the car, waved his hand between the steering wheel and dash, and then looked on the floor between us.

"What's the matter?" I asked.

"There's no gearshift."

I laughed. "It's a push-button transmission, dummy. Look on the dash on the left."

"Oh, yeah. There it is. This is weird."

As we moved down the road, I asked, "How are we going to do this?"

"Sylvia and I will take a pack with us but no more than one pack," said Misty. "When we get to the room, we let them know we can add some kick to the party if they want and offer the coke for twenty-five bucks."

"Spam said to sell it for ten bucks," I said.

"I know, but I think he meant on the outside—you know, up on the boardwalk and that. Anyway, let's try it. If they want to negotiate, we can come down. Remember, these are high rollers. Twenty-five bucks is nothing to them. Delaney, you and Jack keep the supply. If Sylvia and I are going to have another trick, we'll get another pack from you. Same way if we go to that VIP room they mentioned. You guys cruise the bar and see if you can sell any there."

Jack steered the Valiant into the parking lot. My anxiety of the first visit was gone. OK, it wasn't because we had been here the last two nights. No, it was the coke. I was about to do something I'd never done before and never in my wildest dreams expected to do: sell cocaine. I knew I could do it. At least that's what the coke was telling my brain. The four of us walked into the lobby as if it were the living room of our own house. Misty and Sylvia reported to the office behind the registration desk as Mr. Porter had directed. After a few minutes, they returned and Misty said, "No special party tonight. We're on our own until two; then we're to go to the VIP room." With that, we walked downstairs and into the smoke-filled room to sell our wares.

Chapter 43

July 23, 1964
Counting Money

JACK AND I were passed out in the Valiant when the back door opened. We both jumped as if a jolt of electricity had hit us.

"Wake up, guys," Sylvia said with a laugh as she and Misty got in the backseat.

"What happened in the VIP room?" Jack asked.

"We'll tell you on the way. Come on, let's go home. I want to get some sleep," Misty said. Jack started the Valiant and turned south out of the parking lot.

"In a way, it was kinda scary. A lot of big shots," Sylvia said.

"They were big shots, alright," said Misty. "Nobody was using anything but first names, nicknames, and initials, but I recognized some faces from television and newspaper photos. There was no need to be afraid, though. They were there for one thing: sex. And we gave it to them."

"Gave it to them?" I asked

"Well, no," said Misty. "We didn't give away anything."

243

When we got back to the room, we spread out the cash from the night on the bed. Sylvia had had two tricks and Misty one before going to the VIP room, and then both had one each there. We counted five hundred from the tricks. The new rate didn't present any problems. Each trick also sprung for the coke, which added one-twenty-five to the pot. In the bar, Jack sold three packs of coke, and I sold four, which gave us another one-seventy-five. We had eight hundred dollars in cash for one night's work. Sylvia squealed, and Jack started laughing. Then we all laughed until tears were flowing and our sides hurt.

"What'd I tell you, Delaney?" said Jack. "Fat City. I told you we'd be in Fat City, didn't I?"

When we settled down, Misty said, "Let's go get breakfast and then get some sleep. Delaney, this afternoon you and Jack take some of the coke and see what you can sell on the beach. Go up to Ninth and the boardwalk. There are always a bunch of guys hanging out there."

Jack and I woke up around one-thirty that afternoon. We dressed and took a hit of cocaine for a confidence boost. We stopped in at Pyramid Photos and told Mr. D I had another job and couldn't do photos anymore. He said he was sorry to lose me and wished me luck. Luck—that was what I needed, and plenty of it. By two o'clock, we were on the boardwalk and approaching Ninth when Jack made a suggestion.

"Let's do it this way. I'll hold the coke and stand about twenty-five to thirty feet away from you. You make the pitch, collect the money, send them over to me, and I'll give them the dope. OK, how's that sound?"

"OK, but why?"

"Two reasons. First, it reduces the risk of getting robbed by someone, taking both our money and the coke. And second, it might make it harder for a cop to arrest us. But I don't think we have to worry about that."

"Why don't we have to worry about the cops?"

"Well, just look at most of the cops we've seen. They're not trained cops. They're college guys, and this is their summer job. They're no more than bouncers. They just walk around in their uniforms hoping nothing happens. Besides, we're the first people to sell this stuff here. The cops aren't looking for it."

"OK, but why is some kid gonna give me ten bucks and then walk down the boardwalk hoping to get the coke from you? Won't they think it's a scam?"

"Don't worry about that. These kids are dumber than *you*, Delaney," Jack said.

"You know, you have a criminal mind."

"Yeah, I do, don't I?"

"Hey, those four guys over there are from a Virginia Tech fraternity," I said. "They partied with Sylvia a couple weeks back. I'll start with them. Give me your cigarettes and go to the other side of Ninth." Jack handed over a half pack of Camels and continued walking to the north corner of the boardwalk and Ninth Street.

"One a' you guys got a light?"

"Hey, look who it is, the pimp master," one of them said.

Another lit my cigarette off his lighter and said, "Your girl available for a party tonight?"

"Please, the word is manager, but no, she's working a hotel gig. Besides, you can't afford her anymore. She's up to a hundred bucks."

"You're shittin' me."

"No, man. You had a bargain and didn't know it. Now you can tell your friends back at school that you had a hundred-dollar hooker."

They laughed at my comment, but I could tell from the look in their eyes that would be exactly what they would do. And they would repeat the story until their friends were sick of hearing it.

"If you guys are still into partying, I've got something for you to liven it up."

"Yeah? What?"

"Any of you ever try cocaine?"

"You gotta be kidding. You got some cocaine?"

Their eyes grew big with an expression of awe.

"This is a chance to try it for one night of partying, something else to tell your friends back at school."

At that point, a debate the magnitude of Kennedy and Nixon started with three wanting to try it and one holding out. They huddled apart from me for a few minutes and then seemed to reach an agreement.

"How much is it, how much do we get, and how do we use it?"

"Ten bucks for one-sixteenth of an ounce. You call it a sweet sixteen. For the four of you, maybe you should buy two."

"Sweet sixteen," one said with a chuckle.

"So twenty bucks for two sweet sixteens?" asked another.

"Right."

Then they huddled again, and I could see them emptying their pockets and turning cash over to the tallest guy in the group. He approached me and counted out the twenty as a five and fifteen one-dollar bills.

"See that guy across the street looking at us?"

"Yeah."

"I'm holding up two fingers and he's nodding."

"Yeah."

"Go over to him, and he'll give you two bags of coke."

"OK, cool."

It was done, and the next couple of hours went about the same way, with me approaching groups of guys and making a pitch, closing a deal, and sending them to Jack. We weren't sure how we would do, so we had only brought ten packs. When we sold the last one, we went back to the room with our hundred dollars to celebrate our success with the girls. When we walked into the room Sylvia was sitting on her bed painting her toenails. Misty was propped up on the pillows on the same bed smoking a cigarette.

"Another hundred," Jack said, waving the cash over his head.

"Nine hundred dollars!" I said. "We made nine hundred dollars today. Do you realize that? When I was working at The Sands, I made forty-five dollars in a *week*! We gotta celebrate."

"Let's eat at Phillips Crab House tonight," said Misty. "I can't think of a nicer place in Ocean City to celebrate."

"Yeah, man, we've hit the big time," Jack said.

Chapter 44

August 7, 1964
Cuffed

"**S**TEP OVER HERE. Now put your hands against the wall and spread your legs."

I was at Ninth and the boardwalk, and just a few minutes earlier, I had approached a preppy-looking guy and made my usual pitch about having some dust to party with. He gave me a funny look and walked away like his pants were on fire. The next thing I knew, two Ocean City cops were putting me against the wall and frisking me.

"Put your hands behind your back." I did and felt cold steel wrap around my wrists. The cop clamped them tight, pinching my flesh.

"You're coming with us."

Earlier that day, Misty and I had one of our rare arguments. This one got heated. It was about her astrology predictions and her ridiculous fear of new moons. Every day, she went through a ritual of scribbling notes on paper, checking her sun chart, and talking about our birthdates and how that influenced our character and directed our daily actions. Jack was a Scorpio, and as a result, he tended to have willpower and to be stubborn, jealous, and vengeful. I was an Aquarius and therefore loyal and independent but detached, high-strung, and rebellious. I didn't see it, but even if it were true, what were we to do about it? It was written in the stars, our destiny. Yeah, right. But today Misty's forecast took a serious turn. She had wanted us to take the day off.

"Delaney, I don't care if it's a Friday night. Me and Sylvia are not working."

"You and your astrology bullshit. It does as much good as carrying a rabbit's foot."

"Don't make fun of me, Delaney. And if you're smart, you and Jack will stay in and not try to sell any coke today."

"Yeah, well, when have we ever been smart?"

"You got me there. I can't name a time when the two of you ever showed any sense."

Misty and I were going at each other for a while. We were in another new moon phase, and as usual, she was afraid to do anything other than hide in a closet. In the two weeks since meeting Spam, we had pushed hard, working every day and night. Jack and I would hit the boards in the afternoon and sell coke to college kids. We were even starting to get regular customers. For the most part, the regulars were groups of guys rooming together—frat brothers working the beach for the season, like Morton and his frat buddies. These guys were big into partying. We'd work that until around eight o'clock, and then we'd change clothes and go to the Sea Circus with the girls. We'd work that until two or three in the morning, then crash and start all over the next day. Most of it was fun, but it was also a grind. The coke kept us going, and the cash seemed to keep everyone happy—and we were making a lot of dough. It got so that we considered a $500 day a bad day, and hitting a grand was not unusual. Ignoring Misty's warning, Jack and I went out to make some money selling cocaine. And that's how I found myself in handcuffs.

A crowd gathered and stared as each cop grabbed an arm and led me to their squad car. I looked around and saw Jack in the crowd, a blank expression on his face. The look caused me to think of the time he had told me about Jimmy sitting in the county jail at Snow Hill. He didn't give a damn about what happened to him, and I wondered if that was going to happen to me. Would Jack abandon me? What about Misty? They always say you're allowed one phone call, but I had no one to call. I couldn't remember the phone number for the pay phone at the rooming house and wasn't sure they would come anyway. Wendy's father was a lawyer, but he would probably tell them to lock me up and throw away the key.

When we got to the city jail, the two cops took me to a soundproof room with no windows and took the cuffs off. The cop in charge was an older guy, looked to be in his late forties. The other one was much younger, mid-twenties, probably the summer help.

"OK, kid, strip."

"What?"

"Are you fucking deaf? Take your clothes off. Drop them on the floor." I was barefoot, wearing only a T-shirt and baggies, not much to strip down. My clothes fell to the floor.

"Step over here." He pointed to a spot three feet to my left. The older cop was giving all the commands while the young cop stood in the background. I wondered if this was a training exercise. "OK, now bend over."

"What is this, some sort of fraternity-like hazing? Are you going to paddle me?"

"You want your teeth knocked down your throat?" I stared at the cop, naked, vulnerable, and bewildered. "Bend over now." I bent over.

"Look at his ass, George. See anything?"

"No, sir."

Their idea of a strip search, I guess. At least they didn't touch me.

"OK, shithead, put your clothes back on. When we patted you down, we only found seven bucks in your bathing suit pocket and your college ID. We can arrest you for vagrancy, you know?"

We hadn't sold anything yet, so I didn't have much cash on me. At first I thought that might be a good thing. It would be hard to explain a couple hundred dollars, especially if it was all in fives and ones. But now I could be jailed for not having enough money? Really?

"Is that why I'm here? You think I'm a vagrant?"

"Maybe. Were you trying to sell some kind of drugs to that kid on the boardwalk?"

"No. Did he tell you that? It's bullshit if he did."

"What were you talking to him about?"

"I asked him if he knew where any parties were."

"He said you said something about dust for the party."

"Did you check the guy's hearing? I told him I was just looking for a party. I said just, not dust." The cops looked at each other, but it didn't look like they were buying it.

"How'd you get to Ocean City? I didn't see a driver's license."

"I don't drive. I came down with friends from school. We drove down this morning. We wanted to spend the weekend at the ocean."

"Where are you staying?"

"We aren't getting a room. We were planning on sleeping in the car or on the beach."

"Oh, really?"

"Yes, sir."

"We have ordinances against sleeping in cars and on the beach."

"Oh, well, maybe we'll drive up to Rehoboth then."

"Really? What makes you think you're getting out of here tonight?"

That turned out to be a parting comment as the two cops walked out, closing the door behind them. The metal-on-metal sound of the lock seemed like an explosion in my ears. I sat down on a steel bench that was affixed to the wall and surveyed the room. Pale green concrete walls, gray tile floors, white sound-proof tiled ceiling, harsh recessed lighting, a steel door with a slot for an opening, and the bench was all there was. No toilet. It must have been some kind of holding cell. I sat...and waited... and waited. The only sound was a ringing in my ears—not a real ringing but the kind of ringing that fills the void of silence. Five minutes could have passed, or thirty-five minutes, or an hour and five minutes. I couldn't tell. It didn't seem as if they could charge me with anything. I didn't have any cocaine on me and had never mentioned the word to that fink. Maybe they were serious about the vagrancy bit. The locks on the metal door clanged again and opened.

"OK, Mr. Delaney, you're free to go now, but I strongly suggest you find your friends and drive to Rehoboth or Bethany or Dewey Beach. Just get the hell out of Ocean City."

The older cop stepped aside as I walked out of the holding cell door and found my way into the streets of Ocean City. The sun was shining, it was hot and humid, and the ocean air now had a different smell—the smell of freedom. I looked at the clock on a bank, and it said 5:15. The cops had picked me up around 4:30. The whole ordeal had lasted only forty-five minutes, but it had seemed like hours. I wanted to make sure the cops didn't follow me to the rooming house where they would find the cocaine and the money and the car Spam gave us that belonged to God knows who. I walked to the boardwalk and turned north as though going back to Ninth. Then I started to worry that Jack and the girls might take the coke and the money and run, afraid I'd rat them out. I started walking faster, looked around to make sure no one had followed me, then turned on Third and then on Baltimore, going south again. It was in that block that I came to be standing in front of St. Mary Star of the Sea Catholic Church. It was a frame building with a small entranceway, a cross atop the peaked roof, and one atop the bell tower. How many times had I passed this Catholic church without seeing it? When was the last time I had attended Mass, received Holy

Communion, gone to confession? Father, forgive me for I have sinned....Forgive me? I don't think so. There was no room in my new life for this and no expectation of forgiveness. I turned my back on St. Mary's and crossed Baltimore Avenue.

"Delaney, Jack told us what happened. We were so worried," Misty said. She jumped from the bed and ran to me.

"Jack, what the fuck were you going to do, leave me to rot in jail?"

"What? What could I do, Delaney? I had the coke on me. Was I supposed to run up and grab one of the cops so we could make a run for it?"

Misty didn't seem to understand why I was mad. Sylvia, sitting on her bed, started crying, which caused Misty to leave me and go to her.

"What happened after they took you in? You haven't been gone long."

"Nothing. They just harassed me. Threatened me with a vagrancy charge because I only had seven bucks in my pocket." I helped myself to a healthy glass of vodka and gave them the details of the arrest.

"What next?" I asked. "First I had to duck the lifeguards and now the cops. From now on, we sell only to regulars. I've got to stay low."

Chapter 45

August 19, 1964
Problems for Sylvia

Jack banged on the hood of the Valiant to wake me up. Something was wrong.

"What is it?" I was trying to come to my senses. It was close to four o'clock in the morning, and the parking lot and pool area were completely dark.

"I don't know. Sounded like a door over by the pool." Jack was smoking a cigarette, and in the darkness I could see a concerned look on his face.

Half a dozen shadowy figures appeared by the pool, and the sound of muffled voices and stifled laughter floated through the night air.

"Can you see what they're doing?"

"Looks like they're taking their clothes off and going skinny dipping." Jack had no sooner finished than the sound of splashes and laughter replaced the quiet stillness. "Come on. Let's see if we can get a closer look." Jack walked toward the pool, and I followed.

We stopped at the low wrought iron fence that surrounded the pool. In the darkness, it looked like five guys were tossing a woman back and forth like a hot potato in the four-foot-deep water. She giggled and shrieked. It didn't sound like she was objecting. About five minutes into their play, someone turned on the pool lights. Their raucous noise aroused dozens of hotel guests, who were now on their balconies, applauding and whistling at the skinny dippers. The sole woman in the pool was Sylvia, and she was naked. She screamed and pushed away one of the men and climbed out on the pool ladder. She looked around, spotted her clothes, gathered them up, and ran for the door. Her butt cheeks jiggled as she ran while the men in the pool laughed. At the sight of Sylvia's naked body, there was more applause and cheering from people on balconies.

"I guess these assholes are the car salesmen from the party gig of Sylvia's."

"Yeah. Looks like the party's over." I went back to the Valiant.

I was asleep when the back door opened and Misty got in. Jack sat behind the driver's seat, smoking.

"Where's Sylvia?" he asked.

"I don't know. I wasn't with her."

"She was out here skinny dipping with those car salesmen a half hour ago until someone turned on the pool lights."

"Shit! What'd she do?"

"She was naked as a jaybird, grabbed her clothes, and ran inside. Thought she'd get dressed and come to the car. I've been watching for her, but she's never come out."

"Shit." Misty got out of the car and walked back to the hotel.

Ten minutes later, the silhouettes of Misty and Sylvia walked out the main entrance, Misty's arm around Sylvia. Sylvia's head rested on Misty's shoulder. When they got close, I could see Sylvia's head and shoulders bobbing up and down, but I couldn't tell if she was laughing or crying. Together they climbed in the backseat. Sylvia laughed, but it was quickly followed by a sob. Misty held her with both arms.

"What's wrong?" I asked.

"Nothing. Let's go," said Misty.

My furtive glances to the backseat revealed the dark form of Sylvia shaking despite her tight embrace with Misty. She emitted sobs and a soft whimpering sound, interrupted with an occasional sigh. Her damp hair smelled of chlorine.

When we got to the room, Sylvia went to the bathroom, and Misty said, "Delaney, sleep with Jack tonight. Sylvia is sleeping with me."

"I'm not sleeping with Jack."

Misty's nostrils flared, and the fingernail of her index finger stabbed my chest as she said in a *sotto voce*, "I don't really give a fuck where you sleep. Sylvia and I are sleeping together."

Jack raised his eyebrows behind Misty's back and mouthed, "You're not sleeping with me."

Sylvia came out of the bathroom, and Misty, who had changed to her nightshirt, ushered her into bed. Misty showed us her back and pulled a sheet over the both of them as they spooned. I took a pillow, pulled the spread off Jack's bed, and stretched out on the floor. Jack turned the light out, and I heard his bedsprings creak with protest. I tried to think of another sleeping option.

Chapter 46

September 6, 1964
A New Moon

"**I**'M WORRIED, DELANEY."

The sleep was still in my eyes, but my ears were wide awake at Misty's tone. I rolled over in bed and squinted to see Misty at her charts. Jack and Sylvia were still asleep.

"What is it now?"

"Another new moon, plus some other things."

"What other things?"

"Nothing you ever want to hear about. You always blow it off as bullshit. It's the stars, the planets, the alignments."

"What are you two arguing about now?" Jack yawned.

"Misty thinks it's the end of the world."

"Oh, shut the fuck up. Go ahead ignore me; see what I care. We're not working today. Sylvia and me, I mean. And I don't think you two should, either. Don't try to sell the last of the coke. We don't need the money. We have over twenty thousand to split four ways."

"Over twenty-three," I said and reflected on the near-disaster of my arrest. Maybe there was something to this new moon business and Misty's astrology predictions.

"Whatever," Misty said. "That's plenty. We don't need any more. We're leaving town tomorrow. Why take any chances today? No need to challenge the stars."

Jack fired up a cigarette while Misty preached. Sylvia sat up, droopy-eyed, her left breast peeking over her nightgown.

"What'd you say Delaney, $23,000?" Jack asked.

"Yeah, $23,000 and some change...like an additional $279."

"Fuckin' A. Hot damn. We made it. Woo, tomorrow's Labor Day, and we're done in this burg and onto bigger and better places."

"What are you all talkin' about?" Sylvia asked.

"We're not working tonight," said Misty.

"Fine. Suits me just fine." Sylvia lay back down and turned her back to us.

"Jack, your horoscope for today is to avoid confrontation and make peace with old enemies."

"I got a lot of old enemies. Gonna be a busy day making peace with all of 'em."

"Delaney, yours is to find your own way, be independent. Don't follow the crowd."

"That's nothing new. I never follow the crowd."

"That's not true. You always follow the crowd."

The sun cast a yellow glow through the window shade and normally would have raised my spirits, but Misty's doom-and-gloom prophecy gave me the feeling that an ominous gray storm cloud had entered the room. We all should have been happy like Jack—especially me. I had gotten what I wanted, mostly. But the cost was high. We needed to get out of the room and break this gloomy spell.

"Sylvia, everybody, get up and get dressed. Time for breakfast," I ordered.

It took a half hour before everyone was ready, and we made our way over to Melvin's. Harriet filled our cups with coffee and took our food orders. The mood remained quiet and sullen. I broke the silence.

"Misty, I'm not going to let your prophecy get me down. Maybe I won't sell any coke today, but I'm going to have a damn good time on my last day in Ocean City. This is a time to be happy. Look what we did. The money we made. We're gonna celebrate today."

"Damn right we are," Jack said.

"Tomorrow I'm leaving town with more money than I've ever dreamed of having at one time—enough to buy my way back into Georgetown, get my degree, and become a CPA."

"What the hell? Delaney, I thought we would take the money, buy a new car, and drive ourselves to Miami."

"Get off it, Jack. Have you been deaf? I never promised you I'd go to Miami."

"Fuck."

"Shh! People are staring," Misty whispered.

"I don't care." Jack was defiant and pouting, and breakfast remained unpleasant and argumentative. The mood didn't seem any better with the location change. When we finished, I paid the bill, then went to Harriet and gave her ten bucks. She'd been great to us after the episode with Wendy. My reward was a kiss on the cheek. So far, it was the only good thing to happen today.

"Good luck to you, Delaney, and please be careful," Harriet said.

"Let's not go back to the room just yet. Let's take in the boardwalk," Misty said.

We strolled the boardwalk and tried to act like tourists. Jack and Misty played Skee-Ball while Sylvia and I cheered, but they didn't win any stuffed animals. No matter where we went or what we did, Misty was on edge. Even when she was playing Skee-Ball, she kept looking over her shoulder as if expecting someone to sneak up on her. You couldn't see beneath her broad-brimmed straw hat or behind the oversized Foster Grants, but her alert posture, quick movements, and jumpiness at everyday boardwalk sounds said all you needed to know. She was like a cat in a dog pound.

Sylvia's mood bounced like a rubber ball: laughing, cheering at the Skee-Ball game one moment, solemn, tearful-eyed, and glum the next. It was impossible to see any reason for the change. Jack sarcastically suggested that it was her time of the month, but her extremes went way beyond those of a menstrual cycle. Her mood changes were unexplainable and annoying. During her happy times, she was over the top, but in her dark times, she brought all of us down with her. I had always felt sorry for her more than I liked her, and I was glad that after tomorrow, I would probably never see her again.

We neared Ninth Street, and Misty froze. The boardwalk at Ninth was always crowded with young people, typically dominated by college and high school guys with a mix of girls looking for fun. When things were slow at other spots, Jack and I would always come here to find business for the girls or to sell coke. Today the intersection was body to body. You couldn't get through without touching someone or being touched.

"This is a bad place today."

"What, you claustrophobic?" Jack asked.

"No, not that. It's just bad. We don't want to be here."

Sylvia's expression turned sour, and her hand went up to her mouth as if she were chewing her fingernails. "What is it, Misty?" She sounded as if she was about to start to cry.

"Just trust me. I can't say. I don't know, other than that we shouldn't be here."

Jack looked at me with raised eyebrows and a shoulder shrug. There was no point in arguing, so we turned and walked south.

We had been back at our room for a couple of hours. Misty busied herself with her astrology charts, and Jack was reading *On the Road* for the umpteenth time while I was on a Caribbean adventure with James Bond. Sylvia poured her second glass of vodka, returned to her cigarette, and stared out the window—the window with a view of the back of the building next door. I wondered what she saw that we couldn't see. She was sullen and withdrawn. I knew she was going into that dark hole of hers.

We heard the thump of footsteps in the hall, and before there was a knock at the door, Misty said, "That'll be Tony. He's come for the car." She opened the door at his first knock.

"Tony!" She wrapped her arms around his massive body as far as she could reach. It was the happiest she'd been all day.

"Misty, sweetheart!" Tony puckered up and gave Misty a quick kiss on the lips. Sylvia joined them and was rewarded with a lip kiss. Sylvia! With the presence of Tony, she had climbed out of her hole.

"I'm gonna miss makin' my deliveries to yous kids."

"Well, Sylvia and I might see you back in Baltimore."

Vinnie "the weasel," as we called him to his back, came in behind Tony. He had his usual look, as though he had a bad case of indigestion. Nobody showed any interest in kissing him. Tony and Vinnie had been making weekly deliveries of cocaine ever since Spam had put us in business. It was always the same: lovable fat guy Tony and sourpuss Vinnie.

"Yeah, Spam says yous should call him when yous get back in town. He'll set ya up. And he told me to tell Johnny Walker to call 'im when he gets to Miami. Yous still goin' dere, Johnny?"

"Probably. Not sure of anything right now." Jack's jaw was clenched. I could almost hear his teeth grinding. The realization seemed to have finally sunk in. If he wanted to go to Miami, he would have to go by himself.

"Ya got da keys to da Valiant?"

"Yeah, here." Jack tossed the keys to Vinnie.

We said our goodbyes to Tony, Jack and I both shaking his pudgy hand and Misty and Sylvia giving him hugs and kisses as if he were a giant teddy bear. No one said goodbye to the sourpuss weasel, Vinnie. We stood on the porch watching as the big Roadmaster drove off, followed by the little Valiant. We went back in the room and returned to our glum selves. The change was amazing. The presence of Tony was like the arrival of a party; however, as soon as he left, the air went out of our balloons. It was as though we couldn't stand to be alone with each other anymore.

Jack poured himself another vodka, and Sylvia approached for a refill. Misty was back to her charts, and I started sorting my clothes, readying them for packing my suitcase. The radio was playing a series of soft tunes and slow melodies that did nothing to lift our spirits. A new one played, and I heard piano keys open the song, then Johnny Mathis's voice singing "Misty." Sylvia and Jack didn't notice the song. Misty looked up from her charts and stared into space. Then she looked at me with her hypnotic stare and held my gaze until Johnny sang the last lyric. Her stare was talking to me, but I didn't understand what it said, nor did I hear the song's last words. Our gaze broke at the sound of Jack's voice.

"Let's get outta here. This is depressing."

"I'm ready," I said. "What do you want to do?"

"We haven't been to Cowabunga's in ages. Let's go visit Butch. He'll be glad to see us, and the surf music and dancing will be upbeat. It's always rockin'."

"Really? Ya think Butch will be glad to see us?" I asked.

"Sylvia and I aren't going anywhere," said Misty.

"You ain't eating nothing?" Jack asked.

"We might get a carryout and bring it back to the room. But for sure, we're not going anywhere there's drinking."

"Looks like Sylvia's already taking care of the drinking."

"Shut your face, Delaney," Sylvia said. Then she got up and poured more vodka into her glass for spite.

She was now turning ugly and mean—not a normal attitude for her. And she was on her way to being drunk. It's never pretty when a guy gets drunk, sometimes maybe funny, but for some reason it's always worse when a woman is drunk. I didn't want to see Sylvia in that condition. I didn't want to be around her.

"I'm gonna take a hit before we leave." As Jack walked over to the coke, Sylvia picked up a straw and followed him. Misty watched with disdain as they sucked the white dust into their nostrils.

"Be careful. We never cut that leftover shit," I said.

"Yeah, I know. It's a lot better that way." Jack had a big grin, and I knew it was going to be a wild night.

We approached Cowabunga's as the sun was dropping in the western sky beyond the bay. The orange glow drew me to the dock behind the bar, and Jack followed. The sun's golden rays broke through mushroom-shaped clouds, creating a celestial escalator and renewing long-forgotten memories.

"We goin' in or not?" asked Jack.

"Yeah, I was just thinking about something," I said.

"What?"

"See there, where the sun's rays look like something from outer space, like a science fiction movie? Like the rays are pulling something off the earth?"

"Yeah."

"Well, when I was really young, one of the nuns told me that whenever you see that, it means people who have died are on their way to heaven."

"Yeah, really? You believe that shit?"

"Well, Jack, I guess one of us is going to have to die to find out if it's true."

We turned and went inside. "Surf City" by Jan and Dean was playing to a light crowd. Butch was wiping down the bar and waved at us with a worried look.

"Hey, Butch, what's up, man?"

"Jack, where you been? Haven't seen you for a while."

"Been here, there, and everywhere, Butch."

"Delaney, good to see ya. What'll you two have?"

"Gimme a Bud."

"I'll have a High Life."

Butch popped the caps off the bottles, and we picked them up and found a booth along the wall. Jan and Dean finished their song. Jack was still buzzed from the hit of coke when Trini Lopez's rockin' version of "If I Had a Hammer" blared from the speakers. Jack was amped, hopping up and down in the booth and slapping the table after each verse. "This land..." slap. "Danger..."

slap. "Warning..." slap. And singing. He couldn't carry a tune, but he was trying to sing along with Trini and was bouncing his head from shoulder to shoulder. I looked at the bar and caught Butch glancing our way. If Jack didn't calm down, Butch would toss us out.

When the music stopped, I said, "We need to eat."

"Here?"

"Yeah."

"What?"

"Burgers."

"OK."

I caught Charlene's arm as she walked by. "Charlene, how 'bout bringing us two burgers with fries and another round of beers?"

"Sure, hon."

The burgers came, and Jack's edge slacked off as we ate. He was engrossed in his food. Nothing distracted him as he took big bites of the hamburger, making chomping sounds. The french fries went into his mouth by the handful. He was like a vacuum.

"Hungry?"

He ignored me or didn't hear me, I don't know which. I still had half a burger in my hands when Jack finished. He then chugged the rest of his beer, belched, and looked at me with a big grin. He held up two fingers to Charlene, who was across the room. She nodded, acknowledging that two more beers would soon be coming our way. Jack lit up an after-dinner cigarette, stretched back, and patted his belly. He took a deep inhale of the Camel and then blew out smoke rings.

"How the hell do you do that? I've never figured it out."

"Easy, just like this." And he did it again.

Charlene showed up with the beers.

"You musta been hungry, hon."

"Just a growing boy, Char."

She smiled and patted Jack's shoulder. As she walked away, I heard her shout, "Goldie, cleanup at table four!"

I don't think Jack heard her because when Goldie came to the table, it seemed to startle him, as if Goldie had just magically appeared from nowhere.

"I thought you was dead."

"Ah, Goldie, I love you, too."

"Fuck you."

He reached for Jack's plate, and as he did, Jack quickly stubbed his cigarette out on it. All motion stopped as they locked eyes for what seemed like minutes, but in reality it was only a few seconds until Jack broke the silence.

"Hey, Goldie. I got a big tip for you...save your money."

Goldie walked off with Jack's plate and silverware, but he continued to hold Jack's gaze with a look of hate. Jack, oblivious, took a big swig of his Bud and lit another Camel.

"Why do you do that to him?"

"He likes it. He expects it."

"No, he doesn't."

"It's our way of having fun with each other."

"No, it isn't. He hates you."

"Yeah, well, he's not the first."

We finished another round. Goldie never came back for my plate, but Charlene got it shortly after I had finished, giving me a smile that said we shouldn't expect to see Goldie come by again. A glance at the bar told me Butch was keeping an eye on us. But there wasn't much else for him to watch. The place was dead. Very unusual for a weekend night, and one before a holiday at that. Tomorrow, cars would be streaming out of the city, across the bridge, back to D.C. and Baltimore and back to school.

"Finish your beer, and let's get outta here," Jack said. "I can't believe how dead this place is. We need to find some action for our last night in Ocean City."

"Charlene!" I waved. "Check."

She gave the check to me. The bottled beers were forty cents each, the burgers forty-five, and the fries a quarter. The total bill came to $4.60. Jack got up to hit the head, and I dropped a ten and followed him. It was a big tip, but we were rich, and I knew Charlene would share some portion of her tip with Goldie. It eased my conscience, though I don't know why I felt guilty. When I walked in the restroom and stepped up to the urinal, Jack was at the sink taking another hit of coke.

He sniffed it up his nose, saying, "Wooo, that's good shit. Wooo!"

We left the restroom, and instead of leaving by way of the front door, Jack turned and walked past the kitchen and out the back door onto the dock. I followed. Russell, the cook, and Goldie were bent over, staring into the dark water. Under the restaurant's spotlight, Russell was holding a line that led to the water, and Goldie had a dip net in his hand. It looked like they were trying to snag a crab from the dock. This was a spot where fishermen brought their catch to the back of the restaurant, so there was no railing on this portion of the dock. Neither looked up from their task as we came out. Either they didn't hear us or were just intent on catching a crab. I followed Jack. As he passed them, Jack's hip swung into the back of Goldie, sending him off the dock and into the black bay waters.

"What the..." came from Russell.

"Excuse me!" Jack shouted as he looked over his shoulder at Russell and started high-stepping it out of there.

I could see Jack's shit-ass grin in the shadow of the spotlight. I stood frozen, not knowing whether to run or help Goldie out of the water. The water was shallow enough for Goldie to stand up, and he and Russell were yelling curses at Jack. There was no need for me to stay behind.

I caught up with Jack. "Why'd you do that?"

He was holding his side and laughing. "It was funny, man. Besides, we'll never see that asshole again. We're outta here tomorrow."

We got to the boardwalk and went north. When we got to Ninth, the mass of humanity we saw earlier was much larger. Young bodies were everywhere. It was an enormous party. People shared beer, and there was open drinking on the boardwalk. The crowd overflowed to the beach, where several groups held blankets and were tossing girls in the air like they were on a trampoline. We partied with them, and as they shared their beer with us, we shared some cocaine with them. I thought of Misty and chuckled to myself about her goofy fear of this place earlier in the day. A bad place, she'd called it. Too bad she was missing out on a good time. Then the crowd shifted, someone bumped someone, and a fight broke out.

Chapter 47

September 7, 1964
From Bad to Worse

A DANGEROUS MIX OF testosterone, alcohol, and cocaine fueled the crowd. It was after midnight, and there was no sign of the raucous party slowing down. Jack and I were trying to convince two coeds to inhale some white powder when we sensed the mood of the crowd change. We heard shouts and curses, and our first thoughts were that another fight was breaking out. There were flashing lights from the bubble gum top of a police cruiser, and a crush of people pushed us in that direction.

"What's happenin', man?" Someone asked.

"Cops arrested some kid for nothin', no reason," was a response.

"Busted his head with a billy club," came from another.

Beer bottles arced through the sky and crashed on the cruiser. People beat on the cop car, and it started rocking. It gradually pulled away as people moved out of the way. A few climbed on the hood and roof of the car, jumping on it and crumpling the sheet metal like foil. One by one, people either jumped or fell off the cruiser. Gradually the taillights and rotating light turned left on Philadelphia with the siren on and a large part of the crowd that had now become a mob following. Things had turned very ugly very quickly. The mob became a single organism. Information flowed through the crowd like an ant colony, hundreds of people running west on Ninth, following the police car onto Philadelphia, while hundreds of others formed a wave of agitated humanity flowing south on the boardwalk. Jack and I were carried off in the mob following the cop car. The eleven blocks to the police station at Dorchester was mass mayhem. What was four or five hundred swelled to twice that as the mob swallowed up more young people who came out of bars, hotels, restaurants, and rooming houses. Trashcans were set ablaze. Lawn furniture was hurled through plate glass windows. I lost sight of Jack and was simply pushed along as though a tidal surge carried me into an unknown or unknowable fate. I couldn't get away if I wanted to, but the truth was that I didn't want to get away. Adrenaline pumped through my body. I was part of something big, if not great—perhaps disastrous— but still a part of whatever would happen. A boy no older than thirteen put a match to papers in a trash can, and the crowd cheered as it flamed up. A gray-haired lady in a gingham cotton dress walked arm in arm with her husband, a skinny balding man in a wife beater undershirt, who waved a John Deere cap in the air. It seemed everyone wanted to be part of the ugliness. Some had angry faces; others who didn't know exactly what was going on had simple smiles, glad to be in the action. People were on balconies in rocking chairs holding children in their laps as though they were watching a circus parade. Some looked like they were eating popcorn and drinking beer as if this was better than the television shows they had been watching. They were in fact watching a parade, but it was a parade of madness and insanity. Disconnected by the safety of their balcony view, they joyfully watched in anticipation of a disaster happening to someone else.

Near Dorchester, the crowd stopped its forward surge, and people pressed against one another. A group of young men were rocking an empty police car. Jack was in the group, adding his muscle. With enough momentum, the car flipped on its side. Someone set it on fire. Another group bolted to another squad car and began rocking it. I spotted Jack watching the blaze from the first car. I worked my way over to him.

"Delaney! Wooo, wooo! Man, it's the wildest night ever. Yessss."

The people who had split away and gone south on the boardwalk were now coming down Dorchester, adding another thousand or more to the mob. The police station was completely surrounded by rock-and-bottle-throwing crazies. The sound of sirens pierced the air as fire trucks rolled up. The firemen started spraying the burning police cars, and the mob turned its attention on them by throwing things at the firemen. The firemen returned the favor by turning their hoses onto the crowd, which only served to aggravate them. After some time, there was the sound of more fire trucks. Reinforcements arrived from nearby Berlin. The trucks drove through the bottle-throwing crowd and joined with the Ocean City firemen organizing themselves around the police station. They continued to turn their hoses onto the crowd. As they pointed the hoses in one direction, an emboldened group attacked from the opposite direction. Bottles, cans, furniture, pieces of wood, rocks, and stones flew through the black sky, and a few found their mark. I saw an attacker get too close and get knocked down by the water from the high-pressure hoses. Two cops jumped on him, thumped him with their nightsticks, and dragged him into the police station. Then it happened to another guy. It wasn't smart to get too close to the hoses, but fool after fool did so, only to receive a soaking knockdown, a beating by the cops, and a literal drag by leg, arm, or hair into the jail. The mob's assault continued for more than an hour until there was a new wailing of sirens.

"Holy shit!" someone yelled. "Every state trooper in Maryland is here!"

I looked toward the bridge and saw a line of police cars that stretched to the mainland. An army of cops was closing in. Their cars rolled off the bridge and onto Philadelphia, then stopped at Talbot a block north of Dorchester and created a barricade with their cars. The cars just sat there for several minutes, then twenty or thirty Smokey the Bear hats appeared from behind the cars. The troopers were coming forward en masse, and the barking sound told me that they had brought the dogs, the Maryland State Trooper Canine Corps of large, well-trained German shepherds and Dobermans. I had no doubt these were the same dogs that attacked the marchers in Princess Anne, and I knew the damage they could do.

"Jack, we gotta get outta here fast."

"Oh, fuck, let's go. Which way?"

"Let's take Baltimore, see if we can get through that way."

We sprinted the block east to Baltimore and then turned north. The road was clear except for a dozen or so people in front of us. We ran until we approached Talbot, then slowed, thinking there might be cops around the corner. Walking into the middle of the intersection, Jack lagged behind. We looked toward Philadelphia where the troopers had set up the barricade. Our attention focused on two of the troopers coming in our direction. We never saw the tall, thin black man standing a few feet in front of us. He was there to be seen, but the cops had our attention. It was when I looked at Jack to tell him that we needed to go that I saw Goldie. Jack never did. Goldie's hand, holding a hammer, swung in an arc through the air and came down on Jack's head. It sounded like a smashed watermelon. Jack buckled and fell to the ground. Goldie stood over him, hitting Jack's head with the hammer again. And then again, and then, as he was swinging the fourth blow to Jack's head, I heard two loud cracks and saw Goldie's face explode. Two troopers ran to the bodies with their guns drawn. Approaching with caution, one nudged Jack with his boot, and the other did the same to Goldie. When there was no movement, they checked them for pulses.

"This one's dead. You can see his brains."

"Yeah, so is mine. Shit, the bullet took half this guy's face off."

"You had a clean shoot. Don't worry about nothing. He was killin' this guy. Wonder what made him so mad?"

The two troopers were so focused on Jack and Goldie that I was invisible to them. I was in a daze, unsure of what to do. Jack was dead, and there was nothing to do for him, no way to help him. Dreamlike, I wandered toward the beach and remembered the coke in my pocket. I turned the pocket inside out, dumping it on the street, and kept walking. On the boardwalk, people were running north, pursued by troopers. A trooper released his Doberman, and the dog had a kid's ass between his teeth. I dropped onto the beach with no conscious thought of what to do or where to go. I wandered diagonally across the sand for the three blocks to the pier. The repetitive crashing sound of the waves aided my stupor and held me in a trance. Sitting under the pier, I tried not to think about what I'd seen, but my brain wouldn't let me ignore the sight or the sound. The cocaine left my system and was replaced with exhaustion from the adrenaline rush. Eventually sleep found me.

The shock of cold water to my feet jolted me awake. The sun was up and with it the tide. I waded into the surf and dove into a cresting breaker. The cold Atlantic cleared my head. I stood in waist-deep water, hoping the previous night's events had been a dream, but my heart and mind told me that they hadn't been. I walked out of the water and stood under the pier with memories of all that had happened on this spot: Wendy and our kisses; Jack, Sylvia, and Misty plotting our business venture; and Aquarius falling into the ocean. Misty had been right all along.

Misty and Sylvia. I had to tell them. I picked up my shoes and ran across the sand, stopping to put them on at the boardwalk. I noticed that the fresh salt air was lost in the acrid smell of burnt tires and smoldering debris. I ran past the smoke, past shop owners sweeping up glass and boarding up broken windows. I ran to the room, opened the door, and saw Sylvia peacefully asleep.

"Sylvia! Wake up! Jack's dead...Sylvia!"

Her head was raised slightly, propped up with pillows, the chenille bedspread pulled up to her shoulders and around her neck. Her eyes were closed, and her skin was pasty white with a dusting of white power on her upper lip. Her lips were a bluish color. I touched her cheek. Her skin was cold, and there was no pulse at her carotid artery. She was dead. The vodka bottle on the dresser that had been almost full when we left was now empty.

Misty. Where was Misty? Check the armoire. Her clothes were gone, the moneybox hidden in the bottom of the armoire... gone.

"Fucking bitch. Fuck."

I heard a siren, the sound different from all the police and fire truck sirens from the previous night. The scream became louder as it got closer. The sound started to hurt my ears, and then it stopped. It was at the house. I went into the hall and closed the door behind me. It was an ambulance, and two medics were coming up the steps to the front door. Instinctively, I walked toward them.

"Where's room number five?"

I pointed to the doorway to what had been my home for past seventy-one days. I watched them as they gave the door two hard knocks, shouting for anyone who might be in the room and capable of answering, and then turning the handle and entering. A few dozen people gathered around the ambulance. As I passed them, a fat woman in hair curlers, housecoat, and bedroom slippers asked, "You know what happened?"

I shook my head and walked toward Second Street as though I had nothing to do with what was in that room, nothing to do with Sylvia's death, nothing to do with Jack's murder, nothing to do with last night's riot.

On the boardwalk, I sat on a bench, letting the sun dry the ocean from my clothes. Debris was scattered everywhere, and the city's maintenance people were already at work cleaning it up. I now noticed that the storeowners, who were sweeping up glass and boarding up broken windows with sheets of plywood, were giving me dirty looks. Apparently they were guessing correctly that I had been one of the night marauders. It was time for me to leave Ocean City. I counted the money in my pockets: $37.26. I would leave town with less than I came with and only the clothes on my back. My suitcase was back in the room, abandoned along with Sylvia. Going back to the room was not an option. The police would have found the remaining coke by now, and how could I explain Sylvia? I walked to the bridge and held out my thumb.

Three rides got me to Mardela Springs. I stood alongside U.S. Route 50 and looked at the flat countryside. On the way to Ocean City in May, these fields had been green with the new growth of corn and soybeans and the promise of the future. Today, the crops had been harvested, the ground was brown, and a farmer on his red Farmall tractor was plowing the field. Dust kicked up from plowed furrows, and a warm late-summer breeze sent the dust to a home on my sweaty face. The early September sun still carried the heat of August, and it beat on my head, showing me no mercy. I shaded my eyes with a hand, my beloved Ray-Bans a casualty of my retreat. The traffic was heavy, and it flowed fast with everyone leaving the ocean behind them until next summer—folks in cars, in a hurry to get home to tell the tale of what they had seen during the Labor Day riot in Ocean City. No one wanted to stop and lose their place in the line of traffic. I was ready to give up hope when I saw a red Jeep coming, the driver's blond hair dancing in the wind, oversized sunglasses hiding her face. She slowed down as she passed me and pulled to the side of the road. She looked over the back of her seat at me and removed her sunglasses. It was Wendy. She was on her way to Hood for her first semester. I took two steps toward her before she put her sunglasses back on and turned around. The brake lights went off, and she accelerated into the flow of cars and trucks.

My fists clenched until my knuckles turned white. I was mad, but not at Wendy. I could only blame myself.

Aquarius Falling

For Book Club Discussion

1. A theme throughout the novel is that actions have consequences. What were the actions that the characters engaged in that had serious consequences?
2. The characters of Tom Delaney and John E. Walker (Jack) don't seem to have much in common. What draws them together?
3. Tom Delaney was raised in a Catholic orphanage. In what ways do you think this impacts his moral decisions?
4. There are several musical references throughout the novel. Why is the music important to the story? To the characters?
5. Children who are adopted sometimes feel abandoned by their birthparents, and in adulthood they can occasionally have a fear of rejection. Do you see this manifested in the Delaney character?
6. Do you consider the relationship with Delaney, Wendy, and Misty a love triangle? How does the addition of Jack alter a the triangle?
7. Before you read the final chapter, how did you think the story would end?

8. What do you imagine happening to Delaney, Wendy, and Misty after the novel ended? Where do they go and what becomes of them?

The following questions for discussion go beyond the plot and interaction of the characters. These topics address the serious issues of racism, prostitution, drug use, and issues involving victimless crimes.

9. Racism is a strong undercurrent in *Aquarius Falling* and scenes and language portrayed in the novel were common for the time and place. To what extend do you feel racism in America has changed? What has not changed?

10. The fictional characters in *Aquarius Falling* rationalize their involvement in prostitution and cocaine dealing as victimless crimes and nothing more than business transactions between two consenting parties. Discuss the realities of this. Is it true or false and why?

11. One character references the fact that until 1920 cocaine was legal in the United States and was once an ingredient in Coca Cola until 1903. He references the positive financial benefits of legalizing the drug. Do you see more drawbacks to the legalization of drugs or more benefits? What parallels do you see to Prohibition of alcohol in the 1920's and 1930's and our current war on drugs?

Made in the USA
Charleston, SC
08 June 2012